MW01128293

MEDIC UP

Where Criminals, SWAT Teams, and Medicine Intersect

Dennis R. Krebs

ISBN-13: 978-1482312850
ISBN-10: 1482312859

Acknowledgments

My sincerest appreciation is extended to all those who made this book possible. Thanks to my editor Robert Broomall an author and teacher in his own right. Thanks to Dan Rose for his technical assistance on all matters tactical. In addition, recognition goes to the many military, law enforcement, tactical, and fire & rescue personnel who influenced my life—and this text—over these many years. Some have given their lives or have been severely injured in the performance of their duties. Thank you for your service.

Finally, thanks to Jamey, my beautiful wife, for her continued belief and support in this project.

Dedication

In the early morning hours of August 28, 2013
Officer Jason Schneider
of the Baltimore County Police Department died in the
line of duty. Officer Schneider, a member of the
Department's Tactical Unit was serving a warrant when
he was fatally shot. This book is dedicated to his
memory.

CHAPTER 1

The rapid fall of footsteps and labored breathing were evident among the sweat laden bodies running through the suburban Baltimore neighborhood. Residents watched closely as the group passed. The twenty men were in the second mile of a five-mile run. The burn in Danny Weaver's thighs became more intense as they engaged the rolling hills that had been chosen for the course. This was the first hour of the initial day of a three week, physically exhaustive and mentally challenging, SWAT school. And this little jog was the first test to weed out the weakest in the class. Two or three would drop out before the end of the day. By the end of the third week nearly a quarter of the class would drop out on their own request or be asked to leave by the cadre.

Weaver was not just another police officer attending the annual school, he was a fire department paramedic, unusual, but not unheard of.

At 32 years old Weaver was one of the oldest in the class; the physical challenges would be more difficult than for the younger guys. He certainly was not a total wreck; he had been working out for three months in preparation for the school. At 5' 10" and a muscular 185 pounds, he looked like many others in the group—to include the high and tight haircut. But he knew he was not 18 any longer and realized it even more as his feet continued to hit the pavement. Looking around Weaver thought, *I'm in the middle of the pack. Best place to be. Don't want to stand out. Just put one foot in front of the other. Breathe! Deep, steady, breaths.* The moist air was drawn through his nose and deep into his lungs and blown forcefully from his mouth.

He knew he had to get his mind off the distance left to run. Weaver forced his psyche into another, more pleasant, realm. Suddenly, Weaver was jolted back to the present.

"Weaver! Are you with us? Get your ass in gear or go home!" shouted Jack Phillips one of the instructors.

Phillips had been on SWAT for 7 years, was the senior member of the team and thus the team leader. He supposedly had a special operations background in the military, but did not talk about it. Phillips was intense and often had a look that let you know he had been there and done that. He was all business and no nonsense.

Startled, Weaver realized he had fallen behind. He had seen Phillips on occasion but did not know him well. After his scolding, the instructor effortlessly increased his pace and was quickly leading the pack of runners that was now stretched out over 75 yards.

Shit, there's not a lick of sweat on his shirt, thought Weaver as he watched Phillips sprint off. *I hate people like that.* They were passing the fourth mile and he needed to pick up the pace. But, he was still struggling and Phillips kept looking over his shoulder to see where Weaver was. As they rounded the corner back to the training center Weaver was relieved to have completed the 5 miles. He didn't have much get up and go left. His relief was short-lived.

"PT circles, let's go!" Phillips growled as they concluded the run.

The students formed a large circle and were immediately on their stomachs cranking out push-ups.

"One, two, three–*one*; one, two, three–*two*; one, two, three-*three*!" the cadence continued for a full set of 25, 4-count push-ups. In simpler terms they had just done 50 push-ups.

Not missing a stride Phillips yelled, "On your backs, leg raises!"

Groans emanated from each student as they rolled over; each trying to grab just a second of relief.

"Up, apart…, together…, down-*one*!" Phillips yelled effortlessly.

With each repetition it seemed they were keeping their legs off the ground for longer periods of time. Phillips was now on his feet continuing the harsh cadence.

"Let's go, six inches off the ground. Get those feet up!" he exclaimed to no one in particular.

Weaver's strength was fading fast. The blue t-shirt he wore clung to his sweaty torso. His eyes closed as he lay there in the bright sunlight.

Must be a passing cloud, I could use a break from the intense sun rays, he thought as the light dimmed.

"Your feet hit the ground, your feet hit the ground!" Phillips screamed.

It wasn't a cloud at all. It was the team leader's shadow as he stood over Weaver who came three inches off the ground when Phillips barked. Jack was now on one knee with his nose not more than an inch from Weaver's face, his own face crimson and his eyes bulging as he continued, "You let the team down! You let the damn team down! Get your feet off the deck or get off my training ground."

Struggling to get his legs up Weaver thought, *So much for not standing out in the crowd*. The burning in his abdomen was intense—like hundreds of hot daggers permeating every inch of his stomach. PT continued for another 30 minutes. At the conclusion of the session the students were ordered to rally in the classroom for lectures. One of the students asked, "Where do we shower up?"

Phillips bellowed, "What do think this is kindergarten? Get into to your BDU's and get into the damn classroom. We start in 5 minutes."

Oh, thank God I did not have time to open my mouth! I was going to ask the same thing. At least the attention is finally off of me for a while, thought Weaver.

The entire class ran to their vehicles; clothes flying off as they sprinted through the parking lot. Weaver leaped into the back seat of his car pulling off his running shorts while almost simultaneously grabbing his navy blue battle dress uniform pants. As his feet hit the macadam he already had the waist-band buckled. He threw on his boots, grabbed his shirt and was running toward the building in less than three minutes. *Shit, notebook*, he realized halfway to the door. Weaver did an about-face and quickly retrieved the necessary items from his car arriving at the classroom with only seconds to spare.

Bryan Anderson, also known as "Gunny" had the first

lecture on team makeup. Anderson had spent a number of years in the Marine Corps. His rank of gunnery sergeant had gained him respect both in the Corps and on the SWAT team. Anderson spent the next hour lecturing on the duties and responsibilities of each member of a typical team. There were no welcoming speeches by members of the police department's command staff. There was no coffee or donuts to open the session. It was business, hard and fast. Anyone wishing to hold hands and sing Kumbaya could visit the crochet club at the Senior Center up the street. Suddenly, Anderson stopped talking mid-sentence and leered at the back of the room. One of the students, Mike Becker, had closed his eyes. The student beside him gave a quick nudge of his elbow.

"Boring you Mr. Becker?" Gunny inquired. "Gentlemen, do not fall asleep. If you need to, stand up in the back of the room."

Anderson began to lecture once again only to stop and add, "Oh and Mr. Becker, you owe me 50 push-ups at the break."

The students in the class came from all over Maryland. The military had sent two people from Fort Meade and the Delaware State Police also had a few people attending. By noontime most of the students in the class knew Weaver was a paramedic and not a cop. Most thought it was a great idea to have a medic in the class. They provided him with much needed psychological support urging him to, "stay in the fight." However, Weaver knew many were wondering if he would be the first to drop out.

The afternoon consisted of a few more lectures and by the end of the day Weaver was exhausted. It seemed at each break they were doing push-ups because a classmate had screwed-up somehow.

As he left the classroom at the end of the day, he was stopped by Jack Phillips, "Why don't you give this up Weaver and go back to being a band-aid bunny or riding that shiny fire truck or whatever you do?"

Weaver couldn't believe it. He was here to help these guys and the team leader wanted him out. *The years of fighting for this; was it all a mistake,* Weaver thought. His stomach began to churn as he continued past Phillips and walked to his car. Inching through rush-hour traffic he began to weigh his options. He could stay but to what end. If they did not want him there and were not supportive of the entire concept it was senseless to spend three weeks in misery. Yet, he didn't like quitting. His goal was within sight. He picked-up his cell phone and called one of the guys on the team that he could confide in.

"Hello," answered William Brett one of the team's snipers. A former Marine Corps scout-sniper, he was widely known as one of the best in the business.

"Brett, it's Weaver."

"Hey buddy! Having fun yet?" Brett knew the rigors of the first day of the school even though he was not there himself that day.

"PT kicked my ass this morning."

Brett began to laugh but was cut off by Weaver.

"That's not my biggest problem though. Phillips stopped me as I left and told me to quit. What the hell is going on? I thought you guys wanted this?"

With a more serious tone to his voice Brett responded, "Look Danny I can't get into it right now, at some point I'll explain it to you. But for the next three weeks you need to convince him you belong here. After that you need to be a salesman. You need to show him you are a benefit to the team and not just a 'doc with a Glock.'" Brett was referencing an adage that had developed over the years referring to physicians and paramedics who got on SWAT teams because they liked the idea of carrying a gun and having a badge. "After the school I promise I'll fill you in. Until then hang in there. You know Jack is a good guy and he's a good team leader. Danny, you'll do fine."

"Right, hang in there," retorted Weaver. "I hope Phillips doesn't develop chest pains on one of our runs. I might just stand there and laugh at him."

After concluding his call with Brett, Weaver continued the slow commute home. He was met at the door by his smiling wife, Kathy. After a short visit to the hot tub and a cold beer Weaver took 400 milligrams of Motrin for the aches and pains. Retreating to bed his mind kept rehashing the events of the past 12-hours. *Should I quit or have Kathy get the extra large bottle of Motrin at the grocery store tomorrow*, he thought as his eyes closed.

CHAPTER 2

As the sun broke the horizon, Weaver rolled over in bed and assessed the pain he anticipated feeling from the previous day. Surprisingly, the aches were minimal; nothing that another Motrin wouldn't handle. After grabbing a quick shower he hit the road. No breakfast, it would only come back up in the middle of the run. He made sure he was at the training center ten minutes early. *If you're on time, you're late*, Weaver had quickly learned. Class started exactly at 0700 hours sharp.

"Back for more?" Phillips inquired as Weaver entered the building.

"I'm here for the duration," Weaver said. Quietly adding, "asshole" under his breath.

"Two of your classmates elected not to come back. We'll see how long you last."

Weaver was psychologically ready for whatever was thrown his way at the morning PT session. Or so he thought. After a short 5K, 3 ¼ mile run, they again hit the ground for calisthenics.

Without a bead of sweat on his brow Phillips announced, "Grab the telephone polls at the side of the parking lot. Two people to a pole."

The group ran to the edge of the macadam and grabbed the 6 foot sections of wooden telephone pole.

Oh shit! Nothing good can come of this, thought Weaver.

"Alright, pole on your chest. Sit-up position. Let's go!"

"You have got to be shittin' me!" Weaver mumbled. Similar grumblings emanated from the mouths of virtually every other student in the class.

"Fifteen, two-count sit-ups," Phillips instructed. "Up, down —*one*! Up, down—*two*!"

"Am I glad I didn't eat anything. I'd be wearing it right now," Weaver said to his partner, as his abdominal muscles began to spasm.

With physical training complete, the group hustled to the classroom for a lecture on the less lethal weapons currently in use. Weaver learned about bean-bag rounds; rubber bullets; pepper spray; CS and CN gas, typically known as tear gas; and the Taser. After an hour the instructor ordered everyone to the parking lot.

"Everybody in a straight line over here on the grass," Chuck McBride announced, also known as Bones because of his thin frame. With a wide smile Bones said, "By the time I am done you will wish you had not gotten out of bed this morning."

"Sadistic bastard," mumbled an unknown student.

"Okay everyone. Kidding aside, you have already learned that less lethal weapons *can* kill. I don't want any accidents or injuries today," Bones said. He continued to explain the safety measures that would be employed during the exercise and finally added, "Who's first?"

Although Weaver did not want to stand out in the class he figured he would get this over with and thus stepped forward.

Pointing to the padded mat where Brett and Dave Davis, a five-year veteran of the team, were waiting, Bones said, "Danny my boy; our first contestant. Step over to the mat."

"Hey Brett, bet you a buck he wets his pants," Davis laughed as Weaver approached.

"Nah, I think he'll cry," Brett responded.

Not wanting to show his nervousness Weaver said, "Come-on guys, that's just wrong."

Bones explained the sequence of events to Weaver and the rest of the class, "This is the Taser X-26. When I fire the weapon it will shoot two darts that are similar to fishing hooks. They are connected back to the weapon by small wires. Once embedded, you will receive a charge for approximately five seconds. Are you ready?"

Tightening his muscles and contorting his face in anticipation of the jolt he was about to receive Weaver said, "Yes!"

Weaver let out a thunderous yell as the darts embedded into his chest and the electricity coursed through his body. Davis and Brett stood to his side and eased him to the ground. The class roared in laughter; each student knowing they too would have similarly embarrassing reactions.

Weaver regained his composure saying, "What did that commercial say about a 4 hour erection?"

"That was for Viagra you idiot," Bones laughed, "But I would still go to the hospital if that happens."

Looking at Davis as he got up, Weaver said, "I didn't pee myself; you owe Brett a buck."

"Good job, Danny," Brett said.

Weaver received slaps on the back as he rejoined his classmates. The hot poker-like feeling in his body would remain for the rest of the day. *Oh well, Motrin, hot tub, and a beer again tonight*, he thought.

As Weaver turned he noticed Phillips watching him from the office window in the training center. *I know you want me out of here, but I will leap over every hurdle and make it through this school*, he thought.

The remainder of the first week was spent on the firing range. Weaver did not have much experience with firearms and sought out help from a variety of team members in the weeks leading up to the school. So, he at least felt confident that he would not shoot himself, or anyone else, in the foot. Their first range day consisted entirely of practice with the 40 caliber Sig Sauer pistol. They shot hundreds of rounds from varying distances. Each volley seemed to get harder, advancing from basic shooting stances to shooting with their weak hand in case the dominant hand was injured or disabled. Weaver learned to drop an empty ammunition clip and reload in one fluid motion. By the end of the day much of the mechanics of shooting had been committed to muscle memory. His scores began to rival others in the class that had been on the force for years. Although he felt a little like Wyatt Earp, he reminded himself not to get cocky.

11

The second day at the range began with the students practicing their skills at shooting while moving.

"Often times members of a team are engaged while moving through a house or clearing a room. You will be expected to return fire without stopping and planting both feet in a firing stance," Blake Reynolds explained, the 25-year veteran firearms instructor. "That takes up valuable time and you become a target. However, we do not do barrel rolls and come up shooting. We do not sprint 25 yards and hit a bad guy between the eyes," referring to the 2003 movie called SWAT.

"This isn't the movies. I want to see steady, smooth movements. Remember the old military adage, 'slow is smooth, smooth is fast.' Keep your knees slightly bent and don't bounce on the balls of your feet," Blake continued.

Weaver and the rest of the group moved through volley after volley of shooting in the warm sun. He was gaining a bit of confidence back after his run-ins with Phillips earlier in the week.

"Now that everyone is up to speed with their .40, we're going to move on. Next we are going to incorporate the body bunker, or ballistic shield, into the mix," Blake said. "Shields come in a variety of sizes, shapes, and capabilities. The one we use is Level IIIA. As you know it will not stop rifle rounds only handgun. The shield is twenty inches by thirty-four inches and weighs anywhere from twenty to twenty-five pounds and as you can see it has a viewport that is only four inches high. Most of the ones we use also have an eighty-thousand candlepower light on the front that will melt your retina. Hold the shield with your weak hand, left if you are right-handed and right if you're a lefty. It should cover the area from your forehead, just below the brim of your helmet, to about your thighs. In order to fire your weapon you must hold it sideways in front of the shield. It takes practice to be proficient."

"I just hope to hit the target, much less get a center mass kill shot," Weaver commented to the student next to him.

Weaver got the chance to try the combination of pistol and ballistic shield later in the day. Although they initially shot from a stationary position, they were also required to shoot while moving.

"I have problems walking and chewing gum at the same time, you want me to carry this shield, that's heavy as shit, hold a gun in front of it and shoot, all while walking? Not to mention actually hitting something?" Weaver said to Blake as he walked down the firing line preparing for the next volley.

Blake snickered, "Now you know the reason for the running and push-ups. Endurance and upper-body strength. Now shut-up and shoot. Or would you rather run and do a few more push-ups?"

"Shutting-up and shooting sir!" Weaver retorted. *So much for Wyatt Earp*, he thought. The first person on the team through the door of a house was vulnerable. If the shit hit the fan and bullets started to fly, he was the most probable to be hit. The shield provided a bit more protection, but at a price. It was difficult to hold up in front of your upper torso and the small viewport limited visibility. Finally, if someone did engage you with gunfire it took practice to return fire and take out the threat.

Weaver's remaining days on the range involved shooting the team's M-4 carbine. The M-4 is a shorter, lighter version of the older M-16 rifle. It weighs slightly less than 7 pounds loaded and fires single-shot or full-auto of 5.56mm ammunition.

With hundreds of rounds fired downrange Weaver was feeling more confident in his ability. He was gaining strength in his capability to move and shoot both the M-4 and his .40. He was able to quickly and smoothly transition from rifle to pistol when running out of ammo or encountering a malfunction.

Weaver was also just beginning to understand the roles and responsibilities of each member of the team. Something he would need to grasp in order to be an effective medic. Being a member of a SWAT team was physically challenging and required the utmost concentration. Each day he gained new respect for his friends on the team. He was even gaining more respect for the one that did not seem to want him there, Jack Phillips.

With the first week completed, an exhausted Weaver returned home to his loving wife. Kathy met him at the door wearing a smile and not much else. She handed him his robe and a beer and directed him to the hot tub.

"Steak and baked potato okay for dinner?" she asked.

He eased himself into the bubbling water of the tub, being careful not to spill his brew and said, "That's great honey."

Laying his head back and closing his eyes Weaver reflected on the week. He had accomplished things he never thought possible and was proud of his achievements. Slowly he began to worry about the upcoming week. He had had a reprieve from the badgering that Phillips inflicted upon him. The team had a few missions during the latter part of the week and Phillips was not at the range. Weaver feared what the second week might bring. Sore and exhausted he was still unsure if he would make it.

CHAPTER 3

Only a short distance from where the SWAT team was conducting their school, Rick Nash walked outside and took in a deep breath of fresh air; something he had not done for sixty days.

"Rick, over here!" Randy Young shouted, a long-time friend of Nash's. Young's hardcore, inner-city demeanor was strikingly different from Nash's pretty boy disposition. Young sported an array of tattoos that seemed to be a window into his mind and soul. This was not someone you wanted to piss-off.

"Hey, thanks for picking me up. I owe you," Nash said as he approached Young's car.

"How ya' doin'?

"Great now, but I tell you I _will not_ go back. Screw all this. Let's get out of here and get some food. The crap they have in this piece of shit jail would gag a maggot."

"There's a diner just around the corner on York Road. That all right?"

Nash's latest stint in the county lock-up had been for battering a former girlfriend. His record was full of various assaults, handgun violations, and domestic-related offenses. He was 27 years old, 5' 9", a ripped 180 pounds, with baby-blue eyes, and was well groomed. Appearing much younger than his actual age, he preferred dating high-school or college-age girls.

Early on in a relationship Rick Nash was polite and flattering. His young female acquaintances would be treated to flowers, gifts, and dinners at expensive restaurants. Soon however, Nash's controlling personality would take over and he would begin calling at all hours of the day and night. He would stop by the young lady's house unannounced and, if not at home, the girl would bear the brunt of his tirades. He expected her to account for her whereabouts every second of the day. Her total devotion was to him, Rick Nash, and no one else not even other girlfriends.

"Two, please." Nash requested as he and Young entered the diner. The two were quickly seated and began to scan their menus.

"So, what are your plans?" Young asked.

"I'm going to get something to eat," Nash said.

"No, you asshole. I mean, in general—now that you're out of jail. You gonna' try to get back with Lacy?

"That bitch was the reason I was in that shit hole for the past two months. I need to find her and smack the shit out of her."

A young waitress approached the table. "What can I get you guys to drink?"

Nash eyed the girl's name tag, "Christy, could you get us two Buds please?"

17

An almost imperceptible smile crept across the waitress' face as she acknowledged the order from the "hunk" at table 9.

"Nash, you asshole. Don't even think about it," Young laughed, lowering his head so as not to be overheard.

"Hey, it's been two months."

"So, what about Lacy?"

"Screw her. Guarantee you this one will be mine by the time we walk out of here."

Christy returned with the two beers and took their order for a couple of burgers.

Laying on the charm, Nash said, "That's a beautiful necklace you're wearing. Is it from your boyfriend?"

"No, I don't accept gifts from strangers on the first date. That is what you are leading up to, isn't it, a date?" she retorted placing the food on the table.

Young burst out laughing as Nash's mouth fell open. With Nash unable to respond, Christy wrote her number on the back of the check and walked away. Not to be outdone, Nash entered the number into his cell phone and hit "send."

"I'll pick you up at eight tonight," Nash said when Christy answered.

Christy Moore was a freshman at nearby Towson State University. She was an attractive brunette with piercing brown eyes and a slim 125 pounds for her height of 5' 4". She worked part-time at the diner, which was just up the street from the University. Although she was only in her first year of college, she had her eyes set on continuing to medical school. Through the fall semester, she had held a 4.0 grade point average. If she could maintain that level of commitment to her studies, she might very well have her pick of medical schools. Though Johns Hopkins was one of most prestigious, and not to mention that it was right in Baltimore, she wanted to keep her options open. Thus, getting heavily involved with a guy was not in her short-term plans. But there was something about Nash that captured her attention. He certainly was handsome, however it was more than his physical appearance. There was something mysterious about this guy. Although Christy had clearly set goals, she was still a freshman in college with raging hormones.

Nash arrived at Christy's townhouse on Burkshire Road later that night in his black '65 Ford Mustang. A gift from his mother, he kept the car in pristine condition. He looked like any other preppy college student, wearing a blue button-down collar shirt, khaki slacks, and brown loafers. Nash climbed the short flight of stairs to the brick house of 1960's vintage, known in Baltimore as a row house, and knocked on the door.

Christy's roommate said upon answering the door,

"Hi, you must be Rick."

"Yes," Nash said politely. "And you are?"

"Jackie Rogers, I room with Christy. We go to Towson together. Come on in and have a seat. She'll be down in a minute." Jackie and Christy had been the best of friends since their early years in high school and confided in each other on most every topic especially when it came to men.

Christy came downstairs wearing black slacks, a loosely fitting white top, and red heels.

"You look great," Nash commented with a smile on his face, "but you may want to take a sweater. It's supposed to get chilly after sunset."

After retrieving a sweater, the two were out the door and off to the Woodberry Kitchen. Fifteen minutes south of Towson off of the Jones Falls Expressway, the restaurant catered to those expecting good food and good service. The fiery brick oven in the main dining room made the establishment a favorite of anyone wanting a romantic evening.

Christy was sufficiently impressed with Nash's manners—holding doors and helping her with her chair at the restaurant. He was even restrained, only giving her a kiss on the cheek as they parted for the evening. Although Christy did not want a relationship that hindered her studies, she desperately hoped Nash would call again. The following day she returned home from class to find a bouquet of flowers on the doorstep.

Giggling with enthusiasm, she exclaimed to her roommate Jackie, "No one has ever sent me flowers. I can't let this one get away!"

"Well, don't move too fast sister. You don't want to get burned," Jackie retorted.

CHAPTER 4

As Weaver slid his feet from under the bedding, the sun had yet to crest the hill outside his window. He sat on the edge of his bed, ran his fingers through his hair, and wiped his eyes. It was already Monday morning and he needed to get his butt in gear if he was to make it on time. The previous week had been exhausting and although his time spent on the range had been fun, he knew that Phillips would be back in his case today. He was unsure if he could endure both the physical as well as the psychological battering he knew was forthcoming.

Even though many SWAT teams across the country had embraced the concept of tactical emergency medicine, having a medic attached to the team, Weaver was not able to convince his agency the concept had merit. Most of the members of the SWAT team were on board with the idea. They wanted to go home to their families at the end of the day with ten fingers, ten toes, and no leaks. The higher echelons were the ones with their heads up their proverbial asses. Not the Baltimore County Police Department command, the fire department. Weaver had been a firefighter/paramedic for 11 years. He had been asked by a friend on the SWAT team to conduct a short first-aid class years before and started hearing about tactical medics shortly thereafter.

Weaver became increasingly frustrated when asked to help at another medical training class for the SWAT team. They were training on how they could approach and extract an officer shot in his patrol vehicle. Dave Davis—a member of the team—had offered up his Ford Crown Vic for the training scenario. Weaver noticed the picture of Davis' wife and newborn son taped to the dash of the patrol car. That sealed the deal for Weaver; this was one of those things in life you fought for because it was the right thing to do. He would not go down in defeat.

Weaver continued to push the fire department administration at every opportunity. They were becoming increasingly frustrated to the point of holding up a promotion that he was due. Even the police chief was starting to chime-in on the issue. Finally, a deal was struck. One that would rid the fire chief of the thorn in his side, keep the cops happy and it would be a minimal cost. Weaver, at least on paper, would remain an employee of the fire department, but would be assigned to the police SWAT team for a 6-month trial period. With that hurdle behind him the really hard work started.

As he quickly showered, Weaver remembered Brett's admonition to suck it up. He knew, in theory at least, Brett was right; in practice it was much harder to do. *Take it one minute at a time* Weaver thought.

Luckily, he was only minutes from the location for today's practical exercises being held at the Henryton State Hospital in neighboring Carroll County. The long-abandoned complex was in a remote wooded area and consisted of six old buildings and a utility plant. The compound was overgrown and the buildings were in disrepair. The three-story main hospital building was the worst. Its whitewashed exterior had grayed from years of neglect. The roof leaked like a sieve causing the paint on the interior walls and ceiling to peel and fall to the tiled floor that had also started to deteriorate. Some of the other structures were in better condition, but were still dank and dirty. However, the variety of differing building styles made it an excellent location for the type of training the class would need.

As the students fell into formation Phillips asked, "Anyone have problems finding this place?"

There were no, "good mornings" or "how was your weekend?" The second week was about to start as harshly as the first. Everyone knew it was a rhetorical question; Phillips could care less whether anyone did have problems. As quickly as he completed the question he continued, "Excellent! Well, boys and girls, we will be going on a bit of a nature walk this morning? Try to keep up." That fast, Phillips turned and was off running down a trail through the woods.

As they hit the trail, Mike Mund, a student in the class, said to Weaver, "Okay, Phillips is running in his BDU pants and desert combat boots." Mund was an averaged size guy with short black hair and the nimbleness of a runner. A 7-year veteran with the agency, he desperately wanted to get on the team. Mund and Weaver had developed a good partnership at the range.

"He's either nuts or really hard core," Weaver responded.

"Probably both! Anyone who can go out on a casual run in that stuff needs a check-up from the neck up. Hey, did you know this place is an old tuberculosis hospital?"

"Shit, no! So I guess we have a choice on how we'll die.

23

Exhaustion, dehydration, or some half-assed disease." Both began to laugh.

"Weaver! Let's see how funny it is when you are running back up this hill!" Phillips bellowed from the front of the pack.

"Damn, dude. He really rides your ass," Mund said.

"Ah, he loves me. Just doesn't want to show it to the rest of you," Weaver responded.

Phillips was right, the run back up the hill was excruciating. The agonizing pain in Weaver's lungs was nothing compared to the unbearable burn in his thighs. His feet were only coming inches off the ground; it no longer even looked like he was running. Weaver and Mund were still coaching each other as they made the ascent.

As Phillips passed by midway up the hill Mund said, "Hey, are you breaking a sweat there, Jack?"

Leisurely continuing by Phillips said, "No, just splashed my face with some water from the stream while I waited for you light-weights to catch up."

"He wouldn't admit if he was sweating," Weaver gasped after Phillips was out of ear shot. "He must not have a life."

"I don't think he does," Mund said, sucking in air. "Rumor has it he doesn't talk about things outside the job. Nobody knows if he's got kids or is even married."

After completing the day's PT, the students were ordered to get dressed and report, with their gas masks, to the old administration building at the complex. Although most students in the SWAT school had been exposed to tear gas during their initial recruit training, they would get another taste of the chemical agent in the minutes ahead. Still ramped up and breathing heavily from their little woodland run and calisthenics, the group gathered around Bones, the instructor for the scenario. Bones had a wide smile on his face. He knew the CS gas would impact the students more profoundly now that they were sweating and winded. They would soon be very, very miserable.

"Okay, gas time, folks!" Bones said to the groans of those students who had been exposed before. "This is not a big deal. Remember you can work through it; just don't panic. You'll get a runny nose—things will burn—but you're not going to die. I want each of you to take off your mask, state your name and the agency you are with. After that you can replace your mask and clear it."

The process of clearing the mask involved covering one of the valves on the respirator with your hand and then forcefully blowing out what little air you had left in your lungs. This pushed any residual tear gas left in the mask out. The second part was to cover the hole in the filtering canister and breathing inward to ensure the mask was seated properly on your face so that it did not leak.

Weaver and the remainder of the class stood in a circle in the empty brick room. Each of them tightly affixed their mask to their face, periodically pulling on the straps to tighten it even further against the intrusion of any gas. Bones pulled the pin on the tear gas canister. As he let it roll from his hand to the concrete floor, the lever flew from the top of the soup can-like device. A pop was heard followed by what sounded like the hissing of an angry snake. Immediately a cloud of smoke came from the portals on the canister spewing CS tear gas. In a matter of seconds everyone began to feel the burning effects of the gas on the sweaty pores of their exposed skin.

"Alright! Let's do it!" Bones mumbled through his own mask.

Bones pulled the mask from his head and loudly exclaimed, "Chuck McBride, Baltimore County Police Department."

Bones slipped the mask back over his head securing the straps and clearing it in one perfectly choreographed motion. He made the entire event look easy. No coughing, no gasping for air, no runny nose or watery eyes.

It gave the students a false sense of security. *Not too bad in here*, many thought. Even Weaver was feeling a little less apprehensive. He had countless hours wearing his fire department breathing apparatus, however he was used to having a tank filled with 45 minutes of breathable air on his back. Although Weaver was used to smoke, he had never been exposed to gas.

Pointing to the student beside him Bones said, "You're up."

He got his first name out, "Chris" and that was all she wrote. He made the mistake of breathing in prior to saying his last name and was now coughing uncontrollably. His eyes began to tear and his nose looked as if a faucet had been opened. Bones led the student to the door and pushed him outside to the other instructors who were waiting for the inevitable.

The process continued with some students completing the required tasks and properly clearing their mask, while others found their way outside to the waiting arms of the loving instructors.

It was Weaver's turn and, unbeknownst to him Jack Phillips had slipped into the room. "Danny Weaver, Baltimore County Fire," Weaver said.

He quickly slid the mask back over his head. Before he could clear it however, Phillips pulled his own mask off and said, "You didn't complete the exercise right. Try it again, Weaver."

Yanking his mask off, Weaver was incredulous thinking, *I'm tired of this asshole.* "Danny Weaver, Baltimore County Fire Department!" yelling as loudly as possible. Turning to see Phillips standing nearby without his mask on, Weaver defiantly left his off as well and stared straight at him. After 30 seconds the burning in his eyes and throat became unbearable. Long liquid strings hung from his nose. Trying unsuccessfully to get his mask back on he thought, *Oh shit! Who's the asshole now. I just made a fool of myself.*

As he walked past Weaver and out the door still holding his mask in his hand, Phillips said mildly, "Don't try to outdo me, Weaver. You'll lose every time."

It was time to start putting everything together. The remainder of the school would be spent in practical exercises. They would simulate raids and barricade situations in both daylight and nighttime conditions. The Henryton complex had areas where they could simulate everything from apartments to industrial occupancies and business offices.

"Everybody get geared up. Formation in five minutes. Make sure your weapons are cleared and all ammunition remains in your vehicle," Phillips exclaimed.

Weaver and the remainder of the class ran to their vehicles

and donned their heavy body armor and strapped on their pistol belts. Throwing his helmet on his head and grabbing the M-4 he had been issued, Weaver met his classmates at the front of the main hospital building for formation.

"Weapons check," said Phillips adding, "Clip out of both your pistol and your long-gun. Have the breach open as well."

Each student dropped the ammunition clip from each of their weapons to show the instructors they were empty. In addition, the breaches were opened to ensure a stray round was not in the chamber. The last thing they needed was for a live round to go off and injure someone on a training exercise. The instructors took the safety procedures seriously, even patting down each student to make sure there was not ammunition in a pocket or pouch. After the students were complete, the instructors conducted a similar search of each other.

Arriving in front of Weaver, Jack Phillips checked his ammo clips and examined the M-4 asking, "Did you clean this thing over the weekend?"

"Yes, sir."

"It sure doesn't look like it. Fifty push-ups at lunch."

"Yes, sir."

Phillips pushed onward to the next student, not waiting for Weaver's acknowledgment. He was not going to challenge Phillips after the fiasco at the tear gas scenario, even though he had spent an hour cleaning and checking the weapon.

After the weapons check, Gunny split the class into 3 five-man teams; five people had quit since the beginning of the program.

"We are going to begin with the basics. Remember what you learned in the lectures last week. I want everything today to be at a slow pace, do not rush. You will not be expected to know the proper positioning at every door or proper sequence for clearing every room. However, I do not want to see any lasing of other team members, watch your muzzle swing with the long-guns," Gunny said.

Inexperienced operators would tend to sweep the muzzle of their weapon across other members of the team when changing the direction in which they were pointing the gun. In a stressful situation where the group was under fire it would be easy to shoot a fellow team member in the head, chest, or even the back.

"Your first scenario will be a raid at an apartment we have set up on the first floor of the administration building. You can use the blue Ford van as your raid vehicle. Pick your team leader. Once that is done, he can come to me to gather intelligence. I will not volunteer information; the team leader must ask the right questions in order to get all of the necessary intel," Gunny said.

Weaver's group was first up. Keith Miller, a veteran Delaware State Trooper, would be their team leader for the first evolution. Miller had been a trooper for seven years and was considered to be pretty squared away. As the group prepped for the scenario, Miller met with Gunny to gather intel on the raid.

Minutes later, Miller returned. "Okay, we are going to hit an apartment at Number One, First Street, Apartment B.

There is an arrest warrant for a guy wanted in connection with a homicide. Suspect is a twenty-one year old white male. Mund will be on the shield, Nick Hacker will be cover man behind the shield, me, and Ed Muhler. Danny, I'm going to have you take rear guard. Don't want to throw you to the wolves just yet. Gunny said he would give us Bones as the breacher since we only have five people. He will carry the battering ram and take the door."

The group assembled in the van and slowly drove up to the parking lot beside the administration building that had been designated Number One, First Street. The team of students methodically got out of the van and got in their assigned formation with Mund on point with the shield and Weaver assuming the rear guard position.

From the center of the formation, Miller looked to ensure everyone was in place and quietly said, "Stack is tight."

The group moved to the entry door of the building and once inside located Apartment B.

Miller nodded to Bones who moved out of the line and up to the door.

"Initiate," Miller whispered.

Knocking on the door Bones yelled, "Police, search warrant!"

With no answer, the same knock and announce process was done two more times with no response. Bones mimicked using a battering ram to open the door. As the door was thrown open, Mund, with the ballistic shield in front of him and his handgun in front of that, moved rapidly through the first room.

"Police with a warrant! Police with a warrant!" Miller yelled.

The group systematically moved through the apartment not finding a suspect. As last man through the door, Weaver followed the team as they cleared each room. Never having been a police officer, nor having conducted a room-by-room search of this type, he felt ungainly in his movements. He closely watched the actions of his comrades so he could mimic their maneuvers in subsequent scenarios. The students rallied outside to be debriefed by the instructors who had been watching the events unfold.

"Not bad for the first round," Gunny said. "But, a few things to improve on for the next one. Miller, when you gather your intel from the detective running the case, make sure you get a *complete* description of the suspect. Also, whenever possible, try to get information on the layout of the building you're going to hit. You can plan a lot better when you know the number of rooms, floors, etcetera. Which way does that front door swing and is there a storm door? Were there any kids inside? You didn't ask. Need to know whether there are any children or elderly in the house. If there are, you may elect to not hit the house and take your suspect off at another location.

"Everyone, when you exit the van, your weapons should be up and covering the windows and doors as you make your approach to the target location. If your approach is compromised, a suspect can open fire and you may never see him. Keeping that weapon up will reduce your reaction time to a threat.

"Mund, it's not a race. Slow down. Your pace should be

slightly faster than a walk. If you move too fast clearing a room you will miss something and missing things can get people killed.

"Weaver, as rear guard you have a big responsibility to ensure the team is not ambushed from behind. It is not uncommon in an apartment building to have someone from across the hall come out and enter the target apartment after we enter. If that person is the security for a stash we could be screwed. Watch your six.

"Everybody, although each of you has an area of responsibility—an AOR—you need to keep your head on a swivel. Keep your eyes scanning. Watch what's going on around you.

"Overall, good job. There were no suspects in this one. We'll be kicking it up a notch with each exercise."

Weaver and the rest of his team felt good after their first scenario. There had been no major screw-ups; a few tweaks here and there, and they should be good to go. Each of them knew however, that the remaining exercises would test their skills. The instructors would do their best to exploit any tactical weaknesses they could find. In simpler terms, they would try to get them to screw-up. You could bet some knucklehead criminal with a gun would play the same deck of cards, given the opportunity.

CHAPTER 5

Weaver and the rest of the students in his team felt like they were descending into the bowels of the earth. Arriving at the bottom of the staircase in the main hospital building at Henryton, they were met with a dark, wet, mildewed basement area. The filtered light emanating downward from the first floor cast an eerie sense about the room where the students assembled. Richard Rice would be their instructor for the exercise. He was of average height but, like most of the others on Baltimore County's team, he was muscular. Rice had been on the team for 5 years and had taken every tactical training class he could attend; usually on his own dime. He was considered a master at planning out tactics for barricaded subjects and hostage rescue incidents.

"This will be a low and slow scenario. As I explained in class last week, there are times when you have lost the element of surprise and your movements will need to be slow and deliberate. A suspect will have had time to either hide or attempt to ambush you. This morning, you will be required to clear the rooms down the hallway to my left. Obviously, there's not much light down here and on the other side of this fire door it's pitch black," Rice said.

"What about night vision?" Mund asked.

"Other than the feds, nobody has that kind of money to

equip each person on their team with NVG's. We use the alternative high tech method."

Everyone's interest was piqued, expecting Rice to break out a new inexpensive piece of fancy equipment.

"Flashlight. Yeah, nothing sexy, just a high-intensity flashlight. Now, this is not as simple as it might seem. You need to keep a wall of light down the hallway. Someone at the opposite end should be blinded and not be able to see your movements. What do we call that?" asked Rice.

"Concealment," Weaver answered.

"Exactly, but if you screw it up you can actually backlight yourselves and become a very nice target. A good way to get killed."

The lights that Rice was referring to were not the typical buck ninety-eight, hardware store special. Although not as bright as the light on the ballistic shield, they could still illuminate an area with up to 38,000 candela of light. Most seasoned operators carried two lights in case one malfunctioned.

Weaver's team received their remaining instructions and prepared to take the hallway. Rice took up a position at the opposite end about 50 feet from where the students would enter. Leaning against the wall with his arms folded across his chest, Rice would watch the exercise unfold and attempt to see past the blinding light to catch students making mistakes that could be exploited.

As they opened the door, the hallway was immediately flooded with bright white light. Two lights were positioned for maximum effect down the corridor.

With the exception of the sound of water dripping from the ceiling above, there was only silence.

Mund was the team leader and whispered, "Point and point-cover, take the first room on the left."

Weaver had been designated as point man for the exercise, and, once assured the lights were properly positioned and they would not be back-lighted, he nodded to his cover man and moved into his assigned room. Weaver and his partner cleared their areas of responsibility and took up positions to provide long cover down the hallway. Using the door frames as cover in the event gunfire erupted, Weaver aimed his M-4 carbine down the corridor. With his right forefinger on the frame of the weapon just above the trigger, he peered over the sights and watched for any movement in the doorways ahead. The stillness made Weaver feel uneasy. *They sure as hell picked the right place to do this,* he thought. *This is spooky.*

Silently, Keith Miller and his cover man took the first room on the right side of the hallway. After clearing the room, Miller took up a covering position from his own doorway. The high intensity lights were moved forward to provide concealment, and the team stopped momentarily to allow Mund to contemplate his next move. This was just like a chess game, moving one piece at a time. Everything was slow and deliberate.

"Suspect right! Suspect right!" Weaver yelled, breaking the silence. "Last door, white male. Looked out and ducked back in; only saw a small portion of his head."

Shivers went up Weaver's spine. Perhaps the Taser didn't make him pee himself, but this almost did. *Shit, game on*, he thought.

35

"Suspect, come out with your hands up!" Mund announced. After waiting for a moment Mund again ordered the suspect out of his hide.

With no response, Mund decided to have the team continue their move down the hallway. The students would leapfrog from room to room, maintaining their wall of light. Although it was only a training exercise, the tension was palpable. The person at the end of the hallway could very well be their bad guy, but he could also be a scared hostage. The real suspect could be in the next room waiting to ambush the team. The students had to stay focused on each aspect of the operation.

As they were preparing to move to the next room, Miller moved his high intensity light and accidentally hit the switch.

"Shit! What happened, get that light back up!" Mund said frantically.

Once the light was re-established Mund asked Weaver, "Did you hear something when we lost the light?"

"Yeah, but I don't know what it was."

What had once been a well-orchestrated set of tactical movements by this fledgling group of students had quickly turned in favor of their opposing force.

The team continued their methodical march down the hallway. Weaver was again in the position to be point man upon taking the last room. His stomach was in knots and his palms were sweaty.

For his part, Rice, now positioned behind the team, knew this could turn very ugly.

With his M-4 trained on the doorway Weaver was about to enter, the student with long cover whispered, "I don't have anything in that door, Danny."

Weaver was just to his right with his own weapon pointed toward the floor; his point cover man crouched behind him. Weaver lowered his left hand with three fingers extended, letting his partner know they would go on three. He squeezed Weaver's thigh to acknowledge. Weaver closed one finger at a time. On the third, his M-4 came up into position and they quickly moved across the hall and into the room. Weaver's stomach was tight. The only thing he could equate this to was being lost in a burning building and running low on air in your breathing apparatus. Neither situation could be considered fun.

At the same time the long cover man on the opposite side of the hallway concentrated on the last room on the left side.

Something caught his eye, "Suspect—gun!"

He quickly dropped his index finger onto the trigger and squeezed. Everyone heard the click of the firing pin.

Knowing he had a good hit the student announced, "Suspect down!"

Weaver desperately wanted to see what had happened behind him, but knew he still had an area of responsibility to cover. He and his partner finished clearing the room and upon exiting were astounded to find their bad guy in the room across the hall with a wide smile on his face. He had taken full advantage of their blunder.

In his debrief, Rice was calm and analytical as any good instructor should be. After noting a few positive points of their performance, Rice added, "You learn by your mistakes. However, making a simple mistake in this business could get someone killed. You got lucky. Had this been a real incident, accidentally turning off that flashlight could easily have cost Weaver his life. If the bad guy had stayed further back in the shadow he would never have been seen. Being shot from behind, Danny would never see it, or hear it coming."

Trying to lighten the mood after the subtle ass chewing, Rice added, "But then again it was only Weaver and we all know hose-beater firefighters are expendable."

The group gave a light chuckle and patted Weaver on the back. To a person they would never make a similar mistake again.

The group was now in their third week of training and were physically exhausted. However, this was the condition the cadre wanted and expected the class to be in. Anyone not taxed at this point in the program would not have been pulling their weight. A real operational SWAT team could be called upon to function at a barricade or hostage incident for long hours, even days, without relief. The instructors needed to test the group's endurance not only through the tough PT regimen, but also through the endless hours of practical scenarios in full gear. Wearing heavy body armor and helmet along with carrying a weapon for eight or more hours was grueling work.

Although Weaver was far beyond fatigued, his wife loved it. After three weeks he was looking pretty ripped; Kathy thought he was hot and could not keep her hands off of him. His work did not end after his 10 hours in class.

Their final two days in the school would tax them even

further than they thought possible. The group was instructed to arrive at an abandoned veterans' hospital southeast of Baltimore by 1500 hours—3 p.m.—for their final raid scenario. Since they would be getting an early start on the following morning, the instructors suggested they bring a sleeping bag, food, and change of clothes to allow them to remain at the training site.

Following another 5 mile run and calisthenics, Phillips briefed the group on their assignments, "Tonight you will be conducting your final raid scenario. I want them to be flawless. You've been running these for nearly two weeks. No more stupid mistakes. Each student group will need to conduct their intelligence gathering and develop a raid plan. Your team leader will then be responsible to brief me on your plan."

Weaver and his group received the information regarding their exercise. They were to raid a location where a suspect had been selling fully automatic weapons.

"Danny, why don't you take team leader this go round?" Mund asked.

With others in the group nodding their affirmation Miller added, "Yeah! Give it a whirl."

Weaver was happy the group had enough confidence in him to take the position, but he was also apprehensive about screwing up. "I know what this is," Weaver responded with a smile, "you figure I'm expendable at this point, so now you're throwing me to the wolves. Actually, only one wolf—Phillips!"

"Would we do that? We'll be right behind you!" Miller responded.

"Yeah, right! I'm going to turn around and see nothing but dead air."

Weaver gathered intel, while the remainder of the squad began checking weapons and equipment. With their raid plan complete Weaver, with the remainder of the team in tow, approached Phillips for the briefing.

As Weaver approached with plan in hand, Phillips rolled his eyes saying, "You're the team leader? Well this ought to be good!"

Upon finishing, Phillips had little to say. The plan was sound and Weaver had contingencies for most potentialities. "Okay, we'll see how it goes," Phillips concluded with a hint of frustration in his voice.

The group geared-up and conducted weapon checks. Through their intel gathering they had obtained the layout of the apartment they were to hit and decided to run a dress rehearsal.

"Why don't we use some chalk or tape to lay out the diagram of the apartment here on the parking lot?" Miller suggested.

"Good idea! Let's get it set up. We can run the rehearsal from the point that the van stops," Weaver responded.

"I'm going to make a few adjustments on how we are seated in the van. I think it'll make it easier to deploy. Since they're dealing full auto weapons we need good noise discipline on the approach. If they hear us coming it'll give them chance to arm-up and then we're screwed. We need the element of surprise; hit them hard and fast—overwhelming force," Weaver said.

With darkness upon them, the team of students mounted-up in their raid van and drove the short distance to the building they were to hit. Everything had been highly choreographed from where each person sat to where the van stopped. The group deployed and silently made their approach to the second floor apartment. As team leader, Weaver was in the middle of the pack and knew each person on the team had their area of responsibility to watch; he concentrated on the overall progress of the operation. Mike Mund was the point man and had the ballistic shield up with his finger resting on the switch to activate the shield's high intensity light.

At the top of the stairs, the team stopped and listened. Was there any activity inside the apartment? Was anyone talking? If so, how many people? It was less than 30 seconds but it was enough time to gather a bit more intel.

The breacher moved forward and stepped to the apartment door. As the door flew open, Mund stepped across the threshold and lit the room up like it was high noon. By the look on the faces of the role players, they had been caught off-guard.

"Police, get down! Police, get down!" Weaver yelled as they streamed into the target apartment. Mund quickly encountered a stunned role player and pushed him against the wall with his shield. One of the follow-on students would get him to the ground and cuff him. The team quickly cleared each room of the apartment.

With two role players in "custody" Weaver said, "Okay, let's get our secondary searches complete and wrap this up."

In less than 30 seconds the group had two people in custody, cleared a five-room apartment, and had found the weapons they were after. Weaver had a smile on his face. He knew that Phillips, watching the events unfold from a corner in the living room, could find little fault with their op.

As Phillips turned and exited the apartment he mumbled, "Good job everybody."

There were high fives all around the room.

It was 2300 hours—11:00 p.m.—as the students made their way back to their staging area.

"Everybody listen up. Stow your gear, secure your weapons, and grab your sleeping bags. Meet Gunny on the second floor of the hospital building. He'll show you the ward where you can rack out," Phillips announced.

After showing the group to their sleeping area Gunny noted, "Reveille is at 0600. By the way, there is no running water in the building, so figure it out."

As Gunny rejoined the rest of the instructors, Phillips said, "Give them an hour."

CHAPTER 6

Gunny was feeling generous. It had been an hour and 5 minutes when he approached the door to the ward where the students were sleeping. His head was covered in a black Nomex—fire resistant—balaclava hood, his hands were fitted with similar Nomex gloves; standard procedure when deploying a diversionary device. The 6 inch long, black steel, cylindrical device, he held in his hand, was commonly referred to as a flash bang. It had a military fuse on top, that made it look like a grenade. Unlike a grenade however, the bang was not intended to fragment and spew shrapnel about the area.

Gunny pulled the pin on the fuse and held the lever tightly against the side of the cylinder. Slowly, he opened the door to the ward. The clang of metal hitting the concrete floor, as he tossed the bang into the room, went unnoticed. One and a half seconds later, the flash bang erupted with a 175 decibel boom, and a bright 8 million candela flash of light.

Immediately, Gunny ripped the hood from his head, "Get your hands off your cocks and on your socks!

Let's go! Hostage rescue—Henryton. You have 5 minutes to be in a motorcade formation and wheels up."

Weaver, and the rest of the class, were jolted from their restful sleep. It felt like being socked in the chest by some big oaf's fist. Some thought they were being attacked, others thought it was a dream, all had a pulse rate in excess of one hundred. In a daze, they scrambled to grab their belongings and get to their cars.

The column of unmarked police vehicles wove its way around the west side of Baltimore arriving at the dark, secluded, Henryton Hospital at 1:30 in the morning. Instructors, acting as role players, had arrived earlier, and were already secreted throughout the upper floors of the main hospital building.

The line of vehicles turned left off of Henryton Road, into the first drive leading to the parking lot by the power plant. Each car extinguished it headlights as it made the turn from the road. The students slowly, and surreptitiously crept down the drive, and backed into a parking space, as if readying themselves for inspection.

Standing with his arms folded across his chest, Phillips was already waiting for the group as they arrived. He grabbed the first student to exit his vehicle and in a low voice said, "Get everybody together, pick a group leader and have him report to me for a brief."

Within minutes Keith Miller, the Delaware State Trooper, ran to where Phillips was waiting.

"You have a hostage situation at the hospital, start gathering your intel," Phillips said.

"How many bad guys?" Miller asked.

"Three maybe more."

"Number of hostages?"

"At least two."

The questioning continued for another few minutes. Phillips was intentionally evasive with his answers, knowing that in real life, the information you initially received, was limited and quite often completely inaccurate. As Phillips provided bits and pieces of data, Miller scribbled the information down in a pocket-sized notebook.

"Your snipers have already deployed. HNT has made contact and negotiations are ongoing," Phillips added, referring to the hostage negotiators.

Miller returned to brief the 14 remaining members of the class, "Last one guys. We've got to pull together for this final scenario. I know everyone's dead tired, but let's keep our shit together. You know they're going to try and screw with us, so keep your head on a swivel. Keep your weapons up and covering any windows. Rear guard, make sure they don't get behind us.

The group had wondered why they had not run more scenarios in the expansive main hospital building. The only time they had been allowed inside, was for the flashlight exercise in the dank basement. They now realized the instructors wanted to maintain an advantage, and not allow them to see the layout of the building they were about to assault.

"If I recall, the area around the building is open for more than one hundred feet in all directions. That's a pain in the ass for all of us to cross undetected. There may be an area at the rear that backs up to the woods. It might be a slightly shorter distance," Miller added.

Mund who had been tasked as assistant team leader suggested, "If we circle our way around through the woods, and continue down near the stream, we can make our way back up the hill, and stay concealed."

"Sounds good, but I want us to have a foothold in the building before first light. I don't want to be crossing so much open ground in daylight."

"Then we need to get moving. It's going to take awhile to maneuver around and get into position."

The languid group embarked upon their final mission of a three week excursion. Their numbers had dwindled in previous weeks, and each remaining student was fixated on completing this one last hurdle.

The team formed a modified wedge formation as they cautiously patrolled through the woods to their final staging area. With first light only minutes away, Miller moved small groups across the open terrain to the hospital. Once in place, the team would establish a security perimeter, and await the results of negotiations. It was a foregone conclusion that their group would be employed in some type of hostage rescue. Now it was a waiting game—gather whatever additional intel they could—and wait.

Word finally came from Phillips, "Negotiations have broken down. You're cleared to initiate."

The silence on the first floor, where the team had their position, was unnerving. However, it did make Miller more confident that the area was uninhabited and he could quickly clear the remainder of the floor.

"Mike, take your squad and clear the east staircase. My squad will take the west," Miller ordered.

"Okay, once on the second floor do you want to clear eastward down the hall toward me? I'll hold the staircase," Mund added.

"Yeah, that may be the best way to handle it."

Miller took Weaver and the remainder of his squad and began methodically moving up the west-side staircase.

At the same time, Mund and his team were advancing up the other. Once in place, they took up positions so that their suspects could not escape past their location.

At the top of the staircase, Miller's team stopped and listened. There was no talking between suspects, no sobbing from hostages.

"Danny, I'm putting you on point," Miller whispered. "Same drill as we did in the basement last week, but with no lights. Good criss-cross coverage."

Staying low, Weaver slowly opened the door from the staircase to the second floor hallway, just enough to get a visual of the room opposite their position. No movement was noted in either the room or the corridor. With cover man in tow, Weaver moved quickly across the hall and cleared his first assignment.

As he established his cover position looking down the hallway, something caught Weaver's eye. The light from their end of the hall was catching it at just the right angle. He squinted slightly, blinked his eyes to be sure. *Son of a bugger* thought Weaver. Getting Miller's attention across the hall, Weaver held the first two fingers of his left hand up to his eyes and then pointed toward the barely discernible piece of mono-filament line. It was stretched tightly across the hallway about six inches above the floor; one end most likely attached to a booby trap. Miller nodded slightly and smiled. Although the device would be inert—having no real explosive capability—it would probably set off some type of alarm to let the suspects—instructors—know their position. In bypassing the device, they would maintain the element of surprise and keep their opposing force off balance. In a real incident, they would most likely have the bomb squad come in and disable the trap prior to progressing.

The students maneuvered past the booby trap, and continued clearing rooms down the corridor. Miller could see the doors to the east staircase where Mund had his squad stationed. He knew that if he could clear to that point any bad guys on this floor would probably be trapped. But this place was like a maze. There were rooms leading to other rooms and small passageways that could allow someone to flank their position. The entire team of students knew they could not let down their guard.

Suddenly, they heard movement from a room past the east staircase. *Shit, they don't know we're here*, thought Miller. He quickly considered his options. They had the initiative—tactical advantage. The known route of escape was covered, however there might be another path the team had not seen. If they move closer, the suspects may hear the movements and their advantage would be blown.

Electing to seize on the element of surprise Miller announced, "Suspect come out with your hands up!"

Unexpectedly, there was a banging noise and Chuck

Tucker, one of the instructors acting as a bad guy, came running from the room heading for the east staircase. Attempting to pull-up his pants, Tucker tripped and fell face first to the corridor floor with his pants falling to his knees. Unbeknownst to all involved, Tucker had been hiding in the men's room when, at the most inappropriate of times, he actually needed to utilize the facilities.

Surprised by the students advance, and embarrassed by his predicament, he attempted to make his escape to the relative safety of the third floor. The students moved quickly to secure the now red-faced detainee.

"Guys don't do this! I was taking a dump; let me go," Tucker pleaded.

The entire group, with the exception of Tucker, was roaring with laughter. With his pants still around his knees, six students hoisted the 6 foot tall, 200 pound, burly SWAT guy to their shoulders.

"Don't you dare! I'll kick your asses! Let me go!" Tucker screamed.

Carrying him down the stairs and out the door, Tucker was dumped face-down in a small plot of grass.

"You bastards! None of you will graduate!"

With the commotion heard throughout the complex the entire cadre was now outside, their attention directed toward the turmoil near the parking lot. By now everyone was in tears laughing at Tucker's misfortune.

Not known for his sense of humor, even Phillips cracked a smile announcing, "Well, I don't think we will ever recover and continue on with *this* exercise. I say we call it a day." Adding, "Tucker, pull your damn pants up!"

Looking toward Weaver, Mund said, "Buddy, I think that means we're done!"

With a broad smile Weaver responded, "Yeah, and I have the lumps, bumps, bruises, and deformities to prove it."

Mund slapped Weaver on the back, "I think we need a beer."

"They're in the cooler at the house. Let's stow our gear and get out of here!"

The following day was graduation. Kathy accompanied Weaver to the small function at the team's office. She was very proud of his accomplishments. As they walked through the door of the small classroom where it had all begun three weeks ago, Gunny approached Weaver and, shaking his hand, said, "Congratulations doc. Glad to have you aboard."

Although he was just a paramedic the term had its roots in the military where team medics were often reverently given the nickname. Kathy was captivated to see each member of the team approach and offer similar praise to Weaver—with the exception of Phillips.

As the class had started, so did it end, nothing lavish, just a very short and simple ceremony. Each student was called forward to receive a certificate that was held in a padded diploma folio emblazoned with the Police Department's insignia. As is typical, the graduates were called alphabetically with Weaver being the last.

Phillips loosely shook Weaver's hand and presented him

with the certificate saying, "Don't get too comfortable. You're only here for six months."

CHAPTER 7

Nash played it cool and did not call Christy on the day following their date. It was difficult to wait out the 48 hours. On more than one occasion he had the phone in his hand but decided against hitting the send button.

This was a game. No matter what he felt, he knew he had to get Christy's infatuation with him to grow. *Show them a good time and then don't call*, he thought. *She'll be eating out of my hand. Maybe I should write a book someday about how to manipulate women.*

Nash considered himself a ladies' man. He knew he was good looking and had a killer smile. All attributes that younger women—girls—could not resist. He was well aware of what buttons needed to be pushed to get what he wanted.

It had been two days since her date with Nash when Christy retrieved the phone from her purse. Answering on the second ring, "Hello?" She had not recognized the number as she examined the display, but instantly recognized the sexy voice on the other end of the line.

"Hey, gorgeous!" Nash answered.

"I was beginning to wonder if I was going to hear from you again."

"Well, I'm a very busy guy. All this business stuff keeps me hopping," Nash responded wanting to keep Christy intrigued.

He had not actually told her much about himself during their first date. What information he had given had been intentionally vague. Actually, Rick Nash had not had a meaningful job in over 6 months. His last employer had fired him for his poor attitude and unreliability. Most of his money came from his mother, who worked very hard and was more than willing to provide her son only the best, even if he was 27 years old.

"If things go right, I should be free this weekend. Would you like to get together? It's supposed to be great weather," Nash inquired, already knowing he had her on the hook.

"I'd love to!"

"Great, Saturday at eight. See you then," Nash said.

Ending the call, he tossed the phone on the table and slid back into the couch with a wide smile across his face. *College girl, check that one off the list.*

Nash arrived at Christy's house at the agreed-upon time. As Christy opened the door, Nash smiled broadly and held out a single rose.

With a smile of her own, Christy accepted the gift, "You're so sweet!"

What she did not know was that the flower was stolen from a nearby grocery store and the attached note had been recycled. In fact, the money used to buy the roses left at Christy's doorstep after the first date had been stolen from Nash's mother.

It was a warm evening for early spring so the two strolled through the crowded streets of Towson. The restaurants and drinking establishments were frequented by Towson University students. Nash took Christy's hand as they trotted across the busy intersection at York Road and Towsontowne Boulevard.

"How about some ice cream?" Nash asked.

"Love it," Christy said.

Nash opened the door for Christy as they entered Mistey's Ice Cream shop on Alleghany Avenue. Christy could not get over Nash's manners. At the young age of 19 she had never had anyone treat her so nicely. After grabbing two ice cream cones, they walked the busy streets and enjoyed the light conversation and bantering. Finally, they walked back to Christy's house.

"Are you doing anything tomorrow?" Nash asked.

"I work tomorrow morning and I really have a lot of studying to do."

"Come on, you can get together for a little while."

"I wish I could, but I really need to stay on top of my studies."

Nash continued his relentless pressure until Christy acquiesced.

"Six o'clock. I'll fix us a sandwich, but then you have to go," Christy said.

Smiling and making an 'x' across his heart Nash said, "I promise. As soon as we eat, I'll hit the road."

Nash gave Christy a kiss on the lips as he left for the evening, "I'll see you tomorrow!"

The following afternoon Nash arrived at Christy's house.

Once inside the door he gave her a kiss and said, "Hi! I missed you!"

She hugged him tightly, "Missed you too!"

"Where's Jackie?"

"She decided to visit her parents in Virginia."

With Christy home alone, Nash began scheming to get her into bed. At nine o'clock, with his mission accomplished, Nash was in his Mustang and heading home. For her part, Christy was already beginning to question her decisions. She had not completed any study work that was required for Monday's classes. *But what a good looking guy, and he is so good in so many ways* thought Christy as she lay in her bed.

The two began phoning and dating each other regularly. Christy was mesmerized by Nash's small gifts of affection. The dates—picnics, horseback riding, concerts—were so much fun. She was dating a hot guy with a hot car.

One Tuesday afternoon, Christy was leaving the Student Union Building at Towson University.

As she walked the path toward Hawkins Hall she looked up in surprise, "Rick, what're you doing here?"

"You didn't answer your phone last night. I thought something was wrong."

"I told you I had a paper due and needed to finish it up. And besides, how did you know to look for me over here?"

"I saw your schedule lying on the table a while back and knew your next class was in Hawkins. But, that's beside the point. When I call or text you need to answer."

"Rick, there are going to be times that I'm not going to be able to drop everything and answer the phone or go out."

"No," Nash retorted, "we're a couple and couples let each other know what's going on."

"Look, I have to get to class. We'll talk more later."

Christy quickly made her way up the path and into the building for her next class. Nash slowly returned to his car, periodically looking over his shoulder to ensure she was actually going to class and did not have something else on her agenda.

That evening, Jackie and Christy were eating dinner together.

Christy looked up from her plate and said, "You know, Rick stopped by school today."

"Really?" Jackie said.

"He was outside of Hawkins waiting for me. Said he was concerned that I hadn't answered the phone last night."

"And?"

"Well, I told him I had a paper due and couldn't talk. He said we're a couple and I need to answer his calls."

"How did he know where you were going to be?" Jackie asked.

"He said he saw my schedule lying on the table."

"Aren't you creeped out by that, Christy? That he knows your schedule; where you're going to be and when?"

"Well…"

"Christy, this guy is too domineering. You mentioned last week that he's been calling and texting at all hours of the day and night—while you're at work and in class—and he gets pissed when you don't answer! You need to get out of this."

"I know he's a bit controlling, but he treats me so well. I've never been with anyone like him. You just don't understand."

"What do you know about him?" Jackie said.

"He talks about some of the places he's been, some of his cars."

"All superfluous bullshit! What do you know about his background? Where does he work? What school did he graduate from? How about his family?"

"Okay, so I don't know much about him."

"I'm telling you, you need to get out of this or you'll regret it. You and I have been friends for quite a while; I don't want to see you get hurt."

Holding her hands up, Christy relented, "I'll talk to him and try to slow things down."

Jackie wanted her to completely break it off with Nash. Although the guy seemed to be the male version of Emily Post with his manners, and certainly wasn't hard on the eyes, he was also creepy. But she did not want to push Christy too hard and damage their friendship. *I just hope she opens her eyes*, Jackie thought.

That Friday, Christy decided to talk to Nash about their relationship. As Nash drove her home from an Orioles baseball game, Christy got up the nerve to broach the subject, "Rick, I want to talk about *us* for a minute. We've been seeing a lot of each other over the past couple of weeks.

"Yeah, baby. Hope you've been having a good time."

"I have, but…"

Christy saw a change in Nash's facial expression. This was not one that she had seen previously.

With a look of disdain, Nash said, "Don't even think about breaking up with me!"

Scared, she quickly responded, "No! No! No! I'm falling behind on my schoolwork. I think we just need to slow down …"

Nash slammed on the brakes in the fast lane of York Road, nearly getting rear-ended. "Are you seeing somebody else?" he yelled.

Christy began to cry, "Rick you're going to get us killed!"

Tightly grabbing her arm Nash said, "You bitch! If you're screwing around on me, I swear-"

Christy had not seen this side of Nash. The manners, the politeness—they were all gone. Nash was in a rage, and she needed to get away. She was able to pull free and leaped from the car and ran the two blocks back home.

Still crying, Christy ran into the house, closing and locking the door behind her.

Running down the stairs, Jackie screamed, "Christy, are you okay? What happened?"

In between sobs, Christy was able to get out a brief description of the terrifying event, "I tried to talk to Rick about slowing things down. He blew up, accused me of sleeping with someone else. I thought he was going to hit me, so I jumped from the car and ran here."

Jackie put her arms around Christy, "It's going to be all right. You're safe now."

"I'm sorry, Jackie. I should have listened to you from the start."

Suddenly, a loud, horrific bang came at the front door. Startled, the two girls began screaming.

"Christy," Nash yelled, "let me in so we can talk. I'm sorry! I love you!"

"Get out of here!" Jackie screamed.

"Stay out of this. It's none of your business. This is between Christy and me."

"Leave, Rick! She doesn't want to talk to you or see you."

"Rick, leave me alone. Go away!" Christy added.

Lowering his voice to a more conciliatory tone, Nash said, "Christy, I lost my temper. I'm sorry. It was a very stressful week at work. I didn't mean to take it out on you. I love you and don't want to lose you. Let me in so we can talk."

Jackie looked at Christy, shaking her head and mouthing, "No!"

"Rick, I'm not going to let you in. Maybe we can talk in a

---

few days, but you're not coming in here tonight," said Christy.

Infuriated, Nash began beating on the door once again.

"Nash, leave or I'm calling the cops!" Jackie exclaimed.

"That would be a serious mistake. A very serious mistake."

Nash fell silent, looking at the door as if he had x-ray vision and was peering right through the wood and metal portal. His mind was racing. Finally, he retreated to his haphazardly parked car, "This isn't over. Not by a long stretch, bitch!"

CHAPTER 8

Weaver was not quite ready to go operational with the SWAT team. Prior to finishing his three week adventure he had enrolled in a tactical emergency medical services—TEMS —class. The five-day school for paramedics and EMT's assigned to SWAT teams was sponsored by the military. Who better to teach how to provide medical care when you are being shot at?

Over the past three weeks, Weaver's training had focused entirely on the tactics used by a SWAT team to complete their law enforcement mission. By understanding the team's duties and responsibilities he could more effectively complete his own mission—to keep them alive. So this week would be a re-orientation to his primary role of medic.

It was another early morning roll-call. Class was to begin at 0700 on Monday morning. Weaver fought the dreaded traffic on Interstate 495 outside Washington D.C. Still in the "if you're on time, you're late" mode, Weaver arrived at the Uniformed Services University of Health Sciences—USUHS —on Jones Bridge Road and Wisconsin Avenue with time to spare. This was the military's medical school, located on the campus with the famed Walter Reed National Military Medical Center.

The red and white blooms on the azalea bushes at the

front of the school made it a postcard moment. Weaver was already impressed as he approached the main gate. Once his credentials had been checked at the guard post, he pulled into the parking garage below the four two-story buildings that encompassed the USUHS complex. An enclosed walkway connected the top floors of the structures that surrounded a large courtyard.

As Weaver walked through the door of the lecture hall, where the class was to be held, he could immediately sense a stark contrast to the atmosphere of the previous three weeks. He prepared himself a coffee from a large stainless steel urn in the corner of the room. Climbing the stairs, he found a comfortable spot in the middle of the stadium seating and took it all in. Although there were no morning PT sessions, the days would be nonetheless arduous. Examining the schedule in the front of the three-inch binder he was given at the door, none of the days were done prior to 7 in the evening. But, from all appearances the schedule was packed full of interesting lectures and exercises.

Weaver quickly realized there were people attending from throughout the U.S. by looking at the patches on their shoulders. The director of the program, Jim Vincent, even introduced two attendees from London. *If they came across the pond to attend this, it must be good*, thought Weaver.

Following some brief introductions and instructions Vincent said, "Okay, everything off of your desk tops. We will be giving out a 50 question pre-test. You have 60 minutes."

Well, maybe this isn't all that different from SWAT school. The questions ranged from basic medical care to intravenous fluid replacement calculations for a dehydrated patient. There were questions on the forensic examination of gunshot wounds and things like stippling and marginal abrasion.

Weaver was sweating bullets with some of the questions *Am I supposed to already know this stuff? I'm going to look like a real idiot.* He was later relieved to find out that the test was merely a gauge with which to measure their progress at the end of the week.

The initial lectures focused on a medic's responsibility to his team. Weaver began to understand that he was like the team trainer and doctor for a professional football team. He was not only responsible for treating penetrating trauma—being shot or stabbed—but also for the myriad of other illnesses and injuries that could befall a professional athlete. Since the team was responsible for staying in a high state of physical fitness, they often times had the same health issues as a running back for the Ravens, or a shortstop for the Orioles. The medic was even responsible for telling the team what to drink, when to drink it, and how much, in order to stay hydrated. One of the early signs of dehydration was agitation. The last thing the team leader wanted was an operator making poor decisions because he did not have enough to drink. He was even responsible for treating a team member if he ate the wrong thing just before a raid and was now suffering from diarrhea.

The brand of medicine taught here was totally different, and flew in the face of many of the standards that were held in the civilian medical world. One of the biggest was the use of tourniquets. Civilian EMS administrators and educators thought tourniquets to be an instrument of the devil, and did not even teach how to use them to new medical providers.

But the military had been handing them out like candy. Each soldier was issued a pre-formed tourniquet that was carried with them when they went on patrol. If hit in the arm or leg, the black strap of the device could be placed around the injured extremity and tightened with the attached metal rod. It was a hell of a lot better than trying to pack the bullet hole with gauze, and applying direct pressure to control the bleeding. Generally, the bad guys did not politely stop shooting while you tried to treat your partner.

Weaver also learned about some new medications including Fentanyl lollipops for controlling pain. With the exception of aspirin and nitroglycerin, given for heart attacks, paramedics only used injectable medications. *Sucking on a "lollipop" did not seem like something a SWAT guy would take kindly to.* Paramedics throughout the country were familiar with giving morphine for pain. The EMS medical directors generally maintained tight control over its administration. If too much was administered you could stop breathing. Fentanyl, was a pain medication that the military was having great success with. Even the way it was administered was interesting. The lollipop was taped to the injured soldier's forefinger and stuck in his mouth. If he got too much medication, and started to pass-out, his finger would fall from his mouth and prevent him overdosing on the drug. With a smile on his face Weaver thought, *this is some really cool stuff!*

There was also a good lecture on the planning that was necessary for each operation or mission. The SWAT guys themselves planned out each raid they went on, and the medic was responsible to have a plan as well. He was required to develop medical intelligence on the area of operation—AO—in which the team would be working.

Knowing the location of the closest hospital was a no-brainer, but Weaver also learned that not all hospitals are created equal. Taking someone who had been shot three times and had a collapsed lung to a 25-bed hospital in rural Montana was probably not a good idea. But he had to know which hospitals could handle such an emergency. That's where gathering medical intel came into play.

The medic also needed to know what diseases could impact the team. He learned that Lyme Disease could be a problem for the team sniper lying in the Maryland woods, but not a problem for someone in Texas, as it is mostly found in the Northeast portion of the country. The Texas guy just had to worry about snakes and scorpions. More than knowing the problem existed was knowing how to mitigate the issue altogether. Countermeasures for specific problems might include vaccinations, or something as simple as spraying down your clothes with a product called Premethrin, and any exposed skin with insect repellant containing DEET, to repel disease carrying vectors.

Although the "Ten Commandments of Foot Care" was pretty funny, Weaver was unimpressed when it came time to hear about foot disease and extended operations.

Maybe the military stuff is a little overblown. When am I going to worry about our guys having their boots on for too long or their feet being wet? Let's be real.

A question came up from Vincent in the Sensory Deprived Physical Assessment lecture, "How do you tell the difference between blood and urine through the gloved hand, if it's dark and you can't see?"

Weaver's hand shot up, "Taste?"

The entire class let out a roar at Weaver's comment.

"You and I need to talk after the class!" Vincent responded. "Seriously, however, in the situations in which you will find yourselves, using any kind of light to examine your patient, could get you killed. A medic in Iraq was picked off by a sniper when he tried to use a laryngoscope to intubate a non-breathing, injured soldier."

Vincent was referring to a process where a breathing tube is placed in the lungs. The medic had been attempting to use a medical device that had a small 2.5 volt bulb on the tip to allow him to see down the throat.

"Many of you are familiar with the device. The bulb is not much bigger than the head of a pencil. That small amount of light make you a target. You must be able to assess your patient without the use of your sight. You will need to rely on all of your other senses to determine the injuries," Vincent continued.

"We will have a practical exercise on the procedure for conducting such an assessment. You will presented with a patient having at least two injuries, lying in a darkened room. You need to crawl, blindfolded, to the downed person, and determine their injuries. They may be a downed officer or a suspect. They may, or may not, be armed. And, Mr. Weaver, you will not be the first in line for the exercise. I think you need to watch a few others."

"Thank you, sir! Glad to!" responded Weaver to the laughter of the class.

On Wednesday morning the class broke into small groups for a variety of practical exercises.

"Good morning. My name is Mark King. I'm a physician here at USUHS," said Dr. King, a tall Naval Academy Grad with a Texas accent. "We are going to be doing some suturing and skin stapling today. You should have some pigs' feet sitting in front of you."

"Do we get to barbecue these after we're done?" asked someone from the back of the room.

"I get the same smart-ass question every class. I'm thinking not, on the barbecue," Dr. King responded.

Weaver learned the basics about each approach to closing a laceration. The class started with what types of wounds he could close, and which ones needed to be seen at a hospital emergency department. They learned how to debride and anesthetize the area, and then practiced on the pigs' feet. Although he did well in the exercise, Weaver was unsure he could close up a team mate.

"Sticking an IV needle in someone is one thing, this is a whole different level," Weaver said to Dr. King.

"You're right. We certainly don't expect you to be proficient in this after an hour of practice. Get some clinical time in the emergency department of your local hospital and do some suturing. That's the only way you'll get the proficiency you need."

One of the final classes in the week was on dental injuries taught by Tim Barber, a Navy dentist.

"Although dental injuries are not life threatening, they can be disabling, due to the intensity of pain. With every team member being critical to the successful outcome of your mission, you can't afford to have someone incapacitated due to such an injury. We will be demonstrating some simple fixes for the most common dental emergencies," Barber said.

Weaver overheard one of the students behind him whisper, "If I wanted to be a dentist, I would have flunked out of paramedic school!"

Thank goodness, Barber did not hear that comment. Barber would be doing the demonstration on him; even though it was pretty funny, thought Weaver.

After becoming familiar with the anatomy of the teeth, Barber covered the various types of dental fractures, and how you could mix a small amount of clove oil with dental cement to fill the lost portion of tooth. They even learned how to use a paperclip, along with the mixture, to hold a loose tooth in place.

Weaver and the rest of the class practiced their new-found skills on clay models of a person's teeth.

By the end of the week, Weaver was amazed at the skills he had learned. There was a lot more to being a medic for a SWAT team than he had ever imagined. He would now be operating at a level far beyond that of a normal paramedic on the street. Although he hoped none of his friends would become sick or injured, he knew the probability was high that his skills would become useful.

I just have to convince Phillips of my usefulness prior to the end of six months, thought Weaver on his drive back to Baltimore.

CHAPTER 9

Randy Young had not been to the Towson Diner since he picked up Nash, the day he had been released from jail. Towson was not an area he frequented. He was from the east side of the County, and preferred neighborhood bars that could produce a good bar brawl or two on Saturday night.

Finding a booth in the back corner of the restaurant, he plopped down and put his left foot up on the seat cushion. With his left arm over the back of the seat and his right arm resting on the table, Young scanned the area looking for Christy Moore. Nash had told him she would probably be working the evening shift on Monday.

Nash had repeatedly tried to contact Christy, but to no avail. She would not return his calls or text messages and no one answered the door at her house. So, his next step was to have his good friend Young, pay Christy a visit. Perhaps impress upon her that rejecting Rick Nash was just not something that was done.

Leaving the kitchen with a customer's food order, Christy felt someone watching. After serving the food, she turned to notice Young glowering at her.

Approaching, she sternly asked, "What are you doing here?"

"Just stopped by to get a late-night snack," Young responded sarcastically.

"Bullshit, I know better. You and Rick need to leave me alone."

"Hey, Rick loves you. Give him a second chance."

"He showed his true colors last week. That is not something I want to be involved in. I've fallen behind on my schoolwork and besides, I already met someone else."

Christy had not met anyone, but thought Nash might give up and move on if he thought she was dating someone.

Young grabbed Christy's arm. "Not a smart move, Rick doesn't take kindly to rejection. But, then again, maybe Rick would be interested in your roommate. What's her name?"

Pulling away from Young's grasp Christy yelled, "Leave her out of this!"

As Christy ran for the kitchen, the restaurant customers all turned to see what the commotion was about.

"You got a problem?" Young said defiantly to the onlookers.

The manager approached, "Sir?"

Rising from the booth to leave, Young said, "I think you need to teach your waitresses how to treat their customers."

Once in his car, Young called Nash on his cell phone, "Rick, it's Randy. Caught her a bit by surprise, showing up at work like that. But no dice. Still doesn't want to see you. She wouldn't budge."

"She doesn't know who she's screwing with!" Nash answered.

"One other thing. She says she's seeing someone else."

Nash flew into a rage, throwing a glass that shattered against a wall, "That whore! I'll fix her and the little prick she's seeing! I treated her like a queen and this is what I get?"

"Dude, you need to chill. You're going to pop a vessel in your brain or something."

Calming slightly, Nash said, "I may need your help."

"Whatever you need, bud."

"Thanks. I'll call and let you know."

Nash sat staring at the television most of the evening, without really watching it. His mind was racing; his head began to hurt.

He flipped his phone open and dialed Christy's number.

No answer. He threw the phone down and spat, "Damn it!"

Later, he lay awake in bed, looking at the ceiling most of the night. After finally falling asleep, he awoke early with the same splitting headache that seemed to push his eyes outward from his head.

Again, he tried dialing Christy's phone. Still no answer. The rage continued building inside him, like it had so many times before, when things fell apart with other girls. Finally, he could no longer contain his anger.

I'll teach the bitch a lesson, he decided.

Gathering a few things, Nash left his house, slamming the

door behind him. He sped away in his Mustang, heading for Towson.

Slowly, he cruised through the small parking lot at the Towson Diner. Seeing Christy's car Nash said to himself, *There it is. Before the night's out she will be sorry she screwed with me.*

Pulling beside the building, Nash didn't bother to take a parking space, knowing he would not be long. Throwing open the Diner's front door, he quickly eyed Christy.

Hearing the crash of the door hitting the wall, Christy turned to see Nash coming at her, "Leave me alone, Rick!" she said.

Nash spoke not a word. He walked up to Christy, backhanded her across the face, grabbed her by the arm and began heading for the door. Dazed, Christy put up little resistance.

Seeing the assault, the manager quickly approached Nash, "Hey, let her go!"

Without any hesitation, Nash reached under his shirt and into his waistband. With his hand firmly wrapped around a 9mm Glock semiautomatic pistol, Nash methodically raised the weapon to the innocent man's chest and pulled the trigger. Nash exhibited no emotion, the rage he manifested the previous evening was gone. There was merely a quiet resolve.

The 40-year old man fell to the floor. Blood oozed from a hole in his left chest. His eyes were open as if in disbelief; his mouth agape. Within seconds his vital systems ceased to function.

The patrons in the restaurant looked on in horror and disbelief.

Christy began to scream as Nash pushed her through the door, "Stop! You killed him! My God! You killed him!"

Hearing Christy's screams and sobbing, a Good Samaritan in the parking lot tried to intervene as the two exited the building. Once again, without hesitation, Nash raised the gun and fired twice, hitting the young man in the stomach and left shoulder.

Nash pushed Christy to the Mustang and opened the door. Christy began to regain some sense of the events that were unfolding and knew she had to escape. As she began to struggle, Nash smacked her beside the head with the pistol, opening a 3 inch gash on the right side of her head. He pushed her into the passenger seat and slammed the door shut.

CHAPTER 10

Weaver arrived at the SWAT team's office at 0700 hours on Monday morning. Knowing the first order of business would be a good workout with the rest of the team, he came dressed in his PT gear. He stopped momentarily to take in the sign that adorned the entry door.

Breaking News

The pity train just derailed at the intersection of Suck It Up & Move On, and crashed into *We All Have Problems* before coming to a complete stop at *Get The Hell Over It!* Any complaints about how we operate can be forwarded to 1-800-Boo-Hoo with Dr. Sniffles.

Reporting live from Quitchur Bitchin'!

Suck it up cupcake. Life doesn't revolve around you anyway!

The mood in the weight room was light. As Weaver entered, the greeting came quickly.

"Hey, Doc!" said Brett. "Welcome back! How did it go last week?"

Weaver began stretching. "Great class. Learned a good bit that I think can really help you guys. Hey, Gunny! They even showed a video of a Marine having an IV started in a bone in his lower leg."

Stopping in the middle of his pushups, Gunny asked, "What?"

"Yeah, it's called intraosseous infusion—used when you can't get a regular IV started. They use this thing that looks like a small Makita drill. And they drill the needle into the tibia bone in your leg."

"Bullshit!"

"Seriously! Of course they probably paid the dude a six-pack to allow them to do it."

"He was conscious?"

"Yeah, don't know if I could have done it. Probably would have passed out."

"Couldn't have been a Marine. A Marine wouldn't do something like that for less than two sixes. Must have been Army."

The rest of the gym roared in laughter at the banter between the Gunnery Sergeant and the newest member of the team.

Lying on the weight bench to begin his chest presses, Weaver noticed Phillips walk into the room.

Looking at Weaver, Phillips said, "My morning just keeps getting better. Weaver, when we're done PT, I need to see you."

"Yes, sir."

Bones was in the back of the room doing pull-ups and said, "Oh I can just feel the love."

"Knock it off Bones," Phillips responded.

"Talking about my pull-ups, Jack. Just love 'em," said Bones as he cranked out another.

It was a beautiful morning, and the 5-mile run came easy for Weaver as the team members meandered through Towson. They ran as a group and talked leisurely amongst each other. Catching up on family events of the previous weekend, Weaver felt like he'd been accepted as part of the group. Most new members to the team had to gain the respect of their peers. It seemed as though Weaver had already made it over that hurdle—with one exception.

Weaver adjusted his pace to catch up with Brett.

"Hey Brett. The first day of SWAT school you promised to fill me in on why Jack has a hard-on for me. This is getting old, coming in here everyday and having to put up with his attitude."

Keeping up his pace to complete a nine-minute mile, Brett said, "Do you remember the barricade last year on the east side, where the guy came out the back door, put the gun to his head and blew his brains out? It took the medic unit twelve minutes to get two blocks from the command post, where they were staged, to the back of the house where we were. Jack blew a gasket and has not had a warm and fuzzy for paramedics ever since."

"Brett, the medic unit wasn't given the right location by the command post. They went down the alleyway on the opposite side of the street and were blocked by parked cars. You know that; it wasn't their fault. Besides, that gives credence to having a medic right with you. You don't have to depend on anyone else."

"I know that, but Phillips still has a case of the ass over it. The only way you are going to change his mind, is to show him that you're an asset and not a liability. It's going to take time, hang in there. The rest of us are trying to help you as best we can. But in the end, only you can change his mind."

"Brett, I'll do my best. But, this shit is getting old."

After taking a warm shower, Weaver reported to Phillips' office. Knocking on the door frame, he stuck his head in the open door. "You wanted to see me?"

Phillips looked up from the raid plans he had been writing for ops later in the week, and said, "Have a seat, Weaver.

After Weaver was seated Phillips continued, "As I mentioned at graduation, you're here for six months. I must admit, I didn't expect you to make it through the school. And, at the end of the trial period, I also suspect you'll be returning to the Fire Department."

Knowing not to get into a challenge of wills, Weaver just nodded.

"While you're here, you'll do as I say. Do you understand?" Phillips continued.

"Yes, sir."

"Check with Gunny, I believe he has some equipment for you."

"Yes, sir. Thank you. Anything else?"

"No, not right now."

Weaver started to get up from the chair, but sat back down and said, "Jack, I know you don't want me here and I know you dislike paramedics in general. What happened last year on the east side is history. The medic unit was given the wrong location. That's common knowledge. It wasn't their fault and besides, from my understanding, there was nothing anyone could have done for the guy anyway."

"Look Weaver, I don't like my guys being put in that position. Who's going to take the fall for something like that —me and my guys."

"Jack, you're making my point for me. If I'm right there, I can take care of that stuff. It won't be on you and the others. Don't you get it?"

"Weaver, I don't have the time. I've got work to do. You're here for six months and then you're gone."

Weaver shook his head and unceremoniously rose and left the office. As he walked down the hall, Mike Mund approached. "Hey, Mike." Weaver said.

"Danny—how's it going, buddy? How was your medical class last week?"

"Good. What're you doing here?

"They had an opening on the team, and since I was the highest ranked person in the school, they brought me on. I start today."

"Excellent! Having another new guy will take some of the heat off me."

"Thanks. Love you, too."

Following his encounter with Mund, Weaver went down to the equipment area to meet Gunny. "Jack said you had some stuff for me, Gunny."

"Hey, Danny—come on in. I've got your body armor, both the concealable, that has a soft trauma plate, and your assault vest. Here's the plate for the assault vest."

"I feel like it's Christmas!" Weaver said.

"Well, if you say I look like old Saint Nick with a red nose and belly, I'll slug you!"

Holding his hands up, Weaver said, "Didn't hear it from me, but there's been talk."

"All right, smart-ass! Here's your *pistola*. I ought to shoot you in the foot, just on principle. It's the same type handgun as what you used in class. Make sure you know the serial number. Now, sign all this paperwork. You know, for the first day here, you're really pushing your luck!"

Raising his right eyebrow, Weaver said, "Sorry, won't happen again."

"Anything else you need?" Gunny asked.

"Common sense," Weaver said jokingly.

Leading Weaver toward the parking lot, Gunny said, "One final thing. Tucker got new wheels last week, so you'll be using his old Chevy Suburban."

Eyeing up the dark gray, 4-wheel-drive Suburban, Weaver said, "Thanks, Gunny."

"We cleaned it up as much as possible, but you still might

find a McDonald's bag or three under the seat. You know how Tucker can be.

"Better than seeing him with his pants down around his ankles," Weaver said.

"No doubt," Gunny laughed. "It was just serviced. All the lights, siren, and radio are in good working order."

Weaver began gathering the medical supplies he would require to support the team. The Fire Department's quartermaster was able to supply the cardiac medications he would carry, which were similar to the inventory of most paramedic units. However, over-the-counter (OTC) meds like Motrin, Sudafed, and Immodium that he needed to fill his expanded pharmacopoeia had to be acquired at the local pharmacy.

He had also been able to finagle some supplies from vendors at the previous week's medical school. One item he was able to acquire, called Celox, was not available at the corner drug store and was not in the Fire Department's inventory. This hemostatic agent was a granular blood clotting substance that, when poured into an open wound, would stop uncontrolled bleeding within minutes. After reading various studies and other documentation, Weaver had become impressed with how it worked

Late in the afternoon, he began packing medical gear in his various packs and bags. As he slipped tourniquets, Celox, and other life-saving supplies into his pack, he began to reflect on the seriousness of his job and its implications. When riding a medic unit or fire engine, he was able to be empathetic with a patient without becoming personally involved, since the person was a stranger. Yet he began to realize that treating one of these guys would be much more difficult, because they were friends of his. He desperately hoped he would never hear the call, "Medic up," and need to use the advanced life-saving skills he had acquired on any of his comrades.

CHAPTER 11

Weaver was pulling into the driveway at home when his phone beeped with a text message. As he pulled the device from his belt holster and examined the screen, his heart rate jumped.

SWAT Callout; Towson Diner; 718 York Rd.;

Armed Robbery.

Weaver turned on his emergency lights and threw the truck into reverse, tires screeching as he backed out of the driveway. Making his way to Route 140, Weaver headed for Interstate 795 and Baltimore County. *This is unusual. Why would they be hitting us up for an armed robbery?*

Weaver's personal cell phone began to ring. Without looking at the callback number he answered, "Weaver."

"Danny, I saw you pull into the driveway in a Suburban and then you left," Kathy said.

"I can't talk. We have a callout."

"But you worked all day. I have dinner ready."

"Sorry, but I may have to work all night, too. I have to go," Weaver said as he hit the "End" button on his phone.

Immediately his phone began to ring again. Looking at the display he saw it was Kathy calling again.

"I don't need this," Weaver mumbled, and he threw the phone on the dash.

He turned his vehicle-mounted radio to Precinct 6's channel. This was the frequency for the Towson area and the radio traffic was increasingly bad. Weaver listened intently.

"Six-ten to Communications," said the patrol sergeant.

"Go ahead, Six-ten."

"Medic unit on the scene advises both shooting victims deceased. I'm going to need Homicide and the Crime Lab."

"Okay, we'll notify Homicide and the Crime Lab. SWAT is also en route."

"Six-ten, ten-four. Also, I'll have a description of the shooter and the female hostage shortly. It'll be coming out via the on-board computer."

What had started as an armed robbery at the diner was now a hostage situation—a mobile one. One of the worst scenarios a team can face is a bad guy with a hostage on the move. The police are unable to negotiate, because they rarely have an idea of who the suspect is. The SWAT team can't cordon off the scene and deploy, because the suspect will be gone before they even get in the area.

There were already two people dead—the restaurant manager and a male bystander who had tried to rescue the hostage, a young female waitress.

Weaver stepped on the accelerator a little more as the information came across the radio. The drone of his siren continued as he sped toward Towson. The red and blue concealed LED lights above the windshield flashed consistently, moving traffic out of his way. He still had another 30 minutes travel time before he made it to the neighborhood where events were continuing to unravel.

The tactical channel on his portable radio crackled to life. The rest of the team was signing on.

"Phillips is up."

"Brett's on."

"Gunny's up."

Picking up his own radio, Weaver said, "Weaver's up."

The roll-call continued through the rest of the team.

Phillips gave a quick briefing over the radio. "What we have thus far is one suspect—white male, mid-twenties, 5 foot-nine, about one-hundred eighty pounds. No ID on him as yet. The female hostage is a restaurant employee, Christy Moore. She's five foot-four, 100 pounds. They were last seen leaving the Diner at York Road and Lambourne, heading north toward Interstate 695. Patrol is working on the vehicle description. Has anybody heard anything else?"

With no response, Phillips continued, "Let's hope patrol bags this guy. But I'm not optimistic, this isn't starting out well." Radio chatter across the encrypted tactical channels was a little less formal than it was on the standard radio frequencies used by patrol.

With this, his first day of being operational, Weaver hadn't had time to piece together the array of things he needed to accomplish while en route to an incident.

Damn, I feel like Kenny Brooks. His first day as a newly promoted lieutenant on Engine 54, he was faced with a head-on collision between and Amtrak train and a freight train. This is a hell of a way to start out!

Weaver put his mind to the tasks at hand. He had a vehicle-mounted mobile radio, which usually remained on the frequency of the precinct where the incident was occurring. This allowed each of the team members to keep abreast of the situation as it evolved. Then there was the portable radio that remained on one of the team's encrypted tactical channels. The encryption kept the bad guys—and the news media—from monitoring the team's movements. He also had a vehicle-mounted laptop computer, a Panasonic Toughbook, which was critical to his job of gathering medical intel.

Weaver punched the telephone number for the Fire Department's communications center into his phone.

"Communications," the dispatcher answered, "this line is recorded. How can I help you?"

"This is Weaver." He knew the wail of his siren could be heard clearly in the background of his call. "We have a hostage situation in Towson. What do the hospitals look like?"

"Greater Baltimore Medical Center is on by-pass; they've been swamped all night. It's been a little crazy out there."

"What about Shock Trauma?"

"They are still accepting patients."

"I may need to have a medic unit for standby. Once I get to the scene, I'll give you an update."

"Thanks, Danny. Stay safe!"

Weaver never heard the dispatcher's final words; he had

already disconnected. He had quickly become like most of the other operators on the team—he wanted the information quickly and succinctly, no need to include much in the way of bullshit.

Next up was the air medevac service. The State Police handled all scene medevacs, and Weaver knew most of the pilots and medics working the choppers. As with any profession, there were some good crews and then there were some outstanding crews. He knew his guys would only get the best treatment from the air crews.

The state trooper assigned the evening tour as medic answered the call. "Trooper 1, Sergeant Gabriele." Gabriele had been with the State Police for ten years and was one of their best aviation medics. His attention spiked when he heard the siren in the background, even before Weaver got a word out.

"Jim, it's Danny. We have a hostage situation—mobile—in Towson. I'm sure our chopper is in the air for surveillance, but are you guys available for a medevac if it turns to shit?"

"We are right now, but let me know if we should go on standby and hold for your mission."

The medevac choppers did not routinely go on standby for possible missions; their theory was, you either want us or you don't. But for high-threat law enforcement missions, they had an unwritten exception to the rule.

"Not yet, we don't know exactly where this thing is going to end up. I'll give you a call when we have this guy cornered," Weaver said.

Christy sobbed. "Why are you doing this? Let me go. I'll do anything you want!"

Nash seemed to be in a trance as he drove eastward through the streets of Towson. He had originally headed for the Interstate, but at the last minute decided to make the right onto Fairmount Avenue and take the local arteries to avoid the State Police patrols on the major highways.

The wail of sirens now filled the air, as police and paramedics raced to the scene of the carnage he had inflicted upon the unsuspecting diners.

Christy looked at Nash anxiously. The index finger of his right hand rested on the trigger of the handgun. She knew that any untoward action on her part would almost certainly mean her death. She also knew she had to get away from this madman.

Nash knew the police would have a description of his car. *I need to dump this thing and get fresh wheels.* Spying a Toyota Camry at a stop sign at Beaverbank Circle and Cromwell Bridge Road, Nash shot across the intersection and blocked in the unsuspecting motorist with his Mustang. He grabbed Christy by her bloodied and knotted hair and dragged her across the console between the seats.

"Rick, stop! Somebody help!" Christy screamed.

With his left arm around her throat, Nash dragged Christy toward the boxed-in Camry. Nash saw a woman in the driver seat, but did not immediately see the young child beside her. The 32-year old mother had just picked up her son from daycare. The four-year old was in a booster seat beside his mom.

Raising the 9mm toward the Camry's driver, Nash yelled, "Get out of the car! Get out of the car!"

The woman's eyes were wide with fear. Her hands grasped the steering wheel tightly. Her mouth was wide, as if she wanted to scream, but nothing came out.

Nash once again yelled, "Get out of the car, now!"

As much as she wanted to move and protect the young child beside her, the panicked woman could command her muscles to do nothing but contract in fear. Unaware of the approaching danger, the boy continued to play with the toy his mother had brought home from work.

Enraged because the woman would not acquiesce to his commands, Nash raised his gun and fired. The single bullet entered the left side of the woman's head, exiting and striking the child in the shoulder and driving down through his little chest.

Christy began screaming once again. The mother and her child lay motionless in the front of the Camry.

"Shit!" said Nash, realizing he did not have time to throw the woman and child from the car. All the noise was certain to attract the attention of the nearby neighbors. There was no time to remove the seatbelted woman and the child in the booster seat. And, the bloodied interior would have been a red flag to anyone getting near the car. He dragged Christy back to the Mustang and pushed her through the driver's side.

Nash threw the car into gear and sped off, heading for Loch Raven Boulevard and, eventually, Baltimore City. He hoped he could be ahead of the lookout that would most certainly be broadcast to the city police.

CHAPTER 12

The radio communications from the precinct had diminished when the dispatcher suddenly announced a shooting at the corner of Cromwell Bridge Road and Beaverbank Circle. Weaver's mind began to race. He knew that location was just a few miles from the violence and hostage taking in Towson, certainly not a coincidence. This was a suburban area, not the knife and gun club seen in the inner city. With the infusion of patrol vehicles in the area, it was only a matter of minutes before the first officer arrived.

The patrolman screamed into his microphone, "Six-twelve to Communications—I need a medic unit! I have two people shot at Cromwell Bridge and Beaverbank. One's a small child, the other is a woman. She may be deceased."

Weaver was still eastbound on Interstate 695, too far away to be of any help even at 80 miles per hour—maybe 85 now. He knew the medic unit should be there long before he could get to the scene. He also knew he had just lost his helicopter, Trooper 1. If either the child or the woman were viable, they would be flown downtown to the trauma center.

Minutes later, Phillips' voice came across the portable radio. "Phillips to all responding team members. I have some additional. Investigators at the scene don't believe this is a robbery, after all. Apparently, there was no money taken from the store. They were able to piece together that the waitress, Christy Moore, had recently broken up with a guy by the name of Rick Nash. The physical description of the suspect matches Nash almost to a 'T.' Also, the shooting at Cromwell Bridge and Beaverbank is probably related. Witness descriptions match our suspect and the hostage. The female may be injured, witness accounts say her face and hair were bloodied."

In little less than an hour, three people lay dead, a young child was critically wounded, and there was a madman with a gun and a hostage still on the loose. The normally quiet community was now in a state of near panic. County and State police were swarming the area in an attempt to stop the bloodshed.

Phillips continued with his message. "Let's stage at the fire station at York Road and Bosley Avenue. They're setting up a command post there. We can update any info when we arrive."

"Rice, ten-four," answered Richard Rice.

"McBride, ten-four," added Bones.

"Weaver, ten-four."

The remainder of the team acknowledged Phillips' order.

Just down the street from the original crime scene, unmarked Ford Crown Victoria police vehicles were silently streaming into the fire station parking lot. The cars' red and blue flashing lights added to the eerie sense of urgency that was now a part of this chilled night. These were the assaulters. They were the team members who actually made entry into a house to go hands-on with a suspect.

The snipers were also arriving in their Chevy Suburbans and Ford Cargo Vans. The variety of equipment they carried necessitated the larger vehicles. The quiet professionalism of each arriving team member was impressive. As each operator pulled into the lot, he parked beside the previously arriving vehicle. Each car faced the same way, and before the motor was turned off, the pop of the trunk lid could be heard remotely unlatching.

Each operator swiftly exited his unit and disengaged the other systems that secured the array of firearms and equipment in his trunk. Each donned a pair of olive drab, Nomex coveralls that had the agency's patch on the shoulder. The subdued green, black, and red colors would not give away their positions in the dark night. Next came the duty belt with its Safariland tactical holster. The drop-down styling allowed the .40 caliber handgun to rest mid-thigh so that the thick body armor would not hinder the officer from drawing the weapon.

Each operator put on his Level III body armor. Most inserted the ceramic strike plates into the vest to be able to take hits from rifle rounds. Each vest had an array of pouches that could be arranged according to the individual's needs. Most carried a hydration system on the back of the vest, along with a radio pouch. Other pouches on the front of the vest could carry extra clips of ammunition, first-aid gear, and a variety of other small tools and gadgets. Prior to leaving his car, each officer placed his radio headset on and completed a radio check. Once satisfied all of their gear was on and properly functioning, the team grabbed their M-4 rifles and rallied by Phillips.

In the meantime Brett and the other snipers were quickly

shedding their clothes and putting on camouflage BDU's and boonie hats. Each grabbed his rucksack and long-gun and joined his team members for the briefing.

Weaver's kit was noticeably different from that of the others. Although he carried a .40 caliber Sig Sauer pistol and body armor like the other team members, he did not carry a long-gun but an M-9 medical bag. The M-9 was a slim, lightweight black backpack that carried the basics needed for the initial care of the type of injuries he would most likely see on a mission. He grabbed his narcotics kit, a small padlocked hard case, from the onboard safe in the Suburban and threw it into the M-9. Once the remainder of his equipment check was complete and he was suited up, he joined the team for the briefing.

Weaver was nervous, his palms sweaty. *Do I have everything? I feel like I'm forgetting something? Oh, yeah, my flippin' common sense. What the hell have I gotten myself into? Can I handle this? Will I freeze if the shit hits the fan?*

Phillips began the briefing once everyone was within ear-shot. "OK, you all should've seen the updated suspect and hostage information on your computer. We're going to split into two groups and take the two raid vans. Two sniper teams to each van. Weaver, you're with me. Take everything you might need with you, it's probably going to be a long night."

The Ford vans used by the snipers were often used as jump-out vehicles for raids. Weaver sprinted back to his Suburban to retrieve his STOMP bag and oxygen. The STOMP was a larger backpack that carried additional medical supplies. The O_2 was not usually carried when hitting a door on a raid or working a hostage situation. The tank was heavy and cumbersome, and could become a missile if it was dropped hard or was hit by a bullet. But since he was going to be away from his vehicle, it seemed a prudent item to take along.

Everyone loaded into the two vans. Each van contained homemade benches running down the length of each side. Once the team was loaded, the side and rear doors were closed. Phillips was riding shotgun in the lead van with Michael Devonshire, aka Devo, a sniper support, at the wheel. Devo was a wiry 32-year-old, who had been on the force for ten years and on the team for five. With his round, wire framed glasses, he resembled a member of the 1970's new wave band of the same name. Quick witted he was considered the class clown. Dave Davis, Travis Lebo, Brett, and Gunny, all piled in the lead van. Weaver was seated just behind Devo. Russell Jones, Paul Runk, Drew Davidson, Rice, Bones, Mund, and Tucker made up the crew in the second van. Between Jones and Runk, they had a total of 20 years of SWAT team experience. Jones was thin and built for speed; Runk looked like a linebacker for a professional football team and was the assistant team leader. Drew Davidson had no specialized shooting experience when he had come on the team, but since then he had become one of their best snipers.

It was eerily quiet inside the nondescript vans as they pulled onto York Road. Weaver had not seen this demeanor from the team before. This was a highly trained group of professionals. They trained hard and when called upon, they were able to quickly and quietly do their jobs; desperately trying to avoid attention. But this was not the normal raid or hostage scenario playing out this early spring evening.

Weaver could tell by their faces that the other guys were concerned, wondering if they would return home tonight to their wives, girlfriends, and children.

This dirtball has no problem killing, Weaver thought. He could sense that each person in the van knew a gun battle was in the offing.

The local TV stations had broken into the evening's lineup of sitcoms and reality shows to provide breaking news of the murders and hostage situation. A police public information officer provided descriptions of Christy Moore, Rick Nash, and the 1965 Black Ford Mustang they were traveling in. As was normally the case, 911 centers throughout the region were being flooded with calls of sightings of the killer and his hostage. The command post had to wade through the myriad of reports and determine which had promise. Each tip would eventually be followed up, but the command post had to decide which were more likely to be viable leads. The SWAT team was roaming the area but remaining available for any sightings that truly showed promise.

Everyone's attention piqued when the momentary silence on the radio was interrupted. "Command Post to Seventeen-seventy."

CHAPTER 13

Recognizing his call sign, Phillips answered, "Seventeen-seventy, go ahead."

"Seventeen-seventy, we have information on a vehicle matching our suspect vehicle heading to an abandoned house at the end of Powers Avenue off of Sherwood Road. Can you check it out?"

"Ten-four."

"The caller advises they saw a Mustang matching the description, occupied times two. They went back a dirt road at the end of Powers. Caller advises there is an abandoned house approximately a half-mile down that road.

Devo leaned over to turn on the red and blue LED emergency lights. As he made the U-turn on York Road to head North, Phillips flipped the switch to engage the siren.

Through the rear windows, Weaver saw the other van make a similar maneuver. The interior of his van was illuminated with alternating red and blue lights from the trailing unit. The two sped out York Road passing restaurants, gas stations, and specialty stores.

They eventually entered a residential area after turning onto Warren Road and then Sherwood.

The mood in the van immediately changed. They were

now on the hunt. Grips tightened on weapons, and each team member sat up a little straighter. It went from introspection to a process of game-playing potential scenarios in their heads.

Philips said, "Devo, kill the emergency lights and siren once we turn onto Sherwood. We'll dismount and patrol down to the house once we get close. Brett, I'm going to let you and the other snipers lead."

"Got it," Brett answered.

"How far down Powers do you want to stop?" Devo asked.

"The house is a half-mile back off of Powers, so let's edge past Osage Avenue and see what our cover and concealment looks like. I'd like to get somewhat close to the end of Powers," Phillips said as he checked a map.

The house backed up to the expansive Loch Raven Reservoir, an area which was heavily wooded. The watershed covered 218 square miles, and few people knew the house even existed.

Having blacked out just prior to making the turn, the two vans crept down Powers Avenue. Devo flipped a switch that killed their brake lights and dash instrument lights. In this environment, even a small amount of light could give away their position.

With little sound, the vehicle doors opened and the dark-clad operators stepped out and, without direction, immediately formed a security perimeter and took a knee. As they knelt beside the road, their eyes, and their weapons, were focused outward away from the center, looking for potential threats. Nash could have ditched the car, killed Moore, and now be on foot. It would be easy for the team to become the prey if they were not disciplined and careful.

The evening was cool and clear, but without much moonlight. The trek to the house would be slow and difficult. The team only had a handful of night-vision goggles, not enough for each team member.

Phillips looked in Brett's direction and keyed the lip mic attached to his radio. "Brett, take two sets of NVG's with your snipers. I'll take the other two with my guys. Give me a thumbs-up when you're ready."

The team quickly gathered the equipment and stepped off into the darkness. Brett and his crew led the way in a wedge formation.

As they moved out, Phillips said to Weaver, "Stay back and hold security on the vans."

"Ten-four," Weaver answered.

Shit!

However frustrated he might be, it was not the time to have a discussion about the decision, so he merely acknowledged the order. *All the time, effort, and training that I have in this damn program, and I'm left guarding a couple of police vehicles.*

He knew he had to get past the frustration. Nash was still out there somewhere and could very well circle around the team and attempt to commandeer one of the trucks. So he knelt beside some bushes that provided ample concealment, yet allowed him a 360 view of the area. Now it was just a matter of keeping his eyes and ears open while monitoring the radio communications from the rest of the team.

Brett was carrying his .308 Remington bolt-action sniper rifle. He had shot hundreds of rounds through the weapon and spent hours of time on the range learning the nuances of not only the weapon, but also the various types of ammunition that could be used and the effect that wind and heat had on each round and its trajectory. Brett, as with every other sniper, was virtually married to his rifle. Devo—Brett's sniper support—was armed with an M-4. As a sniper support, he was not only a spotter who identified where Brett's rounds were hitting, but was also responsible for security. He was Brett's guardian angel, ensuring no one took out his partner while he was concentrating on his target.

As Brett popped open the covers on his riflescope, he whispered into the lip mic, "Okay, my sniper guys, slow and easy. Stay off the road. Get an eyeball on the four sides of the house and the car."

The primary responsibility of any sniper team was intelligence. Gather as much information as possible and pass it to the command element and the team leader.

"We'll stay about 20 yards behind them," Phillips said. "Lebo, watch our back."

Travis Lebo had been on the team for two years. An exercise nut, Lebo was as hard as a rock with arms the size of telephone poles. The rest of the team had a difficult time keeping up when Lebo led calisthenics. His shaved and highly polished head made him stand out amongst the team.

Each of the operators had a piece of the pie they were responsible for, their area of responsibility. Lebo was being tasked as the rear guard, ensuring that Nash would not flank the team and ambush them from the rear. He raised his M-4 to low ready, the collapsible stock at his shoulder, muzzle at a 45 degree angle pointed toward the ground, and finger pressed lightly against the side of the weapon just above the trigger.

Brett and the remainder of his group moved slowly through the brush. Brett's footsteps fell lightly on the decaying leaves and brush to reduce his own noise signature. His eyes, having adjusted to the ambient light, moved slowly and deliberately from left to right, up and down, looking for any sign of human presence. He was looking for freshly broken twigs or tree branches, even footprints. His senses were in overdrive; an odor of cigarette smoke or woman's cologne could be a sign of Nash's, or Christy's, presence.

Brett drew on all of his training as a former Marine Corps sniper as he listened for signs of the deranged killer and his hostage. The team inched closer to the house. Brett looked to his left and motioned for the other two sniper teams to take up positions at the far side and rear of the darkened house. Looking to his right, Brett again used hand signals to tell the other sniper team to take the front. Each team moved off cautiously to take their assigned positions.

As Brett and Devo got to within 50 yards of the house, they spotted a depression in the ground they could use as a discreet hide and observation point. Slowly and silently, they began to crawl forward. Inch by agonizing inch, they made their way through the underbrush. Arriving at the hide, they lay motionless on the cold ground. No one would ever notice these highly trained professionals lying in the darkness. They could blend into their surroundings with surprising efficiency.

Devo pulled a pair of binoculars from his pack. He painstakingly scanned the area on their side of the house. After checking the yard and finding nothing, Devo's attention turned to the two windows on the first floor.

"No movement outside, no lights on the first floor, checking the second," Devo whispered.

Peering through his riflescope, Brett scanned the area as well. "I've got nothing."

"This is Tucker. I have a car on this side, but it doesn't match our suspect vehicle description. No movement around the vehicle or in the house."

The sniper teams securing the other two sides of the house reported no movement, but would remain in place to provide overwatch for the entry team as they further checked the car and the house.

While the snipers were moving into position, Phillips had his entry team hold their own position further back in the brush. Once the snipers had the overwatch established, Phillips and the rest of the entry team began moving forward.

"Clear the car, then the house," Phillips ordered.

Dave Davis took point and inched toward the car. Gunny, second in the stack, covered Davis with his M-4. Other operators had their weapons trained on various windows and doors, watching for signs of Nash. Davis and Gunny cleared the car while the others maintained their coverage of the house.

"Jack, car's clear," Davis whispered into his mic. The old junker hadn't been moved for months, and the house looked deserted from their vantage point. However, it didn't mean that Nash wasn't hiding somewhere inside, having ditched his own ride somewhere nearby.

"All right, let's take the house," Phillips responded.

Lined-up once again, each operator whispered to the person in front of him, "Stack's tight."

As the team began to move on the house, Phillips advised the sniper teams, "We're moving."

Still on point, Davis made it to the stairs at the front of the house. Normally, he would be carrying a ballistic shield. But with the shield weighing nearly 25 pounds, the half-mile trek through the brush and woods would have been extremely difficult. It was doubtful the team could have maintained their noise discipline with branches hitting the cumbersome shield.

As his right foot touched the first step, Davis quickly raised his left arm and rolled his hand into a fist, signaling the team to halt.

"Door's ajar," he whispered.

Everyone noticed their stomachs tighten a bit. The column continued up the three steps to the front door of the dilapidated house. Davis switched his weapon to his weak hand and slowly pushed open the door with his right. The movements of the team were slow, deliberate, and silent. As they crossed the threshold, Phillips' eyes, and his M-4, were drawn toward the staircase to his right.

Without saying a word, the four members of the team behind him peeled off and began their ascent to clear the second floor. Mund remained behind to take rear guard. Their movements were like clockwork. The team had spent countless hours training for this type of operation. Much of what they did was committed to muscle memory; each knew what the other would do in a variety of circumstances.

Davis, Gunny, Bones, and Phillips cleared a small room just off the entryway. The Surefire lights attached below the barrels of their weapons flickered on and off as they searched the room. The four moved down a short hallway. Davis and Gunny ducked into the next room while Bones and Phillips maintained coverage on the corridor. Hallways were dangerous, often referred to as fatal funnels. If you happened to be in one when a bad guy opened fire, you were screwed. So, the two picked their spot to hold down the hall while Davis and Gunny checked the room. Their weapons followed their eyes as they looked for signs of Nash. Once the room was secured, Bones and Phillips moved out into the hall and headed for the next room, while Davis and Gunny picked up coverage down the hallway.

Jones started his ascent up the stairs to the second floor. The stock of his M-4 was seated in his shoulder; the muzzle pointed toward what appeared to be a bathroom at the top of the stairs. The front sight was just below eye level so it wouldn't impinge his sight line. Rice was literally right on his heels. As his feet hit the second step he began to turn and cover the other areas visible through the railing at the top of the staircase. Runk and Lebo followed, each carefully placing each footstep as they continued the climb. None of the four said a word; each knew his area of responsibility. The key to staying alive was relying on your teammates to do their jobs. Making it to the top of the stairs, Jones and Rice swung into the bathroom, paying particular attention to the drawn shower curtain. Having cleared the area, they turned to see Runk and Lebo leapfrog to the next room and clear it as well.

The process continued for the other two rooms—smooth as silk. Completing their search, Jones radioed, "Second floor's clear."

"First floor, clear," Phillips responded, "Switch it up. Get the secondary done, and let's get out of here."

The team switched areas and completed a more comprehensive secondary search of the closets and other nooks and crannies. Completing the task, Jack pressed the radio's remote push-to-talk, PTT, button on his chest, "Primary and secondary's complete. We're coming out." It was always nice to let the snipers on the exterior know you were about to exit the building. They hated surprises.

The snipers and the rest of the team made their way back toward the vans.

"Phillips to Weaver, we're coming back. Don't shoot us."

"Ten-four," Weaver acknowledged, adding "asshole," after he released the PTT button.

Piss me off enough, I just might, Jack!

CHAPTER 14

Nash sped down Loch Raven Boulevard into Baltimore City. The tree lined road was bordered by the homes of middle income families unfamiliar with the violence of the inner city. Mothers, fathers, and children sat watching their evening television programs comforted by the relative security of their neighborhoods. Their sense of well-being was dashed as the news reports began to filter across the airwaves of the murders only blocks away.

"I've got to find someplace safe to get off the street," he mumbled to himself.

Christy was beside him in the passenger seat, curled in a fetal position, her mind bouncing from thought to thought.

This can't be happening. It's surely a dream. I have to get back to work. Where's Jackie? Blood—where's the blood coming from? Where's my mom and dad?

The mind has difficulty adapting to such radical changes as Christy had experienced in a short period of time. She was not even psychologically capable of attempting to escape. Her mind was not functioning on a level to allow her to formulate a getaway plan. So she lay docile in the front seat of Nash's car as he attempted to avoid police detection.

As Nash continued on Loch Raven Boulevard, he was also

trying to come up with a plan. *There's a flea-bag joint on Route 40. What the hell is the name of it? I'll get a room and figure this out.*

Turning left onto Cold Spring Lane, Nash headed toward the east side of town. At one point he saw a police car in the distance and quickly turned into a shopping center to avoid detection. He eventually turned left onto Pulaski Highway— Route 40.

Should be just over the hill.

Nash pulled into Luke's Motel just outside the city limits. Situated on the original road linking Baltimore, Philadelphia and eventually New York—prior to the construction of Interstate 95—the two-story white motel was a throwback to the 50's. Originally espoused by businessmen and travelers, the motel is now frequented by a seedier crowd.

Nash parked so that the Mustang was not visible from the registration desk. The car's description would be all over the news by now.

Nash drew the Glock from his waistband, checked to see it still had ammo, and pointed it at Christy's head. In her distraught state, she didn't even feel the cold metal against her temple.

"If you as much as move, I swear I will blow your brains out! Then I'll find your roommate and your family and do the same to them," Nash warned.

Christy was too frightened to respond.

Tucking the handgun back into his waistband, Nash exited the car and entered the office. The knotty pine desk, faded artwork and water stained ceiling bore the signs of an establishment long forgotten by its owner.

"Can I help you?" asked the unkempt desk clerk.

"I need a room for one night," Nash responded.

Not unlike others renting a room for the night, or just a few hours, Nash was fidgety and a bit apprehensive.

"The only thing I have is around back."

"That's fine."

"All right. Fifty-six bucks. Cash or credit?"

Fumbling through his pockets, Nash came up with the cash. He didn't want to use a credit card and have the cops track him.

Knowing that very few people used their real name at this type of establishment, the clerk said, "Fill the card out. Name and address."

Nash scribbled a fake name and address on the card and handed it back to the clerk.

"Room 104, around back. Check-out time is 10:00 a.m."

Nash snatched the key from the counter and exited the office. Walking the few yards back toward the car, he scanned the area for any sign of the cops.

After pulling his car around to the rear of the motel, he grabbed Christy's arm and dragged her from the vehicle. Having regained some sense of her predicament, Christy attempted to pull free.

Nash's grip tightened as he said, "I swear I'll kill you if you try to run. Now get in the room."

He pushed Christy to the door and slid the key into the lock, all while looking over his shoulder for any curious onlookers. Once inside, he closed the door and grabbed Christy by the hair, which was now tangled with drying blood.

Nash grabbed a threadbare towel and ripped it into strips, using the first as a gag around Christy's mouth. As she attempted to fight, Nash drove his fist into her abdomen. Christy's eyes bulged and air blew from her nose and mouth. His second blow came in the form of a back-hand to her face. Christy fell to the bed—lethargic. Nash used the remaining strips to tie her to the bed, at which time he proceeded to rape the defenseless young woman.

Although Nash often physically abused his female prey, he routinely used psychological manipulation to have his sexual urges met. Even for a man like Nash, this night's events were indicative of a person who's life was spiraling downward. Nash was at ease both ruining lives and ending lives.

Tears flowed from Christy's eyes as the horrific events unfolded. Her mind was awash with guilt over not listening to the warnings of her roommate. *How could I have let this happen? Why didn't I listen to Jackie?* She sobbed as Nash rolled off of her and fell asleep.

* * *

Weaver could see the team approaching in the darkness. Although their movements were not as quiet and precise as they had been when they had left, they continued to scan the area just in case Nash was nearby. Arriving back at the vans, many in the group either took in water from their CamelBak hydration systems or ate a Power Bar while getting ready to redeploy.

Weaver could no longer contain his anger. He sought out Phillips. "I need a minute, Jack."

"Not now," Phillips said.

"Look, I'm not here to guard your damn cars."

Raising his voice, Phillips said, "I told you, not now."

The argument caught the attention of the rest of the team.

Sticking his head around the corner of the van, Brett said, "Hey, keep it down, you two."

Weaver went on. "Jack, you have a bull on because last year the paramedics were slow getting to you. Well, you just created the circumstances for a similar incident right here. If something had happened up at that house, I would have had to wait for a security team to make its way back here to get me. I certainly didn't know the way to that house, and I wasn't going to come back to you by myself. Then more time would have been wasted trying to make our way back up to you. If someone had bled out, it would have been squarely on your shoulders, because it was your decision to leave your medical asset guarding the flippin' trucks. Explain that one to somebody's wife and family!"

Weaver had said his piece and fully expected Phillips to dump him back at the command post and inform the command staff of his insubordination. It wasn't the time and place for this battle, but Weaver had had enough with Phillips and his attitude. As Weaver walked around the back of the two vans, he felt the eyes of the remaining team members looking at him. He intentionally got into the wrong van, feeling it might be better to stay separated from Phillips for a while.

Phillips quietly got into the passenger seat of the lead van. *He's right. If something had happened, I would have had a lot of explaining to do.*

Brett came up to where Phillips was seated, opened the door and said, "Jack, you know he's right. If something would've happened back there, we would've been in deep shit. We could've called Nine-one-one and gotten a medic unit here just as fast as getting back to the vans to get Weaver up to us. There would've been a lot of questions about that one."

"I didn't want him to get hurt."

"That's a crock. You and I both know it. He was one of the better students in SWAT school. He's squared away and has his head on straight. He can hold his own."

"We've got to get rollin'," Phillips said.

"Think about it, Jack."

Phillips closed the door, and Brett got into the rear of the van with the rest of the squad. Phillips valued Brett's opinion as a senior member of the team, but he also knew Brett was friends with Weaver and might merely be protesting on his behalf.

The team returned to the Towson command post. It was now after two in the morning, and the police were receiving few viable leads on the whereabouts of Nash and his hostage. The investigation was being handled by detectives and the crime lab. The command staff decided to stand down the SWAT team and send them home for the night.

Weaver gathered his gear and stowed it in the Suburban. Getting in the front seat, he heard a periodic beep and remembered throwing his phone on the dash. He grabbed it and noticed he had four missed calls and one voicemail. *I can only guess who these are from. She probably wasn't real happy that I hung up on her.* Punching his password into the keyboard, he awaited the message.

It was Kathy's voice. "Danny, I guess you're working at the shooting that's all over the news. But that's no reason to hang up on me and not answer my calls. You can certainly take time out to let me know you're okay."

First Phillips, now her. I can't win.

Weaver arrived home to find Kathy asleep on the couch in the family room. She stirred and opened her eyes when Weaver entered the room.

Still groggy, she said, "You couldn't call?"

"No, I-"

Before he could continue, Kathy interrupted, "What is that on your leg? Why do you have a gun?"

"In case things turn to shit and I have to defend myself."

"Wait a minute. I'm missing something. Why would you need a gun when you're sitting at the command post?"

"Where did you get the idea I was sitting at the command post? I'm operating with the team. I go where they go." Thinking about his experience earlier in the evening, Weaver mumbled, "Well, maybe not everywhere."

"You never told me you were going to be carrying a gun, and you never told me it would be this dangerous."

"What do you think I spent three weeks in SWAT school for?"

"You told me it was an orientation so you understood what the guys do," Kathy retorted.

"It was, but it does absolutely no good for me to sit at the command post. Damn, you sound like Phillips. That's probably where he would like me to be."

"Sounds pretty smart to me; maybe you should listen to him."

Just what I need – the team leader and my wife thinking the same way.

"It's nearly three. I'm going to sleep. I have to be back in the office in a few hours."

Weaver headed for the bedroom. After setting his alarm for six, he crawled between the sheets and tried to sleep.

CHAPTER 15

Nash stirred as a beam of sunlight broke through a gap in the curtains. After a few moments, he pulled himself from the bed and headed for the bathroom. Turning on the faucet, he splashed water on his face and looked at his image in the mirror.

I've got to come up with a plan. The first thing is to get far away from Baltimore. Who was the guy from Jersey that I bunked with in DOC? Mariano, that's it. Maybe I can get him to hide me out till this blows over. He was supposed to have gotten out shortly after me.

Nash had spent two years in the Maryland Department of Corrections for possession of an illegal firearm. Vince Mariano, Nash's cellmate, had been serving five years on a racketeering charge. Mariano, a Hoboken, New Jersey native, was muscular and heavily tattooed. When Nash had been released, Mariano had told him to call if he ever needed help.

Christy looked at Nash as he walked from the bathroom, hoping he would not rape her again. Still tied to the bed, chills ran up her spine as he approached.

Nash said, "Christy, I'm sorry. I love you, and I know deep down you love me, too. I don't want to hurt you. I have a plan. We can get away from here. There's a guy in Jersey that can help. I think he'll hide us out until things settle down. Then we can live our lives together."

Tears began to flow from Christy's eyes again. *How could he ever believe I would love him after the events of the past few days? He is totally deranged.*

Walking past Christy and the bed, Nash retrieved the remote control and turned the television to the morning news. All three local channels had wall-to-wall coverage of the horrific murders the previous evening in Towson. Three people were dead, and a young boy was clinging to life at Baltimore's Shock Trauma. One reporter from WBAL described the extensive search that was underway for Rick Nash. Film footage showed police helicopters conducting low level searches, along with K-9 units and SWAT teams from Baltimore County and the State Police. The reporter also talked about the high number of calls coming in about the whereabouts of Nash and his hostage.

Finally, the television displayed a mugshot of Nash from a previous arrest and a photo of Christy from her college ID. The reporter said, "If you have seen either of these two individuals, contact 911 immediately. Take no action yourself. Rick Nash is considered armed and extremely dangerous."

Nash turned to Christy. "We've got to get out of here—now."

He grabbed the Glock from beside the television and stuffed it down his pants in front of his left hip. He knew an extra clip of ammunition was in his left front pocket just by the weight of his pants, but he slid his hand in the pocket for reassurance.

113

Untying Christy's feet, Nash said, "I know you love me. We'll be fine."

"I need to use the bathroom," Christy said.

"There's no time. We need to leave."

Nash grabbed her by the arm and helped her from the bed. With his left hand, he pulled the curtains apart just enough to check the parking area for cops and make sure the Mustang was still in front of the room.

Apprehensive about walking out the door with Christy gagged and her hands bound, Nash untied the bonds. Throwing open the door, he said, "We're going right to the passenger side. Hurry!"

As Christy cleared the doorframe, she noticed, from the corner of her eye, a police car coming down Pulaski Highway, approaching Rosedale Avenue and the motel. She jammed the heel of her shoe into the top of Nash's foot and broke free.

Flailing her arms wildly, Christy screamed, "Help! Please help me!" as she ran toward the four-lane highway.

Nash recovered from the unexpected pain and attempted to grab Christy. He was only four or five steps behind her and knew he could overtake her quickly, when he spotted the cop car. Instantly, he turned and ran back up Rosedale Avenue toward a wooded area.

Christy nearly became a hood ornament on a Mack dump truck as she ran into the roadway and attempted to hail the oncoming police car. At the last second, the truck swerved and the driver laid on the airhorn. The patrol car was only feet away when the officer noticed the woman.

Grasping the steering wheel with both hands and standing on the brakes, Officer Jan Brewer shouted, "Are you nuts, you friggin' idiot!"

She skidded to a stop and bolted from her car. Brewer was a petite female, on the job for less than six months. "Are you trying to get yourself killed?" she yelled.

As Brewer focused on the woman's bloodied hair, she recognized the panic-stricken girl from pictures handed out at morning roll call. She grabbed the mic hanging from her left shirt epaulet. "Nine twenty-seven to Communications. Emergency!"

"Nine-twenty-seven," answered the dispatcher.

"Rosedale Avenue and Pulaski Highway. I have the hostage from last evening's homicides." Brewer released the PTT button, awaiting an acknowledgment.

"Ten-four, Nine-twenty-seven," replied the dispatcher, a sense of urgency now evident in her voice.

"Standby, I'm going to get more on the whereabouts of the suspect."

"Nine-twenty to Communications," Brewer's patrol area sergeant said—his siren wailing in the background.

"Nine-twenty, go," the dispatcher answered.

"Start all available units in the area. Notify Precinct 10 in case the suspect crosses into their area. Also, contact Baltimore City and have their cars start searching along the city line."

"Ten-four, Nine-twenty."

"Air One's with you," said the flight observer on the Department's American Eurocopter AS350B3 helicopter.

"Ten-four, Air One," the dispatcher said.

"We're coming from Towson, Precinct 6, Nine-twenty. We'll be to you in less than five."

"Nine-twenty, ten-four."

Brewer got Christy out of the roadway and asked, "Where's the guy that was holding you?"

Trembling, Christy said, "I think he ran back to that road beside the motel."

"What was he wearing?"

"Blue-jeans and a black t-shirt."

"Was there any writing on the t-shirt?" Brewer asked.

"No."

"Nine-twenty-seven to Communications."

"Nine-twenty-seven," the dispatcher answered.

"Hostage advises the suspect last seen heading east on Rosedale Avenue, wearing a black t-shirt with blue-jeans."

"Nine-twenty to Communications. Get that description and route of travel to the City and State Police," the patrol sergeant said.

Nash ran up the slight incline on Rosedale Avenue and through a line of bushes at the end of the road. He crossed two sets of railroad tracks and made a sharp right to head south, parallel to the tracks. A half-mile down the track, he stopped and bent forward to catch his breath. As he sucked air into his lungs, he heard the rumble of an oncoming train. The speed of trains coming south on this stretch of track dropped precipitously as they approached the rail yard in east Baltimore.

Slipping into the tall weeds, Nash waited for the train's engine to pass, hoping not to be seen. As he peered from his hide, Nash spotted an open boxcar approaching. The lumbering train was moving empty cars and coal hoppers down the line. Nash realized he had an opportunity for a quick, undetected getaway. He sprang from the bushes and sprinted down the track to catch up to an empty car. Even at fifteen miles per hour, the train was a challenge to catch.

Nash grabbed the door, pulled himself up and rolled onto the floor of the car. Lying there with his chest rising and falling rhythmically as he tried to catch his breath, Nash contemplated how he would repay Christy's ingratitude.

CHAPTER 16

The buzzing of the alarm clock startled Weaver from a deep sleep. He had been out of it for roughly three hours, but felt as if he had just closed his eyes. Rolling to his left, he noticed Kathy had not come to bed. *Oh, shit. I guess all of my husband points were flushed down the toilet last night.*

Kathy often joked that Weaver gained thousands of husband points when he cooked dinner, cleaned the house, or brought her flowers. However, those points disappeared quickly when Weaver screwed up.

Knowing it was going to be difficult to be back at the office by seven, Weaver quickly brushed his teeth and threw on clean workout clothes. Hurrying down the stairs, he found Kathy asleep on the couch. He kissed her on the forehead and ran out the door.

You're not getting off that easy, thought Kathy as she felt his warm lips on her brow.

Weaver arrived at the SWAT team's office at exactly seven and found Gunny and Devo heading into the weight room.

"Did they ever get a line on that guy last night?" Weaver asked.

"No. Homicide has been working the case all night, but there's been no sign of him or the girl," Gunny said.

"He'll show up," Devo added. "Somebody like that is not just going to fade away."

Devo didn't realize how prophetic his words would be. Midway through the team's less than energetic workout, the weight room erupted with ear-splitting beeps as everyone's phone displayed a text message alerting them for a callout.

SWAT Callout; Luke's Motel; 7905 Pulaski Highway; Homicide Suspect

Sticking his head through the door of the weight room Phillips yelled, "Same as last night. Grab your shit and load into the two vans."

Everyone scrambled, throwing green coveralls over their shorts and t-shirts. Weaver ran to his Suburban and grabbed the same gear he had used the previous evening. From the time of the page, it took less than five minutes for everyone to load up and hit the street.

With less than twenty-five feet between them, the two units screamed eastward on Interstate 695, heading for Pulaski Highway. Weaver and the rest of the team put on their Kevlar helmets, adjusted body armor, and checked weapons as the yelp and wail of the sirens moved cars out of their way.

"Hostage is safe," Phillips said. "Suspect escaped into a wooded area behind Luke's."

By the time the team arrived at the scene, the entire area was awash with County and State Police vehicles. Units were positioned at every intersection in the hopes of controlling a perimeter through which Nash would have little chance of escape. Officers and state troopers watched intently for anyone matching the description of their suspect.

Devo pulled his van down Pulaski to the front of the motel, where a small command post had been established. They were met by the chief of police, Mitch Sherman. Walking to the passenger side of the lead van, Sherman received a salute from Phillips as Phillips jumped from the seat.

Sherman was tall and lean. His deep voice projected the command presence that one would expect from the commander of such an agency. "Jack," he said, returning the salute, "once we have this asshole cornered, do not let him get away."

"Yes, sir," Phillips acknowledged.

"Do you understand the implications of what I'm telling you?"

"Yes, sir."

With another salute, Sherman said, "Stay safe," and walked away.

Phillips knew he had just been given a green light to put a bullet between Nash's eyes in order to stop him from killing again.

Returning to the van, Phillips said to Devo, "Let's pull up Rosedale Avenue to the last place they saw him, and deploy from there."

Pressing the PTT button on his chest, Phillips said, "Seventeen-seventy to Air One."

"Air One," answered the flight observer on the aircraft circling above.

"Have anything?"

"Negative as yet. We've only been overhead for a few minutes and haven't done a full sweep yet."

"Ten-four. We're deploying from Rosedale and Gilmore. Do you have us?"

"Ten-four, I have you. There's another small group of houses directly across the tracks from your position. To my knowledge no one has seen anything in the area. K-9's making a run through there now. Would you want to start working your way south, through the wooded area on the east side of the tracks?"

"Ten-four," Phillips answered.

Everyone exited the two vans and formed up to begin the search.

Lebo ran his hand across his smooth, shiny head.

"Hey, Lebo," Devo said. "Make sure you cover that thing up! You'll give our position away."

Used to the jabs, the big operator dropped his helmet on his head mumbling, "Keep it up, I'll squish those geeky little glasses of yours."

Anticipating that he would again be left behind, Weaver slowly stepped from the rear door and fidgeted with his M-9 medical pack.

Getting a quick head count, Phillips looked around and said, "Weaver, are you coming with us?"

Startled, and trying to stifle a smile, Weaver said, "Yeah, just grabbing my bag."

121

Weaver could tell by the snarl that Phillips was not happy about taking him along.

"Stay beside me and don't move unless I tell you to," Phillips growled.

"No problem."

As they had the previous night, the snipers set out first, to get a foothold inside the tree line. With their faces painted shades of green and black and sporting their ghillie suits, they crept into the tall bushes and weeds. The ghillie suits were made of shredded strips of burlap. The varying shades of brown and green allowed the wearers to become invisible to all but the most highly trained observer.

As the remainder of the team crossed the tracks, Bones lost his footing on the stone ballast used to stabilize the railroad track and fell. Holding his M-4 high with his right hand, Bones used his left hand to cushion his fall.

Feeling a sharp pain in his arm, Bones yelled, "Shit! You son of a bitch!" As he raised his left arm, blood ran down and dripped to the ground.

Weaver looked at Phillips, who finally said, "Well, go do something! That's why you're here isn't it?"

Weaver shrugged and retorted, "You said not to move until you said to."

"Just go!"

Pulling his M-9 bag from his back, Weaver dropped it to the ground and unzipped the kit while looking at Bones' arm. Blood was still flowing from a large jagged gash on Bones' left forearm. "What did you do?"

"I slid and hit a broken bottle," Bones said. "Am I going to live, Doc?"

"I hope so, you still owe me five bucks from lunch yesterday." Weaver raised Bones' arm. "Keep this above your head, it'll slow the bleeding."

Weaver pulled on a pair of black nitrile exam gloves, retrieved an H-bandage from his bag and tore the packaging open with his teeth. "Let me take a quick look and see if there's still any glass in there."

Placing the gauze portion of the bandage over the wound, Weaver wrapped the attached elastic dressing around Bones' arm. "This should stop the bleeding." After tightening the dressing, Weaver pinched Bones' left index finger. "Can you feel that?"

"Yeah."

"Wiggle your fingers. I want to make sure you haven't compromised anything below the wound."

"Can he continue on?" Phillips asked.

"I'm fine," Bones interjected, wiggling his fingers and moving his left hand and arm.

Looking at Weaver, Phillips said, "I wasn't talking to you, Bones."

"He's going to need to get that closed," Weaver said. "But as long as the bleeding remains controlled, he should be good to go. I just wouldn't wait too long to get it fixed."

"You mean stitches—hospital?" Phillips was not happy about the prospect of losing a couple of his operators to go to the hospital and wait for three or four hours to be seen.

Weaver said, "Well, maybe staples. I can do that here—back at the van. It'll take me about fifteen to twenty minutes. I can hold off stapling it closed for a few hours, if you want to continue on with the search. But, if it starts bleeding again, I'll need to stop and close him up."

"All right, let's get going. You heard what the Chief said —'Don't let this guy escape.'"

CHAPTER 17

The rhythmic movement of the boxcar rolling slowly along the tracks sent Nash into a trance as he thought about Christy. He recalled their first date at the upscale Woodberry Kitchen. With his eyes closed, his mind raced through the phone conversations they had. In Nash's mind they were meant to be together. He believed his dogged pursuit of Christy was nothing more than an expression of love and that she simply misunderstood his affections. He could clear everything up in time.

Startled back to reality, Nash jumped to his feet when the train entered the darkness of the Howard Street Tunnel. Built in 1895 and nearly two miles long, the tunnel ran under downtown Baltimore. Nash had forgotten about the tunnel as well as the train derailment and massive fire that had occurred there in 1991.

"Shit, where the hell am I?" he mumbled.

He went to the open door of the car and saw nothing but darkness. *I swear, I will track her down and kill her for getting me into this shit.*

Mood swings were nothing new for Nash. He could be loving one minute, showering a female companion with gifts and affection, then minutes later becoming both physically and verbally abusive—generally, with little warning and over trivial events.

Within a few minutes the train exited the tunnel and Nash recognized the Baltimore Ravens' stadium only yards from the track. The train curved toward the southwest side of the city. *If I don't get off of here soon, I'll wind up in West Virginia somewhere. I've got to find that slut and finish this once and for all.*

Nash looked for an industrial area where he could go unnoticed. He had to make the decision soon, before the train picked up speed leaving the city. A siding ahead, with a line of coal cars, provided the most promise. It appeared to be a transfer point, and one-story concrete block commercial buildings were visible on both sides of the wide track area. If he could lie low until darkness fell, there would be little chance of anyone noticing him.

Nash leaped from the train. Even at fifteen miles per hour, the speed of the train resulted in a hard landing. Nash quickly scanned the area, ensuring that he was not seen. Running across the tracks, he ducked under the coal cars and bolted for the trees.

Lying on the ground, he contemplated his next move. He had no food or water and little cash. He still had his Glock and the extra clip of ammunition. His cell phone and credit cards were useless. The police were certainly monitoring both for any signs of use.

At dusk, Nash emerged from the weeds. Hungry and disheveled, he made his way to Washington Boulevard and found a pay phone at an area convenience store. Dropping coins into the phone, he called the only person he could trust.

"Hello?" Randy Young said.

"Randy, it's Rick."

"Where the hell are you? The cops want your ass bad."

"I'm over on the southwest side of the city."

"How the hell did you get there?"

"I'll explain later. I need your help."

"Sure, whatever you need."

"I need you to pick me up. I'll be at the end of Gable Avenue off of Washington Boulevard, near the tracks."

"No problem. Be there as quick as I can."

"Something else. I need you to go by my house. The cops are probably watching, so you'll have to slip through the wooded area in back. Go into the shed—the key's over the door—there's a black duffel bag inside a container at the back wall. Grab it and bring it with you."

"Rick, why don't I just pick you up and get you out of town?" Young asked.

"I've got something to finish. Then you can get me to Jersey; a guy I know can hide me out."

"Okay. Give me an hour or two."

✳ ✳ ✳

Oh, crap! What have I just done? thought Weaver as the team moved into the wooded area, searching for Nash. *I've never done any stapling on my own before.*

127

Weaver began second guessing his ability to treat Bones' injury. He had already told Phillips that he could handle the job without taking Bones to the hospital. If he waffled now, he would have no credibility with Phillips or the rest of the team. He might as well leave now instead of waiting out the six months.

I passed the written and practical tests. If they didn't think I was capable, they wouldn't have certified me to do it. Get your head back in the game.

With the assistance of the Department's helicopter, the team began searching the wooded area.

"Seventeen-seventy to Air One," Phillips said.

"Air One," the flight observer answered.

"Do you have any areas we should concentrate on?"

"Negative. Saw a few animals, but that was it. Nothing else moving down there."

"We're going to check a few places along the stream where he could hide. We came across them on a search a few months back."

"Air One, ten-four."

The team slowly maneuvered through the wooded area. Pairs of snipers skulked ahead of the main team element. After twenty minutes, they came upon a small stream and checked three cramped caves. Each of the areas was overgrown and undisturbed.

"Seventeen-seventy to Air One," Phillips said.

"Air One, go."

"We checked those areas and found nothing. Do you have anything else?"

"Negative. Foxtrot's been checking their area and has come up dry, as well," said the flight observer referring to the City's helicopter.

"Ten-four. We're going to head back to our vehicles."

The team had been out searching for over two hours. Phillips hated to admit it, but Nash had probably slipped through their perimeter.

As they got back to the tracks, they were delayed by a freight train passing by. Phillips eyed the train intently as the cars rumbled by.

They were met at their vehicles by Chief Sherman. Acknowledging the obvious, he said, "Nothing, Jack?"

"No sign whatsoever, sir. No footprints, broken limbs, nothing."

"Jack, I don't have to tell you, we need to find this guy. The only positive thing is that we have the girl. Her grandfather is the owner of a local bank. It was going to get pretty ugly if we didn't get her back. The guy is a heavyweight in the community."

"Sir, I'm curious about one thing," Phillips said.

"What's that?"

"Did anybody happen to hear a train when this thing went down?"

"No. Nobody mentioned it. Do you think Nash could have jumped one?"

"Well, they're coming through every twenty minutes or so. Anything's possible."

"Friggin' great. He could be halfway to Florida by now. I'll have the Command Post contact CSX Railroad Police. What about Amtrak?"

"Probably not. They move too fast—about fifty-five. There would just be a big red blotch back there if he tried that maneuver."

"Yeah, I wish. That would certainly alleviate some problems," Sherman said. "I'm going to put a marked patrol unit on the girl's house in Towson when they take her home."

"Thanks, Chief," Phillips said.

After the brief meeting with the Chief, Phillips found Weaver and Bones at the rear of the vans.

"Are you going to get him squared away?" Phillips asked.

"Yes, sir. I just have to make a quick call to my medical director to let him know what I'm doing," Weaver responded.

"Let me know when you're done patching him up."

Weaver walked to the side of the van, away from Bones, and dialed the number for Dr. Jesse Whitmire, medical director for the County's EMS system. Whitmire, a former military doc, was well acquainted with the needs of combat medics. Having been the County's medical director for only six months, he was already well liked by Weaver.

His palms slightly sweaty, Weaver waited as the phone rang.

"Doctor Whitmire. Can I help you?"

"Hi, Doc. It's Danny Weaver."

"Hey, Danny. What's up?"

"I'm out with the team and had one of the guys fall. He has a three-inch lac on his left forearm. It's going to need some staples."

"Okay, you should be able to handle that."

"That's just it. I've never done this on an actual person before. I'm not sure about this."

"Look, if you feel that uncomfortable, take him to the Emergency Department, but I think you can handle it. Take your time. Make sure you have everything you need within reach prior to getting started, and do it by the numbers."

"Okay, I'll give it a whirl," Weaver said.

Whitmire said, "I'll be working in the ED at Greater Baltimore Medical Center—GBMC later today. If he needs a tetanus shot, you can stop by."

"Thanks, Doc."

Walking back around the van, Weaver said, "All right, Bones, let's take a look at that arm."

Overhearing Weaver's comment, Brett said, "Hey, somebody grab a camera. Doc's going to sew up Bones' arm."

"Oh, bullshit!" Weaver said. "This is hard enough without you guys leering over top of me, trying to take pictures. Besides, haven't you heard of HIPAA laws—patient confidentiality?"

"There's nothing confidential around here," Rice added.

131

??

"We need two cameras. One for still shots and another for video," Gunny yelled.

"We also need an extra bullet for Bones to bite on," Brett said.

The comments kept coming as Weaver prepared the equipment to staple the laceration on Bones' arm. *What have I gotten myself into? Shit, they weren't kidding about the cameras. Now they're going to take pictures. This just went from bad to worse.*

"Lie on the floor of the van," Weaver told Bones.

"Do I get a lollipop when you're done?" Bones asked.

"Not you, too. Look, I can staple your mouth shut, too, if you like."

Weaver put on another pair of exam gloves and removed the bandage he had placed over the laceration earlier.

"How does it look?" Bones asked.

"It's about three inches," Weaver said. "Probably take six staples—plus or minus ten."

Bones' face went pale.

"Are you okay?" Weaver asked.

"I'm not liking this all of a sudden."

"You'll be fine," Weaver said. *I hope.*

Drawing 10 milliliters of Xylocaine from a vial into a syringe, Weaver asked, "Are you allergic to Novocaine?"

"No, I don't think so."

"This is Xylocaine—sort of the same thing you get at the

dentist. It will deaden the pain around your little boo-boo. It'll be uncomfortable when I inject along the sides of the wound, but it'll eventually go numb."

Weaver cleaned the edge of the cut with Betadine. Then he poked the needle through the epidermal—outermost—layer of skin and began injecting the medication. As he pushed the plunger in on the syringe, he could see the edge of the wound bulge with from the medication.

"Oh, you bastard!" Bones yelled. "You didn't say it would hurt that much."

"Shut-up and lie still," Weaver told him.

Weaver heard the clicking of the digital camera over his shoulder and the snickers from his teammates. He withdrew the syringe and re-entered the skin further up the wound. With one side numb, he began the same process on the opposite side.

While waiting for Bones' arm to numb, Weaver withdrew 60 milliliters of 0.9% sodium chloride, also known as normal saline, into a syringe from an IV bag.

"Next thing I have to do is clean out the lac—make sure there's no crud in there. 'The solution to pollution is dilution.'" Weaver added the colloquialism he had learned in the tactical medicine school.

Weaver squirted the clear liquid into the wound, hoping to expel any bits of dirt or other foreign objects. If not clean, the cut could become infected once he stapled it shut. He reloaded the syringe three more times, each time expelling it into the laceration.

With a pair of forceps in his left hand, Weaver held the

edges of the wound together. In his right was a small white surgical stapler that he would use to close Bones' wound.

"Do you feel any pain?" Weaver asked.

"I can feel you tugging on the skin, but no pain."

"This white thing is the stapler. I'm going to put the first one about midway down the cut. Then I'm going to put one between that staple and the end. I'll continue like that until it's completely closed. You still good to go?"

"Doing good—except for these other assholes."

Weaver pressed the white stapling gun against Bones' skin. As Weaver squeezed the handle, a single metal staple entered Bones' skin and curled around to close the center of the laceration.

Examining the first closure, Weaver thought, *One down. Looks pretty good.* Feeling more at ease, Weaver put the final six staples in Bones' arm. *Damn, just like in class. Not bad, if I must say so myself.* He was done in less than fifteen minutes.

"That's it. We'll put some four-by-four gauze and bandaging material on it, and you're done. You're probably going to have a scar—I'm not a plastic surgeon."

"No problem, something I can show the kids. Thanks, Doc," Bones said.

"If we get back near Towson, we can run into GBMC. Doctor Whitmire can take a quick look and give you a tetanus shot."

As Weaver stowed his gear and bagged the bloody bandages, Brett slapped him on the back, "Good job, Doc."

At that, Phillips came around the back of the van and said sarcastically, "Are we done screwing around? Let's get out of here. We've got work to do."

Weaver looked at Brett and rolled his eyes. *What a jerk!*

CHAPTER 18

Peering from the bushes, Nash watched the CSX Railroad Police Unit, a white Ford Expedition, creep down Gable Avenue. The Expedition approached the tracks at the end of the street, where the driver doused his headlights and sat quietly.

You idiot! Young will be here any minute, and you've decided to take a break in the worst place possible.

Nash watched cautiously for fifteen minutes, his stomach in knots, his hand gripping the cold metal of the Glock, as the police unit sat at the end of the street.

Is this a routine patrol or—they couldn't possibly know I jumped that train. Did somebody notice me running across the tracks? They would have sent more than one cop if they suspected it was me.

Finally, the unit's headlights came on, and the truck turned and proceeded out to Washington Boulevard.

Minutes after the cop had left, another set of headlights appeared. An old Ford pickup truck inched down the road, the driver's eyes probing the bushes for signs of movement. Nash recognized Young's red truck and, as it neared, he cautiously emerged, looking left and then right before crossing the street to jump in the passenger seat.

Young hardly recognized Nash as he approached the truck. He was used to seeing the Rick Nash that was well groomed, smartly dressed, and self-assured. Although Young did not have the same taste in clothes, he liked Nash's smooth talking ways—his ability to have women eating out of his hand. He looked up to the guy. What he saw now was a man in dirty, torn clothes—a Rick Nash who had not seen a razor, nor bathed, in a couple of days. A Rick Nash who looked tired and worn.

As Nash situated himself in the seat, Young said, "Dude, you are scorching hot right now. Your name and picture are all over the news."

"I know. I know," Nash said, "It's all that bitch's fault,"

"Forget about her. Let me get you out of town."

"No, I need to teach her, and everybody else, a lesson."

Nash had been able to dominate and manipulate everyone around him, including Young. To maintain his status, Nash's mind was telling him he needed retake control by whatever means necessary. He could already see the look on Young's face. He could feel the loss of adoration. Nash fed on the servitude of others. To walk away now would mean losing the devotion of followers like Young. He had no choice but to continue on.

"Yeah, you said that before," Young said.

"Look, Randy, you and I have been friends for quite a few years. If you want to abandon me now, go right ahead. Let me out of the truck, and I'll finish this myself."

Nash had actually only known Young for three years—a long time in Nash's world. They had met just after Young's eighteenth birthday. As with women, Nash's male acquaintances were all younger than he, having found it easier to be a guiding influence on someone five or more years his junior. Nash knew the right words to feed Young—*abandonment* being one of them.

Young's father had been stabbed to death over a gambling debt when he was ten. His mother was a crack addict. He had all but raised himself from adolescence. He often told Nash that he felt abandoned by his parents. "Rick, you're my closest friend. I'll do whatever you want, but I'm just saying it may make more sense to just drop the Christy thing."

"Randy, a lesson in life. When you want something, you have to take it. Nobody's going to give it to you. When someone screws with you, you have to pay them back to show all of the other assholes out there that there are consequences to bad behavior."

With hesitation in his voice, Young said, "Okay, dude. Where we going? What are we doing?"

"First, I need something to eat and something to drink. A couple of burgers and a six-pack would taste pretty good. Then we pay my girl a visit."

Nash and Young merged onto Interstate 695—the highway encircling Baltimore—heading northward. They devoured the burgers and fries Young had purchased minutes before at a nearby McDonalds. Nash had waited in the truck while Young purchased the food and alcohol. Each snapped open the pop-top on a cold can of Coors beer.

Young kept his speed below 60 miles per hour and stayed

in the middle lane of traffic to avoid undue attention. They passed the communities of Woodlawn and Pikesville.

Next stop, Towson.

CHAPTER 19

The team had exited Interstate 695, returning to the main command post, which was still located in Towson. Phillips, Devo at the wheel, with Weaver, Gunny, Lebo, Brett and Davis were in the lead van. The remainder of the team was close on their heels in the second.

Drew Davidson, driving the follow-on van, noticed something odd.

"Hey, guys, we've got company," said Davidson, eyeing his side and rearview mirrors.

"What's up?" asked Paul Runk from the front passenger seat.

"I don't want to sound paranoid, but I think we have somebody following us."

"I'll raise Jack on the radio and let him know we need to run a surveillance detection route. Seventeen-seventy-five to Seventeen-seventy," radioed Runk.

"Seventeen-seventy," answered Phillips from the lead van.

"We possibly have a vehicle following us. Suggest we do a SD route to see if they continue."

"Ten-four. Let's go down Dulaney Valley Road through the traffic circle. You go around the circle and continue south

140

on York Road. We'll go into the circle but loop around it an additional time and wind up behind him."

"Ten-four," acknowledged Runk.

With six streets culminating at the traffic circle in Towson, it was considered a maze. The number of cars entering and exiting the rotary made it difficult to navigate, and making it easy to miss your intended exit point. Most drivers familiar with the area avoided the circle at all costs. But for this situation, it met the team's exact needs.

Devo, in the lead van, entered the circle from Dulaney Valley Road and drove counter-clockwise around the rotary. Davidson entered just behind him, but slowed to allow Devo to get ahead. At the exit to York Road, Devo continued around the circle for a second time, while Davidson exited.

Looking into his side mirror Davidson said, "Vehicle's still with us."

"I don't like this," Runk said.

"Devo's coming out of the circle now. He's about a block behind.

Runk briefed the team members in the van on a plan of action if they had to assault the unknowns behind them.

The team members had already begun situating themselves for a vehicle take-down. Helmet chin straps were cinched, ballistic goggles were placed over eyes, gloves were slid on. They had no idea who was behind them, but they were soon going to find out.

"Seventeen-seventy-five," radioed Runk, "we're making a

right on Pennsylvania Avenue. Suspect vehicle turning with us."

"Seventy to Seventy-five," Phillips answered, "we saw you make the turn. We're about a block back. You got a tag number?"

"Negative."

"If you can get one, I'll run it for you."

Phillips was concerned. *Who the hell is surveilling us? Is this an ambush or what?*

Weaver could see the anxious look on Phillips face. Something he had not seen previously. In turn, Weaver began to worry about what exactly might go down.

"Seventeen-Seventy-five," Runk radioed, "now making a left on Washington Avenue. We're going to go down and make a right on Towsontowne Boulevard. If he goes with us, we'll take him out there between Washington and Burke Avenue."

Runk peered through the mirror on his side of the van. *Who the hell is back there, and why are they on our ass?* With the intensity of the past twenty-four hours, everyone was tired. But the adrenaline was now flowing, and Runk's squad was channeling that energy. Each member of the squad was rehearsing in his mind the takedown procedure.

"Seventeen-seventy, ten-four," Phillips said, "We'll hang back at the intersection of Washington and Towsontowne, so we don't get into a crossfire."

The SWAT van continued down Washington Avenue past the County courthouse with the suspicious vehicle only feet behind. Had this been early afternoon, the streets would have been teaming with attorneys, accountants, and government workers heading to meetings or lunch. But now the many office buildings and businesses were dark. The streets were less traveled with the exception of an occasional college student heading to a local watering hole.

Shortly after making the right turn onto Towsontowne Boulevard from Washington Avenue, the SWAT van slid to a stop. The driver in the vehicle had no choice but to slam on the brakes.

Richard Rice threw open the rear doors; at the same time the thud and whoosh of the opening side door could be heard. Rice went to one knee and leveled his M-4 on the driver of the trailing vehicle.

Tucker, his face still painted green and black, launched from the van's side door. His Remington .308 sniper rifle was slung across his back and his .40 caliber Sig Sauer slid from its holster as he moved quickly and smoothly to the passenger side of the suspect vehicle. Russell Jones, Bones and Mund were on his heels, providing cover with their M-4's. Runk and Davidson took the driver's side. Davidson drew his .40, and Runk shouldered his M-4.

"Let me see your hands! Let me see your hands!" Rice yelled to the occupants of the vehicle.

The teenage boy and girl were shaking in fear as six weapons were trained on the windows of their car.

Davidson threw open the driver's door, grabbing the seventeen year-old driver by the arm and forcing him to the ground.

Holding his .40 close to his body, Tucker did the same with the sixteen year-old female passenger, ordering, "Get on the ground!"

Searching the young male for weapons, Davidson asked, "What the hell are you two doing?"

"I was just driving around town."

Runk began searching the car for weapons and heard an odd sound coming from under the driver's area. Reaching beneath the seat, Runk pulled out a police scanner that was monitoring various police precincts in the area.

"Bullshit!" Runk told the teenager. "You were following us. What's with the scanner?"

Almost in tears, the boy said, "I saw the red and blue lights in the back windows of your van and figured you were looking for that guy from last night. I just thought it would be neat to see if you caught him."

Pulling the driver from the ground, Davidson noticed a wet spot in the boy's crotch. Angered at the potential tragedy, he said, "I think you were out trying to impress your girlfriend. You could have gotten both of you killed with this little stunt!" In a tone sufficiently loud enough for the young girl to hear, Davidson added, "Well, she should be real impressed when she sees you've pissed yourself."

The boy desperately tried to hold back tears. "What are you going to do to me?"

"I wish I had the time. I'd be writing you a ticket and having your parents come out here and get you. But I don't. So your little ass is going to get back in your car—with your girlfriend—and go the hell home. I catch you following any other cops around here, and you will go to jail for hindering an investigation. Got it?"

"Yeah."

"That's 'yes, sir,' you little piece of shit!" Runk bellowed.

"Yes, sir," the boy answered humbly.

As the two teenagers got back in their car and drove away, Phillips had Devo pull their van around the corner.

Runk walked over to Phillips' side of the vehicle and said, "Knucklehead kids. Junior thought it would be cool to trail the cops. He pissed himself when we jacked him up."

Shaking his head, Phillips said, "The command post just called. They want us to start toward the east side again. Someone reported seeing a subject lurking around the rear of Nash's mother's house. Patrol's checking the area already. We're going to back them up in case our boy is trying to get back home."

CHAPTER 20

Young took the Charles Street—Towson—exit from Interstate 695. He looked over to see Nash's eyes closed and his head resting against the passenger-side window. He had fallen asleep sometime after consuming his second beer.

Charles Street was one of the pristine gateways to Baltimore City. Large homes of the rich and influential lined the well-maintained boulevard. The lawns were manicured and the shrubbery was sculpted. This was not the place where homicidal maniacs routinely frequented. Yet this community was still reeling from the killings that had occurred nearby only twenty-four hours before.

Young turned left onto Towsontowne Boulevard just north of the Greater Baltimore Medical Center. Passing Towson University, Young saw flashing red and blue lights ahead at the intersection.

Nudging Nash with his right hand, Young said, "Rick, wake up. Looks like cops up ahead. What do you want me to do?"

Nash raised his head just enough to see over the dash, "Looks like they've got somebody sprawled out on the ground down by Washington. Just make a right onto Burke Avenue. We need to go that way anyhow. Take your time and don't draw attention to yourself."

"Rick, those aren't normal cops, they're armed to the teeth. That's the damn SWAT team, man. Think they're still looking for you?"

Nash slowly looked in Young's direction, "That's a dumb question, don't you think?"

As the pickup truck turned onto Burke Avenue, passing the north side of the University, Nash again began to reflect on the earlier days of his relationship with Christy. *I tried to make her happy and treat her nice; taking her to dinner, buying flowers. She didn't appreciate my love and attention—the stuck-up little college bitch.*

"Cross York Road and continue out Burke to Maryland Avenue and make a right. I just want to get a lay of the land," Nash said.

Young followed Nash's directions and wound his way through the small neighborhood just east of Towson University. As the Ford pickup turned onto Maryland Avenue, they cruised by small single-family homes with swing sets and vegetable gardens in back yards. They passed two apartment complexes whose occupancy had changed from older retired couples to young students when the university had expanded. Finally, there were the two streets of old-Baltimore-style row homes where Christy had been living. Circling the area, Young turned off of Aigburth Road and onto York.

"Go up to Burke again and park behind that church just down from Burkeshire," Nash said. "The truck should be out of sight there."

"Okay. What's the plan? We going to grab her and run?" Young asked.

"We'll see how it goes."

"Just answer me one thing. Do I get the roommate?"

Nash's choice for parking the truck was ironic. Nash had never seen the inside of a church, while Young had not been in one since he was a toddler. Young believed in a supreme being but never took the time to pay a visit on Sunday mornings. He attended Sunday school when he was little, but lost religion about the same time he began to smoke and drink. Nash felt that believing in God was a sign of weakness. With a dysfunctional family, he had no religious upbringing and no moral compass.

Exiting the truck, Nash reached into the bed to retrieve the bag that Young had taken from the shed. He threw the carry strap over his right shoulder and adjusted the Glock that was still in his waistband.

Looking over at Young, he said, "Let's do it."

Young didn't answer as he closed the door and fell in behind Nash.

The night was pleasantly cool and streaks of moonlight could be seen radiating past the spattering of puffy clouds passing overhead. Except for the crunch of wintered brown grass, there was only silence as the two men walked across the lawn at the front of the chapel.

Nash was on a mission—his gaze down as he walked the fifty yards to Burkeshire Road, where Christy felt safe behind locked doors. Crossing to the south side of Burke, he peered over his shoulder, checking for police patrols.

Stately maple trees lined the short street. The sturdy brick homes were a testament to the quality craftsmen of the 1950s. Some of the twenty homes were occupied by students, others were owned by working families with one or two children. Each was well maintained and brandished bright white trim around cornices, windows, and doors. Oddly out of place were two stone walls with arches that welcomed pedestrians walking up the sidewalks from Burke Avenue.

As the two began their trek up the incline on Burkeshire Road, Young placed his hand on Nash's shoulder, then pointed up the street. Nash looked up and noticed the white Baltimore County Police patrol car in front of Christy's house.

Nash quietly raised his right hand and motioned for Young to follow. *Well, I know she's here. They wouldn't have the cops here if she wasn't.*

As Nash quietly slid up the driver's side of the parked cars, he noticed the interior light come on inside the cruiser. Nash froze, thinking the cop had seen him and was getting out. Within seconds, he realized the officer's attention was elsewhere and he continued his hushed movements. Reaching in his waistband, he withdrew the Glock and placed his finger on the trigger.

CHAPTER 21

Officer Hugh Reynolds was nearing the end of his shift. As the newest member of his squad, Reynolds received most of the less than glamorous details; the sergeant ensured that. It was monotonous sitting in front of a house for four hours on guard duty. *Thank God I don't have to sit here for an entire eight-hour shift. I'd give serious consideration to gnawing on the end of my gun.*

Reynolds had become a cop only eight months ago. He was not the son of a police chief; his brothers were not police officers. He did not grow-up dreaming of joining the force. Reynolds had been unemployed after being laid-off from a computer software company. He had seen a recruiting advertisement and decided to take a chance. Reynolds was desperate for a job especially since his wife had given birth to a beautiful little girl just one month before he had lost his job.

Since graduating from the academy and hitting the street, Reynolds had come to enjoy the profession and looked forward to coming to work each day—not withstanding having to sit in front of a house for four hours.

There was only so much one could do within the confines of a patrol vehicle. Reynolds had completed all of his logs, as well as reports from incidents at the beginning of his tour. Earlier in the evening, while it was still light, he had watched the neighborhood kids in the playground at the end of the street. Other tikes rode their tricycles up and down the sidewalk under the attentive eye of parents. Now, sitting in the darkness of the dead-end street, there was little to do. Reynolds stretched his arms wide and drew in a deep breath of fresh air from the open windows, hoping to revive himself. He reached up, flipped on the interior light, and pulled a law enforcement magazine from his tan bailout bag. Leafing through the pages of advertisements, he hoped to see an article that would grab his attention.

Reynolds thought he heard something and turned to his left only to see a bright flash of light. He never heard the sound of Nash's weapon discharging, but he did feel a searing pain in his left shoulder. The 9-millimeter round from the Glock drove down through his shoulder, missing the protection of his body armor. The projectile pierced his lung a fraction of an inch from his aorta—the main artery carrying blood to the body.

The rookie cop slumped to his right, the magazine falling to the floor of the car, an article on surviving a gun battle visible on the open pages.

A miniscule amount of blood oozed from the small bullet hole. Almost immediately, Reynolds started having difficulty sucking air into his lungs—it felt as though someone was compressing his left side, keeping him from taking in full breaths. He could feel himself losing consciousness and he fought the urge to surrender. *Fight, damn it! Fight! Don't give up. You can survive this.*

Reynolds knew he had to let someone know he was shot. He tried to reach the red Signal 13 button on his radio. In years past, the words "Signal 13"—"Officer needs help"—sent chills up the spine of every cop who heard it. It meant an officer was in dire need of assistance. He was either getting the shit kicked out of himself or he was being shot at. The cavalry would soon be riding over the hill to help. New technology allowed an officer simply to press a button and get the same result. Linked to a GPS system, the downed officer's whereabouts would be announced to responding units without the officer having to say a word. Many old-timers, however, still grabbed the mic and sounded off the call for help.

Reynolds knew that pressing the button would set off alarms in the communication center and bring every cop in the precinct. But each time he tried to move his left arm there was nothing—no movement, only intense pain. Wedged in the console containing the light and siren controls, he was too weak to roll and free his right arm. He began to think of his mom and dad—and his wife. *Dear God, help me. Don't let me die. Please let someone call for help for me.*

With each attempt to suck life-giving oxygen into his lungs, air was being pulled into the bullet hole. The respiratory system is a closed, complex operation. When that system is compromised by something like a bullet, it cannot function normally.

The air being drawn through the bullet hole wasn't entering Reynolds' left lung. It was being trapped in the pleural space—an area between the lung and a fibrous sac that surrounds the sponge-like organ. The result was a buildup of air that, with each passing breath, was compressing his left lung. Without help, Reynolds' lung would begin to be forced against his heart and his uninjured lung on the right. Because of this pressure, his heart would be unable to pump oxygen-carrying blood through his body. Death would not be far behind.

CHAPTER 22

The calm, quiet early spring night had just been rocked by the sound of a single gun blast. Residents of the tiny street cautiously peered from their windows, not quite sure of what they had heard. Some thought it had been a car backfiring, others believed it to be yet another college student with fireworks.

Young shook his head and, with a smirk on his face, said, "You're an animal."

Nash merely shrugged his shoulders as he marched toward the door of Christy's house. He ripped open the bag on his shoulder and pulled out a Mossberg 12-gauge shotgun with a pistol grip and folding stock.

Holding the weapon at shoulder height, Nash banged on the house door with the butt of the shotgun and bellowed, "Honey, I'm home!"

The ratcheting of the action was unmistakable as Nash chambered a round. He lowered the barrel to the handle and pumped a round into the doorknob. Almost simultaneously, he raised his right foot and kicked open the door.

Christy had cellphone in her hand, attempting to dial 911, when Nash blew through the door. Jackie raced down the stairs frantically. Holding the gun with both hands, Nash slammed the pistol grip into Jackie's right temple. She fell in a heap at the base of the stairs. Young, only steps behind Nash, grabbed the phone from Christy's hand and knocked her to the floor with his left forearm.

"Nine-one-one, what is your emergency?" the operator asked.

Christy was able to get out a scream for help just as Young threw the phone against the wall, where it shattered into small pieces.

"Thought we'd do a double date tonight. So I brought along a friend," Nash said sarcastically.

Seeing the door still ajar, Christy tried to bolt past Nash and Young, screaming, "Someone help! Call the police!"

Nash swung the pistol grip of the shotgun and buried it in Christy's stomach as she ran by. She doubled over in pain and began to vomit on the hardwood floor just inside the entryway.

Kicking the door shut, Nash said to Young, "Find something to tie these two up."

"Rick, let's just grab them and get out of here."

"We will. We will. Just tie them up and then we'll get the hell out of here. I don't trust her not to run."

Young yanked a couple of electrical cords from wall sockets. He grabbed Jackie, still out cold from the blow to her head, and dragged her into the living room. He haphazardly looped the cord around her feet and hands. After knotting the cord sufficiently tight, he tugged to ensure Jackie could not get free.

Throwing his hands above his head, Young said, "I could do pretty good in a calf roping event."

Nash shook his head. "And you call me an animal?"

Young secured Christy in much the same manner.

Sobbing, Christy said, "Why can't you leave me alone? The police are going to be here any second. Just get out."

"I'm not done with you yet, you ungrateful bitch," Nash said. "I show you my love last night, and what do you do? You bolt from me the first chance you get."

Christy was lying on her right side—hogtied—with her hands and feet bound together. Her abdomen was still spasmed from the pain of Nash's blow. Only inches away lay Jackie, unconscious, a knot growing on her head.

"Jackie, I'm sorry," Christy whispered.

"Shut up!" Nash screamed.

Christy jumped at Nash's outbreak and her tears began to flow again. *How could I have done this? I'm so sorry, Jackie. Please forgive me.*

Christy looked just above Jackie's motionless body and noticed the picture of her family that was sitting on the table near the couch. The picture had been taken at Christy's high school graduation. She stood proudly in her cap and gown, with her mother, father, and sister by her side. As she closed her eyes, she wondered whether she would ever see any of them again.

The SWAT team had just left the Command Post and was en route to assist with the search of the area near Nash's mother's house. Phillips was about to switch the radio to the channel for Precinct 11 in Essex, when the communications operator began trying to raise the patrol unit stationed on Burkeshire Road in Towson.

"Communications to Seven-twenty-four," the operator said.

"Communications to Seven-twenty-four," trying again, seconds later.

Phillips could sense by the sound in the operator's voice that something was not right.

"Communications to Command Post—urgent," the operator said excitedly.

"Command Post, go."

"We are receiving numerous calls of shots fired on Burkeshire Road. We cannot raise Seven-twenty-four."

"Command Post—"

"Communications to Command Post," the operator interrupted. "Nine-one-one just had a hang-up call from 54 Burkeshire Road. They report a woman screaming for help prior to the call ending. Additionally, we just received another call that the officer in front of that address is slumped over in his vehicle."

Grabbing for the microphone on the dash Phillips said, "That's our guy! Damn it, I know that's Nash. Devo, get off at Dulaney Valley Road and get us the hell down there."

Devo hit the brakes and swerved to get off at the upcoming

exit ramp. He flipped on the red and blue lights and floored the accelerator after maneuvering around the curve of the ramp.

"Seventeen-seventy to Command Post. We're en route to Burkeshire, ETA less than five."

Weaver sat passively on the bench in the rear of the van. His palms were sweaty and his pulse began to race. *Thank God I haven't had anything to eat, because it would be up around by Adam's apple right now.*

The past two days had been like a see-saw, with adrenaline rushes from the ups and downs of potential sightings of their suspect. The team was getting tired merely from putting their gear on and taking it off. But Phillips knew, as did many of the other members, that this was it. This was the showdown they had been expecting and perhaps, deep down inside, wanting. Nash needed to be taken off the street. It would be Nash's decision whether it would be in cuffs or in a body bag. Silently, most everyone was betting on the body bag.

CHAPTER 23

The sirens—a lot of them—were getting closer. Grabbing Christy under the armpit and slinging the Mossberg over his shoulder, Nash said, "Get them up. We've got to get out of here."

Christy struggled against her bonds and against Nash. Jackie was like a sack of potatoes. Young was struggling to get her off of the floor.

"Screw it," Nash said, "leave her! We don't have time."

He threw open the front door, ready to make a run for the truck. Stepping out the door, he saw a police cruiser, red and blue lights flashing, coming up the street. Nash dropped Christy to the ground, pulled the Glock from his pants, and opened fire on the car—placing three rounds into the hood and windshield. He then grabbed Christy and dragged her back inside, slamming the door behind him.

Seeing the rounds hit the patrol car, Young said, "Good shootin' there, Tex. But now what are we going to do?"

"Back door! Back door!" Nash yelled.

Young ran out the back door from the kitchen, but stopped suddenly when he saw flashing red and blue lights coming from the end of the homes behind them on Burkeleigh Road.

159

Young turned and ran back for the door, pushing Nash back inside, "Cops back here, too."

"Shit!" Nash said. Pointing to Jackie, still lying near motionless on the floor, he added, "Drag her over and prop her up against the front door. If the cops try to come in, they have to go over top of her first."

"Someone help!" Christy screamed. "Help me!"

Nash grabbed Christy by the hair and pulled her head backward. In a flash the Glock was out of his pants. He shoved the barrel into Christy's mouth, cutting her upper lip. "Shut up," he said, eyes wide, "or I swear I'll blow your brains out!"

Christy began to struggle, but Nash tightened his grip on her hair, pulling a few strands out by their roots. Looking at the darkness in Nash's eyes, she knew he meant every word and decided against fighting any further. Nash released her now flaccid body and returned the gun to his waistband.

Young was impressed. Although Nash's appearance was pretty shabby, he had not lost the thing Young most admired —the ability to control a situation.

Nash had a determined look on his face as he pressed the button on the side of the Glock and dropped the magazine from the gun. Tossing the magazine to Young, he said, "There's a couple boxes of nine millimeter ammo in my bag. Fill this up for me."

"You got it."

Nash pulled the extra clip from his pocket and slammed it into the butt of the gun, ensuring it was seated. He pulled the slide back to check that there was still a round in the chamber and slid the pistol back into his waistband.

Young handed the full clip back to Nash. This was an adrenaline rush for Young. He felt alive, the blood coursing through his veins at high speed. Young was not a hardened criminal. He had been hit with some DWI charges, possession of marijuana, and minor assaults for bar fights. His juvenile record also showed a few auto thefts when he decided to use other people's cars for joy rides. His exploits usually netted him an admonition from the judge; waving his finger and saying don't do it again. Young had never seen the inside of the county detention center, and thus had no real sense of any consequence for his actions. To him, this was just the adult version of taking a joy ride in a stolen car. But this was far from a youthful infraction of the law. Things were quickly spiraling out of control.

CHAPTER 24

The two SWAT vans sped south on York Road. Devo kept a watchful eye on cross traffic, looking for other responding police vehicles.

"Seventeen-seventy to Command Post," Phillips said over the radio.

"Command Post."

"Is the APC en route?" Phillips wanted to ensure he had an armored vehicle to use, if necessary.

"Ten-four. They should be arriving momentarily."

Turning to the rear of the van, Phillips said, "Brett, I want eyes on that cruiser when we get there."

Brett gave the team leader a thumbs up to acknowledge the order. Reaching into his rucksack, Brett retrieved his Morovision Gen III night vision rifle scope. He quickly mounted the night optic in front of the Leopold scope already on his .308 sniper rifle.

As the two vans turned onto Burke Avenue, they were faced with a sea of county police cars. The sound of sirens from other responding units filled the air. As the lead van slowed to a stop, Brett leaped from the rear doors and began to search out a location where he could get the best eye on the patrol car that was supposed to be guarding the house on Burkeshire Road.

Phillips climbed from the front seat of the lead van and began walking toward the center of activity, looking for whoever might be in charge. This was typical Jack Phillips. His experience and training told him that nothing was gained by running about frantically. Phillips' deliberate pace allowed him to assess his surroundings and the situation—carefully gathering information by which a sound tactical decision could be made.

Within seconds a young, newly promoted, lieutenant came running up the street toward Phillips. *You have got to be kidding me. This son of a bitch can't be out of diapers yet. He is in way over his head.* Phillips threw a half-hearted salute as he approached. The act of respect went unnoticed by the exasperated lieutenant.

"El-tee," Phillips said, "what do we have?"

Phillips knew he had to calm this kid down if he was going to get anywhere. Phillips also needed the lieutenant to understand he was not in this alone—use of the term "we" was purposeful. The team was there to help stabilize a bad set of circumstances.

"Take a deep breath, sir," Phillips went on, "and start from the top. Do we have any verbal with the officer up there?"

"Negative," answered the lieutenant. "Seven–twenty-three's car was shot up going up the street."

"Okay, I want to talk to him."

"Her."

"Whatever… can we just get *her* up here? Any communication with whoever's in the house?"

The lieutenant said, "I think the gunshots were communication enough, don't you?"

Well I know where my first bullet's going. Shoot this kid in the foot and get him out of here. Trying to control his temper, Phillips said, "Point taken, Lieutenant. So we don't know who the shooter is?"

"Nothing confirmed, but probably the suspect we've been looking for."

"My thoughts, as well."

Phillips tried to gather additional intel from the female officer who had nearly become a second casualty, but she could not provide anything useful.

Brett made his way to the stone wall and arch on the west side of Burkeshire Road near Burke Avenue. He flipped down the two legs of the bipod on his rifle. He rested the device's rubber feet on a four-foot-high section of wall. That would stabilize his gun to give him a better sight picture when he looked through the scope. Settling in to his weapon, Brett peered through the night optics. Everything before him was green and black. Keying his mic, Brett said, "Brett to Phillips."

"Phillips."

"Jack, I've got an eye on the cruiser, but I don't have any movement. I have a heat signature from inside the car. Looks like a body slumped over."

"Ten-four. Anything else outside around the area?"

"Standby."

Brett slowly moved the rifle left and then right. He was looking for anyone else who might be injured, or for someone waiting to spring an ambush. "Negative, nothing else out here."

"Ten-four. We're going to use the APC to get to Seven-twenty-four, can you cover our approach?"

"Affirmative. I'll relocate to provide the cover."

Phillips turned back to the lieutenant and said, "Eltee, one of my snipers has a heat signature in the cruiser. I'd like to use the APC to retrieve him."

"This is your show right now. I just want my officer out of there," responded the lieutenant.

The team had not been on the scene for more than three minutes and was ready to move in to rescue the downed officer.

Returning to the SWAT vans, Phillips said, "I want Bones, Rice, Lebo, and Gunny in the APC. We're going in to get the officer out of Seven-twenty-four. Use the same procedure as in training. Threat should be to the right, but maintain an eye on that left side. I don't know if the windows are up or down in the cruiser. If they're up, just smash the window and get that door open. I want to be out of there in thirty seconds."

Weaver's stomach was already in knots. This was exactly the mission he had been trained for—a downed officer, possibly shot. *Just like at the abandoned house, I'm left behind again. Son of a bitch.*

Phillips turned to Weaver. "Weaver, you're with us, too, but stay in the APC. Do not get out with the rest of the squad. Once he's inside, he's all yours."

"Got it. Do we know if the state police medevac chopper is in the air? I want him downtown to Shock Trauma ASAP."

"If not, I'll make sure they are."

The knots in Weaver's stomach did not disappear. The reason for the uncomfortable feeling merely changed. He was now going to be in the thick of it and would have to perform.

Phillips quickly checked with the lieutenant to request the chopper while heading for the APC. The Lenco BearCat armored personnel carrier had been on the department's inventory for less than six months. The four-wheel drive, black, armor-plated, truck could withstand multiple hits from small arms fire. The previous unit had been a military surplus hand-me-down, originally built in the seventies. It was in poor shape and parts were next to impossible to locate. The new truck had twice the interior space as the old unit. But, the team had had only one training session on performing a rescue of this type. There was no time to run a rehearsal. The injured officer, if still alive, might not last that long.

Weaver grabbed his M-9 medical bag and headed for the APC. Phillips had already climbed into the right front seat and would command the rescue from there. Bones and Rice were the actual rescuers and sat across from each other toward the front of the APC. Lebo and Gunny were both carrying M-4's and would provide cover. They sat near the rear doors. Weaver took a seat in the middle of the truck just behind the driver and Phillips. He faced the rear of the truck, enabling him to treat the injured officer once they got him inside.

"Everybody good to go?" Phillips asked.

Getting five thumbs up, he looked toward Bob Murray, the driver. "Let's go get our boy back."

Murray was a fifteen-year veteran of the agency, currently working out of Headquarters. He had been involved with writing the specifications for the armored vehicle and watching its progress as it was built. Murray was very territorial about the truck; few people could even touch the thing without his permission. He was considered to be a near expert on what it could and could not do, but he had never put the truck to the test in a real incident.

Murray grasped the gear shift tightly and put the truck in drive. The APC slowly moved down Burke Avenue headed for Burkeshire.

"You want to go dark?" Murray asked.

"Yeah," Phillips answered.

Murray hit a few switches, and every light on the unit went out. There were no headlights, no clearance lights, no instrument lights on the dash. The brake lights would not even come on when Murray stepped on the brake pedal. The smallest bit of light could illuminate the truck or, more importantly, one the team members when they made the rescue.

As the APC made the right turn onto Burkeshire Road, Weaver briefly thought about what he might face. These circumstances were so out of the ordinary for most EMS providers. EMTs and paramedics arrived at an emergency in a big red and white ambulance with a wailing siren and lights flashing. Generally, they were met at the door by concerned family members or friends of someone who was sick or injured. But tonight he found himself in body armor and helmet, with a gun strapped to his side. It was too dangerous to get out of the apparatus. In fact, it was so dangerous, his ride was armored. *Maybe Kathy was right. Is this lunacy?*

Weaver closed his eyes momentarily and refocused. *Get your shit together. Okay, protocols. Head trauma? Chest trauma? Abdomen?* Within seconds he had run through the basic and advanced techniques he might need to keep this officer alive. If he *was* still alive.

* * *

Every inch of Christy's body was in pain. The electrical cord that served as her bindings cut into her flesh. Her head, arms, legs, and abdomen throbbed. She was tied in an unnatural position, with her hands nearly touching her feet behind her. The muscles in her arms and legs felt like they were being torn. She didn't know how long she could endure the contorted position she was in.

As she lay on her left side in the middle of the living room floor, Christy was frightened at the prospects of when, and how, this would end. She knew Nash was unstable, but it seemed that with each passing minute he was becoming more unglued, more prone to outbursts of violence. *How could one person hold so much rage inside of them?* At any moment, she expected him to walk up, put a gun to her head, and blow her brains out. Every time he came near, her muscles involuntarily tensed. And each time she tensed her muscles, the pain became unbearable. She could not stand this much longer.

Christy looked across the floor and saw her friend Jackie lying motionless. She had yet to completely regain consciousness after being hit in the head by Nash. Noting the rise and fall of Jackie's chest, Christy was relieved to see she was still alive. There was little more Christy could do for her friend other than pray.

They had been having a typical college dinner—pizza— when the violent invasion occurred. Jackie had just run upstairs to retrieve a friendship card she had purchased for Christy earlier in the day. Half-eaten slices of pizza still sat on the table in front of the couch. Two partially consumed glasses of chardonnay sat beside the pizza box. The half-empty wine bottle had toppled over on the floor when Young dragged Jackie to where she now lay.

What had started out as an intimate welcome home party for a terrified friend had turned into another violent night at the hands of a madman.

CHAPTER 25

Weaver sat facing the rear doors of the APC. It was cramped, and would be even more so when the injured officer was loaded aboard. He unzipped his M-9 medical bag to expose the lifesaving gear he might urgently need. Bones and Rice readied the backboard, a device usually used by EMTs at the scene of motor vehicle accidents when a victim has a possible neck or back injury. The board would be used to load Reynolds into the back of the armored vehicle.

In training, the team had attempted to simply grab their victim by the ankles and elbows and heave him into the back of the APC, but they had found that the board made the process faster and easier. It also reduced the possibility of additional injuries to the person being rescued.

The four team members in the rear of the APC glanced at Weaver, knowing this was his trial by fire. Not one had misgivings about his capabilities.

Burkeshire Road was only the length of a football field and the travel time to the patrol car was a matter of seconds. The team had little time to think about the mission they were attempting.

Turning to the rear of the unit, Phillips reminded the two rescuers, "Thirty seconds, guys."

The APC quietly crept up the street—a stealthy approach might not draw unwanted attention from Nash. Once Murray saw the rear doors were past the patrol vehicle, he slowed to a stop. The rear doors opened, and both Lebo and Gunny stepped out onto the six-inch-wide heavy metal bumper and propped their M-4 carbines over the top rear corner of the APC. Lebo aimed his weapon at the houses and cars on the east side of the street. Gunny kept his trained on the houses to the west

"Show your face, asshole," Gunny mumbled. "I'll take it off."

Right on their heels, Rice and Bones jumped from the truck with the backboard in hand. They rested one end on the ground and the other on the bumper of the APC.

Reaching the side of the cruiser first, Rice reached through the open window and opened the driver's door. Bones dropped onto his hands and knees between the door and the frame of the car. Rice reached over top of him and grabbed the injured officer by the top of his body armor and pulled him upright. He heard the gurgling noise coming from Reynolds' airway and knew he had to get him to Weaver fast. He reached under the officer's armpits, grabbed his wrists, and yanked him from the driver's seat. Bones could feel the weight of Reynolds' body sliding over his back. When the officer's legs fell free of the patrol car, Bones stood and grabbed his ankles. It was smooth and flawless—as if they had done it countless times before.

Bones and Rice concentrated on getting Reynolds into the APC. They knew Gunny and Lebo had their backs. If anyone posed a threat, their cover would engage and keep them safe.

The concept of relying on your team was borne through years of training together. It was a basic concept that each person needed to be comfortable with—putting your own life in the hands of another team member.

Rice and Bones carried Reynolds the couple of feet to the rear of the armored vehicle. Rice laid Reynolds' torso on the upper part of the board closest to the doors so that his head would be the first part of his body to go inside. Once Bones had dropped Reynolds' feet onto the backboard, he moved opposite Rice. Looking at each other, they picked up the backboard, slid it into the APC, and jumped inside.

Gunny and Lebo continued to scan their areas of responsibility for threats. They never looked behind to check what the two rescuers were doing. Hearing Rice and Bones slide the backboard inside, Gunny and Lebo ducked in the APC themselves and closed the rear doors.

In less than twenty seconds the team had retrieved the downed patrol officer and delivered him to Weaver. As Reynolds was slid into the rear of the APC, Weaver saw a blue tinge around his lips. *Shit! He's not getting enough air.* Weaver fought the urge to jump right in and begin treating Reynolds' breathing problem. Unlike the traditional ABC's of medicine—airway, breathing, and circulation—battlefield medicine dictated the medic check for severe bleeding first. Reynolds could last four to six minutes without oxygen. However, if he was shot and severely bleeding, he could die from a loss of blood in about two. Even though it had been nearly ten minutes since the team embarked for the scene, Weaver wanted to be sure the officer was not bleeding out. Dragging him from the patrol car could have caused the bullet to move and knick an artery.

Weaver poked his hands under Reynolds' back and slid them down toward his waist. He held his palms up as he pulled them out. *No blood—that's good. No blood pooling around his legs. Didn't see blood all over Bones and Rice when they got into the APC. He must not have any major leaks. Get to his breathing! Bullet hole in his shirt near his left shoulder.*

Next, Weaver pulled the Benchmade tactical knife from the thigh strap of his pistol belt. With one hand, he flicked open the three-and-a-half-inch blade and sliced open Reynolds' blood-stained uniform shirt and body armor. Using a knife was a lot faster than trying to cut the material with a pair of scissors. More dangerous—especially if you slipped—but faster. Coupling Reynolds' breathing problem with the bullet hole Weaver now saw near the officer's clavicle, he knew he was dealing with a collapsed lung—a pneumothorax. He also knew that time was precious. If he did not act quickly, the collapsed lung would begin pressing against Reynolds' heart.

Pointing up the street, Phillips told Murray, "Take the alleyway ahead and curve around behind the houses on the east side of the street. That will give us some cover."

Murray engaged the transmission and stepped on the gas. Suddenly, the team heard gunfire and three rounds struck the side of the APC. Everyone ducked instinctively even though the unit would stop most small arms fire.

"Go! Go! Go!" Phillips yelled.

Murray slammed the accelerator to the floor and sped up the street.

"Son-of-a-bitch didn't have balls enough to engage us when I could have lit his ass up!" Gunny yelled.

173

Rocking from side to side as the APC careened out of the kill zone, Weaver, kneeling on the floor, held Reynolds' head between his knees in an attempt to keep his airway open. Weaver's butt was between the driver's seat and Phillips. The entire crew compartment was bathed in red light meant to maintain the team's scotopic vision. At the same time, he reached toward his M-9 bag. Without looking, he withdrew the long cylindrical tube that carried a 14-gauge IV needle.

Weaver had memorized the location of each piece of medical equipment in his bag. Working alone, he might not have the ability to take his eyes off of his patient. If operating at night, he might not have enough ambient light to see. He had to be able to grab the right piece of gear without looking or using a light.

Holding the tube in his right hand, Weaver popped open the top with his thumb and withdrew the three-and-a-quarter-inch long needle. This was an enormous needle to have penetrate the skin. Paramedics often joked that you needed a hammer to get this thing through.

With the first two fingers of his left hand, Weaver felt down Reynolds' rib cage. He pushed down firmly and found the space between the second and third rib just above his left nipple. He pressed the needle against the skin just above Reynolds' third rib and pushed. The skin of Reynolds' chest stretched slightly and was finally pierced by the sharp needle. Weaver continued to push its full length into the near lifeless man's chest. A sudden hiss of escaping air from the needle let Weaver know he was in the right place and had just saved the officer's life. The air building in Reynolds' chest had been relieved—he now had a fighting chance at making it to the trauma center.

Weaver withdrew the needle from the plastic catheter that would remain in Reynolds' chest.

Dropping the needle, Weaver said, "Needle on the floor!"

In all emergency departments and ambulances, used needles are immediately placed in a red plastic container. This safety measure helps to keep a doctor, nurse, or paramedic from being stuck with a dirty, contaminated needle carrying blood-borne diseases. But the back of the APC was not an ambulance, nor was it an emergency department. At that moment, Weaver felt safer dropping the thing on the floor and covering it with the toe of his boot rather than attempting to put it in the small container in his M-9 bag.

The four team members in the back of the APC looked on in awe as Weaver worked feverishly to save the life of the injured officer. His actions were methodical, as if he didn't have to think about what needed to be done. None of them wanted to be in Reynolds' position, but each felt comforted that if they were injured, Weaver was there to help.

Continuing his examination of Reynolds, Weaver hollered, "How long to the LZ?"

"Thirty seconds to the landing zone. Trooper 1's on the ground," answered Phillips, looking over his shoulder.

Still having a few seconds until their arrival at the landing zone, Weaver reached in his M-9 bag and retrieved a nasopharyngeal airway. He ripped open the pouch of Surgilube that he had taped to the device and spread the clear lubricating jelly on the flexible rubber tube. Weaver slid the airway into Reynolds' left nostril. He continued to advance the tube until the flange at the end of the tube seated at the entrance to Reynolds' nose. The airway would help keep Reynolds' tongue from dropping to the back of his throat and occluding the flow of air into his lungs.

Weaver heard the roar of the helicopter blades cutting through the air as they approached the LZ—a grassy plot on York Road in front of the university. As the APC ground to a stop, Gunny and Lebo threw open the rear doors and jumped out. Rice and Bones grabbed the backboard with Reynolds on it on their way out the door. Weaver leaned over, grasping the other end of the board and helped Rice and Bones. Jumping from the rear bumper of the APC, Weaver noticed a county fire department paramedic in his peripheral vision.

"Hey!" yelled the paramedic, "Did you needle that guy's chest?" attempting to be heard over the noise of the aircraft.

"Not now," Weaver said.

"I don't know who you think you are, but you don't do that kind of shit on your own. Why isn't he on oxygen?"

Clearly, the fire department medic did not know who Weaver was. With over one thousand people in the agency it was hard to keep track of who was who. Of course the helmet, body armor, and gun didn't help. This guy was not expecting one of his own to be jumping from an APC in this kind of getup.

The paramedic tried to push his way between Bones and Weaver as they were heading to the chopper in an attempt to examine the injured officer.

To Weaver's surprise, Phillips, his M-4 carbine in hand, stepped in front of the paramedic and said, "Take a hike. He's got it under control."

The paramedic thought twice about pushing past a guy with a rifle across his chest. He fumed as he turned and walked back to his ambulance mumbling, "The medical director will hear about this."

Carrying Reynolds feet first toward the black and green state police EuroCopter Dauphin medevac helicopter, Weaver saw the trooper-paramedic open the side doors to the rear section of the aircraft. Even with the helmet visor down, Weaver could tell it was Sergeant Jim Gabriele, and he knew the injured officer was in good hands.

The three ducked their heads slightly as they approached the aircraft. The whoosh of the blades was unnerving to those unaccustomed to working around helicopters. Both Gunny and Lebo ducked down a little further as they heard the blades spinning dangerously close overhead.

Gabriele came in close to Weaver's left ear and said, "Danny, what've you got?"

"Bullet wound," Weaver yelled over the noise of the helicopter. "Left chest near the clavicle. Possible pneumothorax. Needled his chest—good air release—and dropped a nasal. That's all I had time for."

"No problem," Gabriele said as he laid his hand on Weaver's back.

Gabriele knew this was Weaver's first mission, and it was one that would be talked about for years to come. He knew his friend was probably nervous as hell; he would be if he was in that position.

As Gabriele closed the doors of the aircraft, he turned to

Weaver with a thumbs up and said, "Good job, Danny! Stay safe."

CHAPTER 26

Nash heard the motor noise of the armored personnel carrier creeping up the street. At this time of night, noise carried farther than it did during daylight hours, when the din of a busy metro area rendered individual sounds indistinguishable.

"Randy," Nash said, "hit the lights. Cops are coming up the street in an armored car."

Young jumped to the front door and flipped down the light switch for the first-floor living room. "What the hell's going on, Rick?" Although he had been on board with having a little fun, Young was increasingly worried that he might have gotten in over his head.

"Chill, we've got the upper hand. They aren't going to come charging in here when we've got these two as hostages."

Looking at Christy as he was speaking, Nash noticed the change in her facial expression on hearing that the police were coming up the street. She thought she was about to be rescued.

Christy relaxed ever so slightly. *Dear God, thank you! Please let them get me and Jackie out of here.*

Nash knelt on a chair positioned near the two living room

windows. With two fingers, he spread the slats of the mini-blinds and watched the large black truck plod up the street. He noticed the perspiration building on his hands and tightened his grip on the cold black steel of his handgun. Seeing the heavily armed cops grabbing the officer from the patrol car, Nash knew they weren't coming after him—at least not yet.

Nash turned toward Young. "Hey, told you not to worry. They're just getting that cop from out front."

Seeing the police retreat back into the safety of the armored vehicle, Nash said, "Watch this. I'm going to have a little fun."

Silently sliding the window up, Nash stuck the muzzle of his handgun out and fired three rounds. Laughing, he exclaimed, "Look. They're running like a pack of scared rats."

For Christy, Nash's words were the psychological equivalent of his burying the butt of the shotgun in her stomach again.

With a sinister laugh, Nash looked at Christy and said, "You thought they were coming for *you*, didn't you? They're worried about their own buddies and not about you—you spoiled little bitch. See, the world doesn't revolve around you."

Christy was devastated and once again began to sob.

"Shut-up!" yelled Nash, and he bolted from the couch, raising the gun as if to pummel her head.

Before Weaver could get back to the APC, he heard the whine of the twin gas turbine engines build as the chopper pilot increased power to the rotor blades. Within three to five minutes of lifting off, Trooper 1, carrying Officer Reynolds, would be landing on the rooftop helipad at Shock Trauma in downtown Baltimore. There was no better place in the world for the officer to be treated.

Head down, Weaver walked slowly back to the armored vehicle. The time he had to treat Reynolds had been mere minutes. *Did I do the right thing? Should I have at least attempted to get an IV line in place? Shit, I didn't even get a pulse and blood pressure. No time. Didn't have the time to get anything else done.* Weaver's mind raced through all of the treatment modalities he should have performed if he had the time.

"Weaver," Phillips yelled, "let's go. This isn't over yet, we've got work to do."

Drawn back from his thoughts, Weaver trotted back to the APC, his heavy body armor bobbing up and down on his chest. He climbed into the rear of the truck and took his seat. Gunny, Lebo, Rice, and Bones climbed in behind him. As he stowed the gear in his M-9 medical bag, Weaver said a short prayer. He asked for God to watch over Reynolds and grant him a speedy recovery, and he also asked for the strength and ability to get through the next few hours.

As the APC lumbered away from the landing zone at the university, Phillips pressed the PTT button on his chest and radioed, "Phillips to Brett."

"Brett to Phillips. Go."

"Have you started to deploy your snipers yet?"

"Starting to move out now. I'll have each team give you a sit-rep once they're in position."

"Ten-four," Phillips acknowledged.

The APC turned onto Burke Avenue and came to a stop at a small bank parking lot that was now serving as a staging area and command post. Gunny threw open the rear doors of the truck and climbed out, with Lebo, Bones, and Rice close behind. Weaver slid his arm through the right shoulder strap of his M-9 bag and crouched down as he walked toward the rear doors. As he stepped down to the macadam of the parking lot he saw that Phillips had already made his way to the side of the mobile command post vehicle.

It was a surreal scene. Alternating flashes of red and blue light coming from a multitude of marked and unmarked police cars bathed the entire street. Periodically, the circling police helicopter with its thirty-million-candlepower light would immerse the area in a blue-tinged, artificial radiance. The roar from the orbiting aircraft drowned out all other ambient noise. Officers posted at nearby intersections directed vehicular and pedestrian traffic away from the scene.

Something caught Weaver's eye. His wife, Kathy, was standing in a small crowd of people on the other side of the yellow police barricade tape.

Son of a bitch! This is not what I need right now. I cannot believe she would come down here.

Weaver was already tired and hungry. He had just treated a guy who was near death. There was an idiot with a gun and maybe a hostage barricaded in a house around the corner, and now his wife decided to come by for a visit. Weaver was feeling the pressure. There had been no easing into this job with a few in-and-out raids or a short-duration barricade. He had his butt handed to him straight out of the gate. Weaver knew he had asked for this assignment. Actually, he had fought incessantly for it. To cave under the pressure would ruin his entire career. But he did relish the simplicity of a blazing structure fire or cardiac arrest.

Looking around to see if anyone was watching, Weaver stepped to the yellow tape that fluttered in the breeze.

"Kathy, what the hell are you doing here?" he said.

"I'm worried about you. You haven't called, and I heard on the news–"

"Let me explain it one more time. This is not a game. I can't just stop everything and call. Other people and events dictate my actions, and they don't generally allow for coffee breaks to call family and friends. Now, go home."

"I can't sit at home and wonder where you are and what you're doing. I could deal with your shifts at the fire department, but you running out the door and not coming back—I can't deal with that."

"This is what I've been wanting to do for a long time. And now I have the opportunity to do it. Don't you understand that?"

"I'm not going to live like this."

Weaver was pissed. He turned to walk away, but knew he had to keep his home life from crumbling. Before he had taken his first step, Weaver added, "Love you."

Kathy's eyes were visibly wet when she whispered, "Please be careful."

Weaver turned to see Phillips looking in his direction. *Shit. That's all I need is to now have him on my ass.* He quickly walked back to where the remainder of the team had gathered. Phillips eyes bore through Weaver, "Who was that?"

"Nobody," Weaver answered.

"I don't have time for you to be screwing around. You either keep your attention on this mission or you go the hell home."

Weaver wasn't going to argue. He was about as pissed as Phillips was right now, "Got it."

Phillips turned his attention back to the team and said, "Everybody gather round. To our knowledge, the suspect is still in 54 Burkeshire Road. He shot at us about five minutes ago, so I would take that as a good indication. No one has been observed leaving the residence. No contact with him as yet, so we have no confirmation that he has a hostage. But I would certainly make bet on it. Once the snipers are in place, we'll move up the street and get set up two doors down from our target location."

As if on queue, everyone heard Brett's voice in their earpiece, "Brett to Phillips."

"Phillips. Go."

"Taking side Alpha," said Brett. "I'm attempting to use a residence directly across from the target. Where can we send the occupant?"

The team would designate each side of the house with a letter from the military alphabet. The front of the house being Alpha, continuing clockwise with Bravo, Charlie, and Delta.

"We can't force them to leave," replied Phillips, "but obviously it's in their best interest. We don't know how long this will take. If they decide to leave, send them back to the command post."

"Ten-four. I haven't gained access to the residence as yet. I'm trying to get someone to the rear door now."

Brett knocked on the rear door of 55 Burkeshire Road a third time.

"Police!" Brett yelled, "Come to the door."

He did not go to the front door of the house for fear of arousing Nash and drawing gunfire.

A woman in her mid-sixties finally opened the door. She looked as if she was ready to retire for the night. Her jaw dropped when she spotted the six-foot-two-inch sniper standing outside her entryway. Clad in camouflage BDU's, with his face still painted, and an awfully large gun in his hand, Brett was not what someone might expect to see on an early spring evening. The woman's eyes grew large and she could not speak. She was sorry she had opened the door.

"Ma'am, I'm sorry to scare you. I'm with the county police SWAT team. There is a man barricaded in the house across the street. He has already shot and killed a few people and he shot one of our officers tonight. Can I use your house?"

Brett's words spewed from his mouth quickly and by the look on the woman's face, he was not sure she had understood the message. He was about to repeat the request when the information made its way past her eyes and ears and into the depths of her brain. She stammered slightly but finally was able to think clearly and answer.

"Ah, how do I know you're really—" the woman began.

"Ma'am. How many bad guys run around town dressed like it's Halloween? Can we please come in? I don't have much time."

"I guess," the woman answered.

Before the second word had been fully spoken, Brett started through the door, "Thank you!"

Turning to see his partner coming through the rear yard, Brett said, "Devo, get her squared away while I get set."

Brett, with his rucksack on his back, ran up the stairs to the second floor and found the front bedroom.

Devo entered the rear door and stopped near the bewildered woman.

"Ma'am, I would suggest you get out of here," Devo said.

"Where am I supposed to go? I don't have any family nearby. Besides I'd need my medicines and–"

"Gather your medicines real quick and head down the alley to Burke Avenue. Go to our command post in the bank parking lot. I'm sure they will have an evacuation center set-up."

"But…"

With a sense of empathy, Devo said, "Ma'am, I can't kick you out of your own home, but it is not safe for anyone on this block. You really should leave. We'll take good care of your house."

Devo helped the woman gather a few essentials and called for a patrol officer to ensure she made it to the command post safely. Brett had already begun establishing his observation post when Devo arrived on the second floor.

"Give me a hand moving the furniture," Brett said.

The two rearranged the room to meet their specific needs. They needed to be able to observe the house where Nash was barricaded, but they did not want to be seen. A reflection from a rifle scope or a light from another window silhouetting their profile could give away their position.

A similar situation was unfolding on Burkeleigh Road, where Tucker and his sniper support Randy Greco were setting up another sniper hide. Greco had been Tucker's partner for over five years. A native of New York, he was often teased about his accent.

The family at the Burkeleigh house was insistent about not leaving. They would remain in the basement of the residence for the duration.

"Brett to Tribe's," radioed Brett.

"Tribe's to Brett," Tucker answered. "I've got my oh-pee established on the Charlie side of the house. Should have a good eye on anything at the rear of our target."

"Ten-four. We are up on the Alpha side. I've got an oh-pee on the second floor. Davidson and his support will be setting up on the first floor momentarily. No activity as yet."

"Brett to Phillips," came the next transmission.

"Phillips. Go."

"Your overwatch is established. Let us know when you're ready to move."

Phillips concluded his briefing. "Let's gather our gear from the two vans and get ready to move out. We'll stack at the stone wall at the corner of Burkeshire."

The department's large command van was just arriving. Seeing no other senior command staff on scene yet, Phillips sought out the precinct lieutenant he had dealt with earlier. Phillips tried to stifle a laugh as he noticed the young lieutenant's name tag—Rambo.

"El-tee," Phillips said, "the assault team is about to deploy. My sniper teams are already in position."

With a concerned look on his face, the lieutenant responded, "Can you do that before the captain or the major get here?"

"Lieutenant, I think they would be rather pissed if we didn't have this place locked down real soon."

"Okay, do what you think is best."

Weaver trotted back to the van to retrieve his STOMP medical bag. The rucksack carried extra medical gear he might need if the operation continued for an extended period. Among other items, the kit included additional intravenous fluids and medications, bandaging supplies, airway and breathing equipment, skin stapling materials, and a small dental kit. The combined weight of the STOMP and the M-9 was over forty pounds, but Weaver did not want to find himself isolated and short of needed supplies.

Weaver was not the only person carrying extra equipment. Jones carried a pack containing the team's six-round, forty-millimeter, semiautomatic Sage Control Ordinance projectile launcher. The weapon shot CS gas and smoke projectiles, as well as less lethal rubber baton rounds. Although the thirty-four-inch-long rifle only weighed eleven pounds, the ammunition brought Jones' pack weight to nearly twenty.

Runk had strapped on a pack carrying an array of breacher tools weighing nearly thirty-five pounds. The rig carried a pair of bolt cutters, a maul, and a pry tool known as a Halligan. The three tools gave the team the ability to force their way through doors, windows and walls.

Everyone moved slowly under the weight of the extra gear. The lack of food, water, and rest was taking a toll.

The team gathered near the stone wall at the corner of Burke Avenue and Burkeshire Road.

"Brett, any change?" Phillips radioed.

"Negative. One light on the first floor, but shades are drawn. No activity.

"Ten-four. Tucker?"

"Tucker has nothing on the Charlie side."

"Ten-four."

With the target location being sandwiched between two other row homes the Bravo and Delta sides were not watched by the marksmen.

Phillips wanted the sniper teams to be aware of his intended movements. He pressed the PTT button on his chest and radioed, "Let's stack up along the stone wall. We'll move to the corner house and regroup there. Our end point is the Delta side of number 58 Burkeshire—two doors away from our target."

"Brett. Ten-four."

"Davidson. Ten-four."

"Tucker's Okay."

The group lined up along the short wall. Bones was in the lead, with Davis behind, providing cover. Weaver tucked in behind Phillips. The remainder of the team fell into the formation, with Mund as the rear guard. Each person squeezed the thigh of the person in front and said, "Stack is tight."

Phillips radioed, "We're moving."

The bicep muscle in Bones' left arm contracted as he raised the ballistic shield to cover his head and torso. Simultaneously, his right hand pressed the release on his holster and he slid the .40 caliber Sig from its berth. Snapping around the corner of the wall, Bones and the rest of the team had fifty yards of open, moonlit ground to traverse. With his handgun just below the viewport of the shield, Bones kept a watchful eye on the houses ahead. As each person cleared the wall, his M-4 carbine swung up to cover a window, door, or car.

Weaver's stomach was once again in knots. Their first point of cover—the side wall of 68 Burkeshire—seemed a world away. In the scheme of things fifty yards was not a great distance, except in football or when being shot at. Weaver had had the misfortune of having a ricochet zip past his head while on the range during his initial training. He would never forget the sound and did not want to relive the moment if Nash decided to open fire. Although the snipers could take Nash out, the assault team would be sitting ducks.

Slow is smooth, smooth is fast, Weaver remembered from his training as he fought the urge to sprint to the safety of cover.

The team silently maneuvered across a small alley to the side of the house. There were five homes to a group, and Nash was in the middle house of the second group.

"Everybody good to go?" Phillips asked.

With a thumbs up from each person, Phillips continued, "We'll move to the corner house of the next group. If he comes out and opens up, Bones and Davis will engage. Everybody else, find a window or door and get it open. I don't care how. But get us the hell out of the line of fire."

Each member of the squad gave a thumbs up, acknowledging Phillips orders.

"Sniper teams, any change?" Phillips asked.

"Nothing on the Alpha side," Brett radioed.

"Charlie side quiet," Tucker added.

"Ten-four. We're moving."

Bones swung around the corner of the house, leading the team on their trek to the next point of hard cover—the side of 58 Burkeshire. Each person concentrated on his mission to the exclusion of all else. A momentary lack in concentration could be disastrous.

Midway up the group of houses, Weaver heard a bang to his right side as a dog ran to a window and began barking. *Son of a bitch! Damn it!* Weaver nearly wet himself as he jumped to the left about two feet. Rice and Gunny, positioned directly behind him, stifled a laugh. Everyone had similar events where they had been startled. Rice reached up and squeezed Weaver's shoulder; at least he had not let out a yell.

The team made it to the side of the second group of houses. Just two doors south of their position, Rick Nash was barricaded—possibly with a hostage.

"Bones, maintain coverage on the front. Mund, cover the rear," Phillips said.

Bones dropped to one knee at the corner of the house and rested the ballistic shield on the soft earth. He kept a watchful eye on the front door of number 54 through the shield's viewport. Mund kept a watch on the rear of the house from his own vantage point.

Weaver once again found himself in eerie silence. The normal sounds of a bustling metropolitan area were missing. The sounds of buses picking up and delivering passengers had ceased. All traffic and other activity within blocks of the incident had been shut down. Even the police helicopter had pulled away from the area. He heard only the noise of his own lungs filling with air and eventually releasing it back to the chilled night.

Phillips turned to Runk and in a hushed tone said, "Bones and Davis will be your cover. Check the front door. If it's locked, then we'll go for the rear. If that's locked too, we'll have to force our way in."

Runk nodded to acknowledge the plan.

Bones, Davis, and Runk cleared the corner of number 58

and silently moved toward the front door of the house. The three stepped through a small unkempt garden filled with wet, moldy leaves and dead bushes. A ten-by fifteen-foot cement porch sat in front of the entryway. Bones and Davis took a position just past the door to provide cover for Runk. Davis moved a foot to his right and leveled his M-4 toward the front of the house where Nash was holed-up.

Runk stepped up onto the concrete pad and reached for the doorknob. Slowly, his black-gloved, right hand turned the knob. *Shit! Locked. Nothing is ever easy*.

Leaning forward to Davis, Runk whispered, "Locked."

Davis laid his hand on Bones' shoulder to let him know they were retreating back to the corner. The three cautiously moved backward without ever taking an eye from the potential threat before them.

As the three backed around the corner, Runk caught Phillips' eye and shook his head.

Gunny immediately stepped up and took over coverage of the front of the row of houses. He leaned his right forearm against the corner of the brick wall and rested the barrel of his M-4 in the palm of his hand. His left forefinger rested lightly on the frame, just above the trigger. Gunny scanned the area through the EOTech Holographic Weapon Sight mounted atop his rifle. The HWS system was unlike previous laser systems that placed a red dot on the intended target. The new system produced the same precision shots, but did not have the telltale red dot signature.

Although Gunny was right-handed, he had switched to his left side in order to use the brick wall as cover. As with most of the team, he practiced off-handed shooting incessantly and was nearly as good with his left hand as he was with his right. If Nash stepped out to fire, he would only see a sliver—one to two inches—of the former Marine.

"Tucker," Phillips radioed, "Breaching team will be checking the back door."

"Ten-four. No change," Tucker said.

As Bones, Davis, and Runk approached Mund's right shoulder, Mund lowered his M-4 so he wouldn't sweep his teammates. Bones stepped around Mund and immediately felt his right boot sink into a pile of dog excrement. *Son of a-,* Bones thought. Not missing a beat, he stepped around two overflowing trash cans. The small grey-painted porch leading to the rear door was only steps away. Bones and Davis took a position beside the structure, knowing there was insufficient room for all three.

Runk checked the rear door, but it too was locked. Reaching over his left shoulder he slid the Halligan from the backpack. The forcible entry bar had been a mainstay in fire departments across the country since the 1940s. There was a blade, or adze, at one end with a tapered pick protruding at a ninety-degree angle from it. The other end contained a two-pronged fork. The tool could be used for prying, twisting, striking, or breaking doors, windows, and locks.

Runk slid the forked end of the bar between the door and doorframe just above the lock. Firefighters would use a maul or the flat end of an axe to strike the Halligan and seat it into place. However, Runk knew any noise would give away their position. He would need to muscle the tool into place. Runk pushed and pulled on the bar until he was able to spread the door far enough to allow the lock to spring from the strike plate mounted in the frame. The door swung free and Runk radioed Phillips the shortest of messages, "We're in."

Now the team had a foothold only feet away from Nash. And there had been no indication that he knew they were there.

CHAPTER 27

Phillips had the team complete a sweep of the house to ensure no one was home. Runk and Davis took the second floor; Gunny and Rice checked the basement.

Mund, the last person through the door, looked around the room and said, "What a shit hole."

"I've seen worse," Weaver retorted.

"Doc, there's shit growing on the dishes in the sink. My feet are sticking to the kitchen floor. I've been in some nasty places, but damn ..."

Weaver shrugged. Over the years he had responded to fires and medical incidents at homes that were deplorable. Most often, the conditions were the result of personal neglect and not the result of the family's being poor. There were many families who had little money but were able to keep their meager surroundings neat and clean. Others were just slobs. He had been to a variety of neighborhoods and found the good and bad in each—roaches, rats, you name it. Kitchen cabinets hanging from the walls, garbage and junk strewn about—these were the types of houses that Weaver responded to routinely. Most people ignored the existence of such filth. It wasn't something that was depicted on the evening news.

College students could be right up there on the slob list.

With a Towson University Tigers flag hanging on the wall of the living room, it was obvious they had stumbled into a student rental unit. Returning from the second floor, Runk said, "Found some weed laying out on a table upstairs."

"Yeah," Phillips said, "there's a couple of pipes down here, too. But we've got more important things to worry about right now."

Walking in on the conversation, Gunny said, "They must do some heavy partying here. There's six cases of beer and a tap for a keg in the basement."

"Just make sure those six cases are still there when we leave," Phillips said. "Now, I want eyes on our target. One person at the front door and one at the rear. Switch it up every thirty minutes."

"I'll take first watch front," Gunny said.

"I got the rear," Mund followed.

Phillips depressed the PTT button and said, "Brett—Tucker, I'm going to maintain watches at the front and rear doors of 58."

"Brett. Ten-four."

"Tucker. Okay."

Gunny opened the front door of the house and switched his M-4 to his offhand just as he had done earlier at the front corner. He braced his right boot against the door frame and rested the barrel of his weapon in his right hand, which was also braced against the same frame. His sight picture was just above the EOTech. Thirty minutes was a long time, he wanted to be at least somewhat comfortable.

Mund positioned himself at the rear door and kept a watchful eye on the dimly lit rear of their target.

Phillips gave a nod to Runk. "We need to get a rescue plan together in case we have to move in the next few minutes."

"Okay," Runk said. "I'll start a schematic of this place—I'm sure the layout is the same as in 54—then we can start working on a plan."

Runk pulled a small pad of paper and a pen from a pouch on his body armor. Starting on the second floor, he sketched each room. He plotted where each window, closet, staircase, and door was located. He even noted which way doors swung and the distance from the window sills to the floor. Nothing could be left to chance; every piece of intelligence was valuable. If a rescue attempt became necessary, the more intel they had, the greater the chance the hostage could be extracted alive.

After Runk had diagrammed the first floor and the basement, he and Phillips put their heads together to devise a quick plan. Over time they could revise the procedure, but if something happened, at least they had a basic plan to work with.

Watching Phillips and Runk work on their plan reminded Weaver he needed to work on his own medical intelligence and threat assessment.

He slid a four- by six-inch spiral-bound book from the bellows pocket of his BDU pants. Weaver had purchased the book while in his tactical medical training only weeks before. The *Special Operations Mission Planning Field Guide* used a type of laminated paper that would allow him to reuse the book on subsequent missions. The small green and black guide was a template for documenting Weaver's medical intelligence data. The front portion of the manual could be used by the other members of the team for their own planning and reference. He hadn't had the time to pass it around before all hell broke loose.

Weaver pulled a felt-tip pen from his shirt pocket and began filling in a few of the blanks on the medical threat assessment template page of the book.

Primary hospital is Saint Joseph's; they're only about a mile away. GBMC is the secondary hospital. Shock Trauma is the primary trauma center. I'll use the same landing site we just used to fly Reynolds out. I also need to get some basic medical history from each of the guys on the team—allergies, medications they're taking, and any pertinent medical history. This would have been so much easier if I'd had the time to do it at the office and not out here.

Since this was protected medical information, Weaver needed to be discreet in talking to each guy on the team. Not something that would be easy in this environment. But it needed to be done. The probability of something going wrong was painfully obvious—they'd already had one cop shot this evening.

After tactfully, and quickly, gathering as much medical data from each of the guys as he could, Weaver approached Phillips.

"Jack, I need you for a minute."

Slowly looking up from some notes he was making at a grungy kitchen table, Phillips said, "What do want?"

"I've gotten medical history from all of the guys. It's not the best time, I know, but I haven't really been able to handle it before now. Do you have anything significant history—meds, allergies—that I might need to know? Everything will be kept confidential."

"A positive."

A questioning look came across Weaver's face, "I'm sorry…"

"A positive," Phillips repeated, "my blood type. That's all you're getting. Now leave me alone, I've got to call the command post."

Weaver noted the information in his book as he walked away. *Jackwagon! He is not going to change.*

Everyone was tired but still on edge. It had only been thirty minutes since they had taken gunfire while rescuing Officer Reynolds from the cruiser. It had been quiet since then, but there was no telling when violence would erupt again.

* * *

Christy felt like she was riding a rollercoaster. Her emotions had been given a boost when she heard the police were coming up the street, only to be dashed once again when they left without her.

Psychologically, Christy was having difficulty coping with such a rapid change of situation. An hour ago, she and Jackie had been sipping wine and eating pizza. Now she and her friend were bound, injured, and possibly facing death. Her mind could not accommodate such radical shifts. *Why haven't the police done anything? My God! Don't they know we're here?*

Christy was not only worried about her own well-being but that of her roommate, as well. Although Jackie had regained consciousness, she was still lethargic and not fully aware of the direness of the situation. Her eyes were open, yet she was still only able to get out a few clipped phrases.

Nash looked at the two women dispassionately. There was no remorse for the injuries he had inflicted on them. He was still enraged over what he felt was Christy's abandonment of him. He believed the entire issue was of Christy's making, including the involvement of the police.

Walking across the living room, Young said, "Rick, what's the plan?"

Nash had been recalling the events of the past few weeks and the prospects for his future when Young approached.

Running his hand through his hair, Nash said, "They're probably expecting us to make a break for it, so I say we wait another hour or two. There's that little playground at the end of the street; only fifty yards or so away. We'll head out the back—it's darker than out front—and beat feet for it. I think if we can make it to the playground, we'll have a pretty good shot at getting away."

"What about those two?"

"We'll play it by ear," Nash said, nodding in Christy's direction. "If we can drag her along, great. I want to make her life as miserable as possible. Screw the other one—leave her behind. If this one becomes too much of a distraction, we'll dump her."

Shoving a piece of cold pizza in his mouth, Young mumbled, "Works for me."

CHAPTER 28

Phillips pulled open the Velcro flap of a pouch on his duty belt. Sliding out his cell phone, he pressed the speed-dial number he had programmed for the command post.

"Hi, Steve Rambo," came the answer.

Phillips pulled the phone from his ear and looked at it for a second. This was not the typical way he would expect the command post to answer the phone.

"Lieutenant?" Phillips said.

"Yeah, Lieutenant Rambo."

"El-tee, is the major there yet?" Phillips spoke with a bit of exasperation in his voice.

"He just got here. Hold on."

I swear I'm going to walk back down the street, put my hands around his throat, and squeeze.

After a few seconds of silence, Phillips heard a familiar, raucous voice. "Major Gittings."

Major Chris Gittings had been on the force for twenty years. His service as a lieutenant in the Army Airborne carried into his no-nonsense leadership style. Many of the SWAT team members loved him because of his kick-ass approach.

"Phillips, sir. Good to hear your voice. I can give you a sit rep when you're ready."

Reading between the lines of Phillips' message, Gittings said, "Understood, Jack. I can only imagine. Yeah, give it to me."

Phillips closely followed standard military format. "The assault team is currently located in number 58 Burkeshire. I have sniper teams deployed on side Alpha in number 55 and on side Charlie in number 55 Burkeleigh Road. You're aware of the small arms fire we took making the rescue?"

"Ten-four."

"We've had no other suspect activity since that time. Currently, I have assaulters covering both the front and rear of the target. We have no injuries, and I think we have everything we need logistically. We're developing an initial assault plan in case we need to make a rescue in the near term."

"Whatever you need, Jack," Gittings said. "Make it happen."

"Ten-four."

"Anything else?"

"Negative," Phillips said.

"Very good. The crisis negotiation team is getting set up. I'll have them talk to you directly when they're ready. Have your guys had any food?"

"Negative, sir. No time."

"It's been a busy day. We'll try to get something down to

you. Also, I was just informed that Reynolds will be okay. The trauma center says that that medic of yours—Weaver— saved his life by putting that needle in his chest."

With a bit of tension in his voice, Phillips said, "Well… I'm glad to hear he's going to be okay."

"Jack, I know you don't like having Weaver on the team. But he just proved his worthiness."

Phillips concluded the call with Major Gittings. Although he shared the rescued officer's condition with the rest of the team, the second portion of the major's update never passed Phillips' lips.

The major kept his word and sent two boxes of donuts to the house where the team was staging. Having not eaten all day, the group devoured the sweet, fattening globs of dough in minutes.

"Hey, Jack," Rice said, "didn't they send any coffee? Who eats donuts without coffee? And besides, how the hell am I supposed to stay awake?"

Even though Weaver had partaken in annihilating the donuts, he knew the sugar spike would be followed by a sharp drop. Eyelids would become heavy shortly thereafter. It had been a long couple of days, and it did not look to be ending any time soon. The team needed to be put on a rotating schedule of work and rest in order for them to maintain peak efficiency. If a rescue was to be attempted, everyone would have to be on his game.

Weaver had come to learn that approaching Phillips about letting the guys get some rest was not going to be easy. His words would need to chosen carefully, otherwise Phillips would have a second snack—chewing on Weaver's ass.

Weaver approached Phillips and said, "Jack, I have a limited number of over-the-counter caffeine pills, since they didn't send any coffee. If you like, I can give a few to the guys keeping watch at the front and rear."

"I don't know about giving these guys any pills."

"Yeah, I understand," Weaver said sympathetically, "but it's nothing more than what you would get in a couple cups of coffee. Besides, those donuts are going to hit bottom pretty soon, and they'll be nodding off."

"Okay, give them to the guys holding cover. I'll tell the others to close their eyes for a few minutes and get some rest."

The corner of Weaver's mouth turned upward ever so slightly; he was proud of his accomplishment. Learning to manipulate Phillips might just be the ticket to a long relationship.

Rice and Jones were now pulling watch at the front and rear doors. Having been given caffeine pills, the two were able to keep their weapons up and their eyes open. The same could not be said for the rest of the assault team. Bones had found a rickety old wooden chair to call his own. Still clad in armor and helmet, with his M-4 across his lap, Bones rested his head against the wall behind him and closed his eyes. Lebo sat on the floor and ran his hand across the stubble on his normally smooth head. With his rifle between bent knees, he lowered his head to the front grip of the barrel. The remaining guys followed suit, finding whatever small uncluttered area they could find.

Weaver leaned against the staircase leading to the second floor. He felt a slight breeze coming from the open doors where the two black-clad assaulters stood watch. He looked around the cold, dark room and took in the silence. It was surreal. This was like something out of a war movie where troops huddled in a combat-ravaged house. Worn soldiers using whatever down time there might be to catch a quick power nap before their next battle.

The stark reality of the situation was not lost on Weaver. Anything could happen at any moment. Having never dealt with an incident like this, he had no point of reference. Weaver knew he could control the fear. He had done it countless times on fires. Being lost inside a burning, smoke-filled building or being trapped beneath a collapsed roof was his routine—he had been doing it for years. However, this was wildly different. There was a whack job up the street who had no problem killing people. Whatever Weaver was feeling, he had to lock it away. This was not the kind of job where you could pick up the phone and call your mentor for guidance.

After the moment of reflection, Weaver sat on the small landing where the steps made a ninety-degree turn near the bottom of the staircase. For the past two days he had been moving at high speed. The sudden slowdown hit him just like it had every other member of the team.

He was torn, try to tough it out, or relent and close his eyes in the hopes of recharging his batteries? His intellect told him he was no better than the others in the room. Actually, they were probably in better physical condition than he and more adept at managing the rigors of long standoffs. He had just encouraged them to get some rest, yet he felt the need to do the exact opposite. *Let's not listen to my own medical advice.*

Weaver realized his turmoil was rooted in his conflict with Phillips. He did not want to appear weak. Phillips was still awake and moving about the house—inspecting his equipment and checking on the guards at the front and rear doors. But if the shit hit the fan in an hour or two and Weaver couldn't keep up with the team, or he made a stupid mistake, he was screwed. Phillips would push to get rid of him—and for good reason.

Weaver took off his Kevlar helmet and lay back against the wall at the bottom of the staircase. His eyes slowly shut and he drifted into a state of lassitude. His mind subconsciously registered the sounds and movements in the room, but he was able to otherwise rest. It wasn't like crawling between the sheets of his own bed next to Kathy, but it would have to do. Weaver's respite lasted for nearly thirty minutes, when he was suddenly jarred from his slumber.

Weaver was awakened by a vibration at his right leg. He had forgotten about having thrown his cell phone in the bellows pocket of his BDU pants. Weaver had been undecided about carrying the device after the repeated voicemails from his wife on the previous day. With the intensity of the operation, he had decided it would be wise to have a second means of communication if all hell broke loose.

Still groggy, Weaver answered, "This is Weaver."

"Danny," responded Doctor Whitmire, Weaver's medical director. "It's Doctor Whitmire. Are you okay? It almost sounds as if I woke you up."

"Actually, you did."

Confused, Whitmire asked, "You aren't at the hostage incident?"

"Yeah, I am. We're two doors down from where this guy Nash is barricaded. The team leader agreed to put most everyone down for some rest. I took advantage of it myself and closed my eyes for a few minutes."

"Glad to hear it. You're not of much use to anyone if you can't function."

"Ten-four. I wasn't able to stop by the ED to have the staples checked on my guy with the laceration."

"Not a problem. Just clean the lac every twenty-four hours, put some antibiotic ointment on it, and cover with a clean dressing. If it appears to be infected at any point, let me know and we'll start him on a course of oral antibiotics. You've got some in your bag right?"

"Yeah, I'm carrying Cipro, Keflex, and Ancef."

"Good," Whitmire said. "I don't anticipate you'll have a problem, though."

Weaver rubbed his forehead with the palm of his hand. He was developing a headache. "Since you're on the line—I completed a threat assessment. There are a couple of things we need, but I haven't been able to reach out to anyone as yet."

"Give it to me."

"I'd like to have two medic units on standby at the Command Post. One needs to be strictly dedicated for any injured police. The second would be for anyone else. Also, can you see if the state police would be willing to leave a chopper standing by at the university LZ site for the duration?"

"I wouldn't think either one would be a problem. Anything else?" Whitmire responded.

"Yeah. A quick end to this."

"I hear you. Well, if there's nothing else—I'll talk to you later."

After completing the call, Weaver rummaged through his M-9 bag and pulled out two, 500-milligram acetaminophen tablets. He took a swig of water from his Camelbak hydration system after popping the pills in his mouth. Weaver then leaned back against the wall and closed his eyes in the hope of reducing the throbbing in his head.

Phillips had just finished rotating the guards at the front and rear doors when his phone began to vibrate.

"Phillips."

"Jack, it's Pete Mitchell," answered the seasoned detective. Mitchell had been with the department for fifteen years and had been a crisis negotiator for ten. Tonight he was operating as the intel officer for the group; gathering every bit of information about Rick Nash that was available.

"Have you had any contact with this asshole yet?" Phillips asked.

"No, we're still trying to get a handle on what we're dealing with."

Hostage situations develop in stages, the first of which is the capture stage. The hostage taker is nervous and trying to gain control of an unsettled situation. He is very prone to violent outbursts.

The potential for violence continues into the transport stage. A hostage might be moved from one room to another, one floor to another, or clear across town. The hostage taker might resort to restraining, blindfolding, and gagging his captive.

Knowing this, the police let the situation, and the hostage taker, settle down prior to making contact.

Mitchell continued, "The information we do have is not good. This guy Nash is very unstable. He's been on a path of destruction since he was a kid. Nash's father was a heavy drinker and would beat his mother right in front of him. To make matters worse, he would then throw the empty cans and bottles at Nash.

"We also have reason to believe that at the age of eleven or twelve our suspect began torturing animals. Later, as Nash started dating, he was quick to follow in his father's footsteps and began to abuse his girlfriends. Everybody we talk to says this guy can be polite one minute and unbelievably violent the next.

"He's been in and out of jail on all sorts of charges, including possession of an illegal firearm. We're still trying to check into any psych history. Jack, you know this type of scenario doesn't usually end well. We'll do what we can, but you need to be ready at a moment's notice if he goes off the deep end again."

"Thanks for the upbeat information, Pete," Phillips said. "And by the way, you're off my Christmas list.".

"Yeah, right. Well, wish us luck. We're making our first call to Mister Nash in just a few minutes."

CHAPTER 29

Christy was startled as the old, tan, push-button phone on the kitchen wall began to ring. She had finally been able to calm herself—as much as anyone could while being bound and held captive. It took a few seconds for her to focus on the sound and its whereabouts. *I never had home phone service connected when we moved in. How …?*

Gun in hand, Nash was able to cover the short distance between the living room and kitchen in less than six steps. Eyeing Young, he picked up the receiver on the fifth ring. Covering the mouthpiece with his fingers, Nash remained silent as he held the handset to his ear.

"Hello? Hello? Anybody there?" a voice asked.

"Who's this, and what do you want?" Nash answered.

"My name's Tim. I'm with the police. Can—"

Nash slammed the receiver back into its cradle, disconnecting the call.

"Who's that?" Young asked.

Walking past him back into the living room, Nash answered, "Wrong number."

The phone began its rhythmic tone again. Young took a step toward the kitchen, saying, "I got it."

"No!" Nash yelled. "It's the cops. Leave it alone."

The phone continued its incessant, annoying ring for nearly thirty seconds.

"Rick, do you think it's a good idea to just hang up?" Young asked. "We're up to our ass in cops. We can't just ignore them and hope they'll go away."

Annoyed, Nash barked at his friend. "You don't get it. We talk on my terms, and when I'm ready." Reaching down and grabbing Christy by the hair and pulling her head from the floor, he continued, "I've got the control, and I've got the collateral. If they don't know that, they'll soon find it out."

Young quickly threw his hands up. "Chill, man. I'm with you—I'm on your side."

Nash threw Christy's head to the floor like he was spiking a football. A sickening thud could be heard throughout the room.

The gray matter of her brain sloshed back and forth within the confines of Christy's skull. The intense pain came on her like an Amtrak Acela Express. The young girl's eyes rolled back in her head as she fell silent.

Moments later, Young noticed an unexpected stream of light coming from the edge of a drawn curtain.

"Rick, something's going on outside," Young said.

Nash leaped from his seat and doused the living room light as he headed for the window.

Pulling the drapery back slightly, Nash said, "It's hard to see past the lights, but it looks like that same truck that was out there earlier."

"This is the county police," came the voice across the PA system of the armored personnel carrier. "Someone inside number 54 Burkeshire pickup the phone. We want to make sure everyone is okay."

The same message was repeated two more times. At the conclusion of the third repetition, the APC began its retreat back down the street. Within seconds, the phone on the wall of the kitchen began to ring again.

Nash stuffed his pistol in the waistband of his pants and sauntered toward the kitchen. He rubbed his hand across his face, stopping momentarily at his eyes.

Slowly lifting the handset from the cradle, Nash said, "What do you want?"

"My name's Tim. Who's this?" asked the voice.

"You don't need to know my name. You just need to know that I'm the one holding the cards right now."

"I understand what you're saying, but it just makes it easier for us to talk if I have a name that I can call you by. Anything, it doesn't even have to be your real name."

"Rick."

"Okay. Do you normally use Rick or Ricky?" the voice asked.

"Never call me Ricky!" Nash yelled, "My father called me Ricky. Never, ever, call me Ricky!" Enraged, Nash slammed the phone down once again.

Nash fixated on the two girls lying on the floor as he slowly paced the room. He cradled the gun in his two hands as he moved about. It was as if the cool steel gave him comfort as he contemplated his predicament—and a way out.

* * *

Weaver watched and listened as the APC, with its bright white rooftop lights, inched up the street and began to broadcast its message.

Phillips had warned the team to expect the maneuver. He had received a call from the command post indicating that Nash had hung up the phone with little more than a few syllables being uttered. Although it wasn't uncommon to use the APC or a bullhorn to make an initial contact, it was another indicator that things weren't going well.

Minutes later, Phillips could be seen on his phone again. In a hushed tone, as the team gathered around, Phillips gave a quick briefing on the status of the operation.

"Our suspect," Phillips said, "refuses to play well with others. He's hung up on the negotiators twice in less than thirty minutes. That's probably a record."

"We can solve the, 'not playing nice issue,'" Bones interjected, raising both an eyebrow and his M-4.

"Since you're so anxious there, Bones, you're coming with me. Lebo—you, too. The command post wants us to retrieve the keys and shotgun from Seven-twenty-four. It would look pretty bad if Nash was able to escape in one of our own cars with a weapon still inside. I'm sure Brett would have a shot from across the street long before he made it to any of the cars, but… we'll play it safe. The negotiators are hoping to reestablish contact with our suspect—keeping him busy while we make our move. Bring the tire spikes. We'll need to spike each car out there so he can't use them for escape, either."

Phillips continued refining the specifics of the operation with the assault team and the snipers. After another ten minutes of planning, Phillips said, "Any questions? Good, we move out in five. We need to be back in here prior to sunrise."

Lebo stepped out the rear door and dropped to his right knee; his M-4 trained on the rear of their target house.

The utility company had been ordered to cut power to the lights in the alley and on the street. The trio's movements would be concealed by the darkness and shadows. The lack of light had little effect on the assault team. They had been sitting in darkness for hours. Their visual acuity was at its peak. Phillips knew he and his men had the tactical advantage.

Phillips and Bones were next out the door. Bones, the last of the two, lightly touched Lebo's shoulder as he passed, to let him know he was the last man moving by. Bones stopped at the corner of the house; the same place they had set up a cover position earlier, upon breaking in. Phillips peered over the EOTech sight on his M-4 as he watched the street from the front corner of the house.

Hearing two clicks across the radio—a pre-arranged signal that Bones was in position to provide cover—Lebo stood, spun on his heel, and headed for the corner of the house.

As the trio slipped out the rear door, Weaver plopped his Kevlar helmet back on his head and secured the chin strap.

With his M-9 bag in hand, he stood near Rice, who was keeping watch at the front door.

Chills ran up Weaver's spine. It was hard to tell whether this was the result of the cool temperature of the early spring night or the potential violence that could erupt if Nash spied the team moving about the line of cars. *Shit! If this escalates into an all out gun battle and one of them is hit, they'll be screwed. I won't be able to make it out to the street, and they don't have as much as a damn band-aid between them. If I would've had time to work all of these things out beforehand, we'd be a lot better off. Deal with what you're given, Weaver.*

Phillips, Bones, and Lebo stepped out from the corner of 58 Burkeshire Road, where they had been staged. As each left the cover, and safety, of the brick wall, he swung his M-4 up and pointed the weapon at the house two doors away. Aiming a rifle while swiftly moving from one point to another is a practiced skill. The three appeared like black holes in the night. Their movements were seamless, akin to a well-choreographed ballet.

Reaching the relative safety of a blue Mazda, Phillips took up a position of cover behind the front wheel and motor. Leaning against the small car, he covered the remaining two team members with his carbine as they crossed the open expanse.

Without a word spoken, Bones reached into a pouch and dropped a tire spike under the rear wheel of the car, where it would go unnoticed. Known as caltrops, the spikes were made of five-sixteenths of an inch of hardened steel. The device had four two-inch-long prongs, each with razor-sharp edges. When thrown, one prong always landed facing upward. If Nash attempted to escape in the car, the tire spike would instantly flatten the tire.

Lebo crouched down and passed Phillips, heading for a Jeep parked in front of the Mazda. Taking up a position beside the front wheel similar to that of Phillips, Lebo assumed cover, allowing the other two to leap-frog forward.

Lebo dropped a spike in front of the knobby tires of the four-wheel drive vehicle. *Some college student is going to be really pissed if his tires get flattened. Oh well, expensive or not—needs to be done.*

Bones took up a position in the gutter behind the rear wheel of the Jeep, where he would be well concealed. He slid his rifle up just above the curb. It would take someone with a real good eye to pick out his position. He gazed through the EOTech and positioned the hologram on the front door. *If Nash comes out that door with a gun in his hand, he'll be Swiss Cheese.*

"Davidson to Phillips—stop!" Davidson transmitted across the radio.

The three froze in position. Lebo drew his M-4 tighter into his shoulder, anticipating that he would need to squeeze the trigger at any moment.

"I've got movement at the front of the target," Davidson continued. "Stand by."

Positioned at the front door, Rice tightened the grip on his weapon and dropped his eye to look through the reticle of the EOTech. There was a sudden surge of adrenalin in everyone operating on the radio net. Even Weaver felt like there were a thousand tiny needles piercing his skin. The entire team's concentration piqued.

After nearly sixty seconds of silence, Brett radioed, "Davidson to Phillips. The curtains on the first floor started to move. May have just been the heat coming on. Did not get a visual on anyone opening the curtains. Probably safe to proceed."

"Ten-four," Phillips acknowledged dispassionately.

Phillips was as cold as ice; nothing seemed to excite him.

According to plan, Phillips dropped to his belly and low-crawled across the street. With his M-4 laying across his arms, he slithered on his knees and elbows to an old VW. After placing a spike in front of the rear tire, he continued to a Beemer just ahead. With each of the cars on the east side of the street spiked, the team could be relatively sure Nash would not be able to successfully breach the perimeter and escape—at least in a vehicle. There was one last vehicle to secure—Seven-twenty-four.

Phillips made his way back to the opposite side of the street, where Bones and Lebo were providing cover. The three moved to the abandoned patrol car. Bones once again crawled into the gutter at the rear of the cruiser, while Phillips covered the front.

Lebo slowly opened the driver's door and was immediately hit with the stench of coagulating blood. For a second, he thought about what it must have been like for Reynolds as he was ambushed. Even more disconcerting was the thought of lying there, dying, and not knowing if help was on the way.

Lebo pushed the thoughts to the back of his mind and proceeded with the mission at hand.

The interior light was disabled, allowing Lebo to open the door and not be bathed in light. He quickly found the button that released the lock for the shotgun. Lebo grabbed the twelve-gauge from the rack on the heavy wire screen behind the front seats. Before backing out of the car, he took the keys from the ignition and scanned the car to ensure there was nothing else that needed to be retrieved. Lebo slung the shotgun across his back and silently closed the vehicle's door.

In his peripheral vision, Phillips saw Lebo exiting the car. "Phillips to Brett and Davidson. We're done—heading back the way we came," he radioed.

"Ten-four," came the response from both elements.

The three began the process of leap-frogging back to the Mazda. As Phillips passed Lebo, he tapped him on the shoulder to let Lebo know he was now last in line. Phillips dropped to a knee at the front of the Jeep to provide cover. The process continued; Lebo tapped Bones as he went by and then made his way to the rear of the Jeep. Ten seconds later, Bones pulled himself from the gutter at the rear of Seven-twenty-four and tapped Phillips as he made his way back to the front of the Mazda.

Eight minutes later, the three made there way back to their forward operating base. In the east, the first signs of dawn could be seen on the horizon. They had made it back to safety with little time to spare. A new day was about to dawn and they were no closer to ending the standoff than they had been the previous evening. No one knew what this day would bring.

CHAPTER 30

The phone on the wall began to ring yet again. It had been thirty minutes since Nash's previous bout with the cop on the other end of the line.

Young could barely make out Nash sitting in the darkness. Only a spattering of light was coming through a small pane of glass at the top of the front door. Nash stared into space as if fixated on some unknown object. Young wondered if he even heard the noise. Ten, eleven rings. The darkness, along with the otherwise silent room, made Young think of the drone of a foghorn at a coastal lighthouse. It was ghostly.

The ringing stopped, only to begin again within a matter of seconds. Finally, Nash stood and slowly walked to the kitchen and picked up the receiver.

With no inflection in his voice, Nash said, "What do you want?"

"Rick, it's Tim again. Can we talk?" the same voice as before asked.

Nash's answer was short and clipped. "What?"

"First, are you okay?"

Nash was somewhat surprised at the question. He thought the first words from the cop's mouth would be that he was surrounded and should surrender.

"I'm fine," Nash said.

"How's everybody else?"

"I just wanted to talk and the two of them had to put up a fight."

In the police command post, Tim Bolz looked over at his partner, Ray Finessey, with an eye of concern. Bolz was the primary crisis negotiator—the person tasked with making contact and talking with a hostage taker. He had been on the team for little over two years, and this was his most challenging incident to date.

Finessey was acting as the secondary negotiator. The two complemented each other when working together as crisis negotiators. This was a piece of intel they did not have previously. Everyone surmised that Christy was being held hostage. They did not realize that Nash was holding a second person. It would certainly complicate the issue.

Bolz remained silent. Active listening was the cornerstone of being a good negotiator. They needed to build a rapport with the guy. He knew it was not going to be easy. He wanted Nash to pour his guts out so he could find an opening to end this thing peacefully.

"I was defending myself," Nash went on. "They're bruised up, but they'll survive. That won't be the case if you try to come in here."

"No one's coming in there, Rick," Tim said. "I just want to talk."

"If I see one cop coming toward this house, somebody's going to die."

"Rick, I hear what you're saying, but we can talk this out and end it safely for everyone. That is my main concern here tonight—that everyone, including you, comes out of that house safely."

"Yeah, right. I know there's a bullet out there with my name on it. It's just which one of you trigger-happy bastards is going to deliver it."

With that, Nash placed the receiver back in its cradle and slowly walked back to his seat in the darkness.

CHAPTER 31

The morning was crisp but clear, the air fresh and clean. Birds chirped in the newly budding trees that lined the neighborhood streets and a spattering of daffodils and crocuses sprouted from gardens that fronted the brick homes. It was a typically beautiful early spring morning.

A snapshot of Burkeshire Road would betray nothing of the drama that was playing out in this Towson, Maryland neighborhood. The collection of pixels captured on electronic media would not reveal the contingent of assaulters who sat silently in a house awaiting the next move in this chess match. Nor would it disclose the snipers who kept careful watch through their high-powered scopes, continually sweeping their areas of responsibility, looking for any sign of movement. Similarly, it would not show the two helpless young women bound and beaten, lying on the floor while two thugs—one of them mentally unstable—watched over their every move.

For the small cluster of onlookers a block away, the tension in the air was palpable. There was a constant hum of generators powering huge command vehicles and media satellite trucks. Orange cones blocked streets, and large, flashing traffic arrow boards detoured commuters around the area. Police officials scurried back and forth, while law enforcement vehicles of all shapes, sizes, and colors arrived and departed the staging area.

The light shining through the dirty front windows of the forward staging area made Weaver's stomach turn. *Shit hole is too nice a term for this place. Holy crap!* What they had missed in the darkness of the night was the two small clumps of dried animal feces on the floor—luckily no one had stepped or sat in them. There was a pot on the stove with an unidentified food product gracing the bottom. A colony of ants had decided it was still a viable nutritional supplement. In addition, Weaver began noticing a foul odor throughout the house—and it wasn't someone's lack of personal hygiene.

Although he had seen homes just as bad, he never had to live in this kind of filth. He arrived at such places to treat a patient or put out a fire and left within thirty to sixty minutes. Weaver got the impression they were going to be staying put for a while. The current situation was just not going to float. Weaver was a bit of a neat freak, and he was already getting the heebie-jeebies. *I've got to do something about this place. I'm going to go bonkers, and somebody else is going to get a serious case of the creeping crud.*

Weaver found a piece of cardboard and gingerly scooped up the dried dog dung. Carrying the makeshift shit shovel at arm's length, he scrambled to find a trash can in the kitchen. Opening the cabinet below the sink, Weaver was overcome by the stench.

"Oh, dear God!" Runk moaned, "What's that smell?"

Fighting back the urge to vomit, Weaver said, "I think something died in the trash can."

"Well, get it the hell out of here."

Weaver pulled the can from the cabinet and watched as half-a-dozen roaches scurried up his arm.

"Son of a bitch!" Weaver yelled, nearly dropping the feces.

"Hey!" Phillips said in an agitated, but hushed, tone. "Noise discipline, you idiots."

Weaver shook his arm, allowing the vermin to fall to the floor. The dance that followed was accentuated by the popping noise heard as each critter met his maker.

"Weaver," Phillips snapped, "what the hell are you doing?"

"Trying to clean this place up."

"You can trade those BDU's in for a maid outfit, if you like."

Keeping with his previous attempt to manipulate Phillips, Weaver said, "I don't want to see somebody get sick due to hygiene issues and wind up with a case of the shits. Murphy's law says it'll happen when you need them most."

Phillips was quite familiar with things going wrong at the most inopportune times and couldn't challenge Weaver's thought process. All he could muster was a clipped, "Well… keep the noise down."

Weaver fought off a few more roaches as he pulled the plastic bag from the can. He tied it securely and headed for the rear door, where Davis was holding cover.

"Doc," Davis said, "why don't you toss it out the side window between the two groups of houses? Our little friend up the street might hear you if you toss it out back."

"Good idea," Weaver acknowledged, and he headed for the window.

Weaver continued with his self-imposed chores, cleaning both the kitchen and the second-floor bathroom. It wasn't perfect, but at least no one would get sick. From his tactical medicine training only the week before, he knew that eighty percent of casualties in war result from disease and not bullets or bombs. If someone was to get sick from the unsanitary conditions in their little home away from home, it could affect the overall mission.

Weaver was now getting hungry and felt confident everyone else was having the same pangs. However, another round of donuts was not going to do it. The team needed food that was going to keep them functioning and not put them to sleep.

Weaver fished his phone from the bellows pocket of his pants and hit the speed dial.

Answering on the first ring, Doctor Whitmire said, "Hey, Danny. What's up?"

"I'm sure someone is going to start talking about sending food up here again. These guys are going to need something better than donuts," Weaver said.

"What did you have in mind? Mickey D's?"

"Tucker might like that, but I don't think so. We could do some egg white sandwiches on whole wheat bagels. Perhaps oatmeal or some granola bars or protein bars, if they can't come up with that. Oh, yeah—some apples and bananas."

"When did you become Mister Nutrition?"

"About a week ago. Sitting in that tactical medicine class last week, I never saw the relevance of some of the lectures, especially the ones on extended operations."

"Never say never, Danny boy," Whitmire responded. "That's where people get screwed. They think, 'it can never happen here,' or 'it won't happen to me.'"

"I'm quickly learning that lesson—anything can happen in this little soiree."

"Is there anything else you need?"

"Yeah—common sense. Whose idea was this?"

The doctor laughed and said, "Another adage, my friend—watch what you wish for."

Weaver chuckled. "I just wasn't expecting to be knee deep in this so early. No, nothing else right now."

"Good. I'll get to work on this. Call if you need anything else."

Pressing the *End* button on his phone, Weaver contemplated Whitmire's words—"never say never." Anything could happen over the coming hours, and Weaver needed to be prepared for it. In some jobs, a lack of attention to detail might cost your employer a few bucks. Weaver knew that such a mistake here could cost someone his life.

✳ ✳ ✳

The white dry-erase board in the command post was

covered with pieces of information. There were names, places, dates, and much more. Pictures taped to the board reminded all involved that real lives were at stake. Each piece of data was critical to understanding the current situation and where it might lead. Arrows marked relationships between pieces of intel.

Tim Bolz, Finessey, and their intelligence officer, Pete Mitchell, sat staring at the board. The small conference room in which they were located was at the rear of the nearly forty-foot-long vehicle. The massive black truck was as long as some tractor-trailers, but its array of flashing red and blue LED lights left no mistake that it was an emergency vehicle. With the unit's updated communications systems, they could talk to almost anyone in the country. The large satellite dish positioned on the roof would probably extend that reach to most of the world. There were eight separate work spaces in the truck, each with a bank of radios and computers. Today, the desk just outside the conference room was being occupied by Bolz and the rest of his team.

"I'm not buying it," Tim said. "He's killed three and wounded a couple others, and the two hostages are only bruised?"

"Yeah," Finessey added, "that's not consistent with his recent history."

Mitchell chimed in. "From the information I have thus far, it's evident he can go from being kind and caring one minute to agitation and violence the next. It's possible that, in his affection for Christy, he did hold back and has not seriously injured her. He's had ample opportunity to kill or seriously injure her prior to last evening."

"But that was before she escaped from him at Luke's," Tim responded. "His whole frame of reference may have changed. We need more information about what's going on inside, but he keeps shutting down on us and hanging up. We don't have the rapport built yet to where he'll open up."

"There is one option," Finessey said. "The team has that new medic. We put him on the phone and see if Nash will give anything additional about the well-being of the hostages."

"Absolutely not!" Tim fumed. "You know the policy. Nobody talks on that phone but one of us. We have no control of what comes out of someone's mouth once they get on the phone. It could make matters a lot worse than they already are."

"That policy is meant for friends, family members, clergy, and the busybody standing on the corner. This guy is part of the team. And on more than one occasion, members of the SWAT team have needed to enter into direct face-to-face negotiation with a hostage taker. It's not like it's uncharted territory. You've read the documentation where a medic has provided medical direction across the phone in similar circumstances—medicine across the barricade. He's a neutral party and may be able to confirm that both girls are not severely injured."

"You're right, but it's never been done here. Now isn't the time to try something new. Besides we've never even met this guy. We have no idea who he is."

"Then what's our next move, Tim?" Finessey asked.

"I try again. If I can't keep Nash engaged with the next call, and we don't get a better feel for the welfare of the hostages, then I'll consider using the medic."

The three negotiators continued strategizing on how to approach the next telephone conversation with Nash, agreeing on a range of contingencies. At the end of the session, Bolz noticed Chief Sherman enter and begin talking to Major Gittings.

Tim overheard Gittings provide the Chief a briefing on the second conversation with Nash. The Major described the two pieces of substantive intel they had been able to obtain—the fact that there were two hostages, and that they had minimal injuries. He also relayed the negotiator's concerns over the veracity of the second piece of information.

Tim, however did not hear Sherman's part of the conversation.

Looking toward the floor, Sherman said to the Major, "I have some information that's going to complicate the situation even further. Christy Moore's grandfather is the CEO of a local bank. He's been on the phone for the past hour with the County Executive, pressuring him to get his granddaughter out sooner rather than later. The County Exec just phoned me."

"And?" Gittings asked with a raised eyebrow.

"I told him he needed to keep the guy off my ass."

A smile crept across Major Gittings' face.

"Don't get too smug. This guy has a lot of pull in this town. I told the Exec we need to be able to solve this without any outside influence or pressure. Right now things are stable, and the more time that elapses, the better our chances of ending this thing peacefully."

"Normally I would agree with you, but I don't think there's any guarantees with this guy, Nash. He seems too at ease with killing."

"I know. Just keep trying to talk him out. But have the team ready to move if things turn to shit."

"I talked to Phillips earlier. They were already working on rescue plans. I'll get an update."

Patting Gittings on the back, Sherman said, "Thanks. And don't share that piece of info about the grandfather."

Nodding his head toward the rear of the Command Post, Sherman said, "It's hard enough trying to mitigate this thing. They don't need the additional pressure."

CHAPTER 32

In an attempt to allay any fears on the home front, Weaver pulled his phone out and began typing a text message to his wife. *The last thing I need is her showing up here again. Don't think folks would be real happy if she knocked on the door of the Command Post asking for her hunka, hunka, burnin' love. A short text will keep her happy and me out of the doghouse.*

Tired & hungry— but safe. Miss U.
Luv DW

Within seconds the phone vibrated, indicating a return message.

When will u b home? Dinner with my parents. Remember?!

Weaver sat on the steps leading to the second floor. His head dropped into his cupped hands as he read the message. *Love it when a plan comes together. I can't believe her—like I can just pack up and leave. She does not have a clue.*

Weaver's two thumbs began typing again.

Will call bad guy & have him speed it up. DW has plans tonight!

Kathy responded,

Thanks! Reservations @ 7

Jesus keep me near the cross, Weaver thought as he looked upward toward the ceiling. I can't catch a break.

Slipping the phone back in his pocket, Weaver noticed Bones sitting nearby and remembered he had not checked the laceration he had closed the previous day.

"Bones," Weaver said, "let me check that lac on your arm. How's it feel?"

"A little throbbing periodically, but not too bad," Bones said. "To be honest, in the heat of things, I had totally forgotten about it."

Weaver cut the bandage on Bones' left arm with a pair of bandage scissors to expose the wound. He carefully examined the staples holding the laceration closed, as well as the injury itself, for signs of infection.

"There's no purulent discharge—" Weaver said.

"No what? Speak English," Bones said sarcastically.

"Pus. There's no pus. I'm trying to sound like I know what I'm talking about, Bones. Remember, baffle 'em with bullshit. A few well-placed ten-cent words can go a long way."

"Just what we need," Bones said, "a comedian for a Doc."

Weaver spread antibiotic ointment on the wound and

covered it with two four-by-four-inch gauze pads. He then wrapped the area with a roll of gauze to keep the wound clean and the pads in place.

"Keep this thing clean. That's going to be a tall chore in this shit hole. If you start to have any problems, come see me. Should it get infected, we'll have to start you on a course of 500 milligrams of Keflex—an antibiotic."

"Don't they usually give a round so you don't get an infection?" Bones asked.

"Not anymore. Bugs are becoming too resistant. Mainly because they've been overusing the damn things."

"Thanks, Doc. I'll keep an eye on it."

As Bones turned to walk away Weaver smiled. "Sorry, but I was all out of SpongeBob bandaids."

"Screw you, Weaver."

Weaver repacked his STOMP medical bag and noticed Phillips coming toward him. "Weaver, the Command Post wants you."

Weaver looked at Phillips quizzically. "Are they on the phone?"

"No. They want you down there at the CP. Maybe they wised up and will finally get you out of my hair."

Weaver's face went flush, and he immediately started to perspire. *Why would they want me back there? Did I do something wrong? No... Would Kathy actually show up at the command post? Shit.* Weaver's thoughts reverted to the sparring he engaged in earlier.

"Did they say why?" Weaver asked.

"No. And I didn't ask. I just follow orders. Now get going. Take the front door. Lebo will cover you as you head down the street."

Not wanting to let his dejection show, Weaver mustered a strong, "On my way."

CHAPTER 33

Weaver cinched the chin strap on his helmet and bent over to pick up his M-9 bag. In the hope that he would return, he left the STOMP medical bag behind.

At the front door, Lebo said, "I'll cover you as you head down the street, Doc."

Laying his hand on Lebo's shoulder, Weaver said, "Thanks. I'll let you know when I'm past the stone wall at the end of the street."

Lebo gave Weaver a thumbs up, then raised his M-4 to a near horizontal position to cover the medic's withdrawal.

Weaver crouched and hurried across the open space between the two groups of houses. He would re-trace the team's advance up the street the previous evening. He hugged the brick wall of the houses as he began making his way down Burkeshire Road. Weaver stopped suddenly. *Dog— which house had the dog? Damn thing will probably break through the window and maul me to death.* He proceeded quietly past the final three houses.

By the time Weaver made it to the door of the Command Post, his stomach was in knots. He felt as if everyone had been looking at him ever since he had exited Burkeshire Road. *Everyone knows what the hell is about to happen except me.*

My ass is toast. What the hell did I do? Was it Kathy? Perhaps the administration of the fire department changed their minds and has ordered me off the scene?

Everyone's eyes had been on the black-clad SWAT team member, but for a different reason than Weaver's own perceptions. From the uniformed patrol officer directing traffic, to the civilian bystanders, to the media—everyone knew how volatile the situation was. The small patch on Weaver's chest and medical bag that read, "MEDIC" was not lost on those who eyed his rapid pace to the black, bus-sized vehicle. Many believed the worst had already occurred and the medical provider was delivering the bad news in person.

Weaver hesitantly rolled his right hand into a ball and knocked on the door of the command post. Immediately, the door swung wide. *Shit, they're waiting for me.*

Major Gittings stood just inside the door. His facial expression was stone cold.

"Come with me," Gittings said.

"Yes, sir," Weaver said sheepishly.

The two stepped briskly down the aisle past the many workstations. Weaver could feel everyone inside the truck staring at him. Gittings opened the door of the conference room at the rear of the unit.

"Danny, do you know any of these people?" Gittings said.

"No, sir."

Weaver's stomach tightened even further. Having never met the individuals in the small room, he could not imagine the reason for his involvement. His mind searched for any recollection of the faces, but he was coming up empty.

Gittings began the introductions, each of the three men nodding as his name was conveyed. "Tim Bolz, Ray Finessey, Pete Mitchell. This is Danny Weaver, the team's medic.

Weaver simply nodded in return and waited for the hammer to fall.

"We have a problem," Tim began.

Here it is, Weaver thought, *it's going to be quick. They didn't even ask me to sit down or to take off any of my gear.*

"You know this guy Nash has two female hostages. By his own admission, Nash has roughed them up. We need to find out the extent of their injuries. Are they minor or severe? The commanders need the intel to determine whether we need to initiate a rescue operation or continue with the attempt to negotiate."

Weaver's facial expression gave away his surprise.

"Weaver–" Tim said, "are you with me?"

"Yes, sir. I...never mind."

Bolz looked toward Finessey. *I knew this was a bad idea.*

"Okay, well, get your shit together. I don't have a lot of time."

"Are you familiar with medicine across the barricade?" Finessey interjected.

"Yes, sir. I've been trained in it."

Gittings squeezed Weaver's shoulder, "Lighten up, Danny. You don't have to say 'sir' every two seconds."

Weaver relaxed ever so slightly.

"Why don't you take your gear off and have a seat," Gittings added. "How about some coffee?"

"That'd be great, Major."

Weaver took off his helmet and body armor. It was the first time in nearly twenty-four hours he had been out of the heavy protective vest. He shrugged his shoulders in an attempt to release the tension that had built in his muscles.

Gittings returned with a steaming cup, handing it to Weaver as he took the only empty seat in the room. Weaver grasped the cup with both hands and took a careful sip. *Rice will have my ass if he finds out about this*, Weaver thought, reflecting on his teammate's rant the previous night.

"What we need," Finessey said, "is for you to provide us with questions to ask—"

"I will ask the questions, not you," Tim interrupted.

Finessey looked at Tim, somewhat annoyed, and continued, "Medical questions for *us* to ask that will enable us, and you, to determine how badly injured the two girls are."

"Easily done. I can have a few basic questions written in a matter of minutes. I'll provide follow-up questions as he answers the initial ones."

For the next ten minutes, Weaver and the three negotiators worked on the medical questions that Bolz would attempt to ask during the next call to Nash.

Tim Bolz slipped the padded earphones over his head and positioned the small black microphone near the left side of his mouth. Weaver and Finessey donned headsets of their own and plugged them into the workstation next to Bolz. Getting nods from the other two, Bolz pressed a small red button on the console before him.

The phone in 54 Burkeshire began to ring. A member of the police department's technical services branch had wired the phone in the house directly to the command post. Nash could talk to only one person when he picked up the receiver of the wall phone—Bolz. While up on the telephone pole, the technician had also severed the residence's cable connection. Nash had no access to cable TV or the Internet—he was isolated.

The periodic buzzing noise in their headsets stopped when Nash answered on the fourth ring. "Yeah?"

Bolz pushed another button on the console that opened the mic and allowed him to talk, "Hi, Rick, it's Tim again. How you making out?"

"Okay, I guess."

Tim could sense a change in Nash's tone of voice. He was more soft spoken and not as agitated. Bolz knew this would be his best shot of developing rapport with the killer on the other end of the phone.

"Anything I can do for you?" Tim asked.

"I'm really getting hungry."

"How 'bout if I send some food up for you, Rick? What would you like?"

"Some eggs, bacon, maybe toast," Nash said.

Weaver grabbed a pen and quickly began to write on a legal pad nearby. As he finished scribbling, he slid the pad in front of Tim and pointed the pen at the question he had written. Tim looked up, and a short smile crept across his face.

"Rick," Tim asked, "should I send enough for the girls, too?"

Finessey didn't understand the significance of the question or of his partner's enthusiasm. Looking at Weaver, he said, "I don't get it."

"If he answers 'yes,' we know the girls are conscious and breathing. They can't eat, otherwise. Those were the first two questions on my original list—'Are they conscious? Are they breathing?'"

"We gather intel, and he's none the wiser," Finessey said.

"Yeah, send some extra," Nash said.

Weaver began writing again and pushed the note in front of Tim.

"Okay, Rick. I'll send enough for everyone. Oh, by the way. You said you had a little bit of a scuffle, do you need any band aids or any other medical stuff?"

"Hey, I didn't mean to hurt them. I love Christy, and I think deep down inside she really loves me, too. It's just been a little crazy recently. If we can just get away somewhere and talk, it'll all be fine. I know it will."

"I understand, Rick. We can all talk through this, and it'll work itself out. So do you need any bandages?"

Tim turned off his microphone and looked toward Finessey. "I think he's starting to cry."

"No," Nash said. "They're not cut, I just hit both of them in the head earlier. Believe me, I didn't want to. I guess maybe I lost my temper a bit."

"I've lost my temper, too, on occasion. Are they both awake? Are they going to be able to eat?"

A bit more agitated, Nash said, "I told you they were fine. Jackie has a knot on her head, but both of them are awake and looking at me."

"That's great, Rick. I'll give you a call back when I have the food and I'm ready to send it up."

Tim disconnected and looked at Weaver and Finessey. "What do you think?"

"That's a drastic mood swing from when you talked to him earlier," Finessey said.

"No shit," Tim answered, "You must have been a detective before coming over here. Weaver—medically, how do we look?"

"Well—A's, B's, and C's. If they're awake and can eat, then I say they have an airway, are breathing, and they're circulating blood. That's the good news. I'm concerned about him knocking them out. I'm especially concerned with the one that has the knot on her head."

"Jackie," Tim interjected.

"She could develop a subdural hematoma, which could be life threatening. You'll need to make sure she doesn't lose consciousness. It's a late sign, but it's a sure indicator that she's going south. Maybe you could think of a way to talk to her later. If her speech is slurred or she's not answering appropriately, it would be an earlier indicator that something's not right."

"What about Christy?"

"Same thing for her. If she loses consciousness, it's a problem. She may only have a mild concussion. But without knowing specifics about how she was knocked out, it's difficult to give you anything definitive. Sorry I can't give you a clearer picture of their status. Right now they both appear stable. We just need to monitor their progress."

"You've been a big help," Tim acknowledged. "I'm going to let you get back to the team. Before you leave, however, give your cell number to Mitchell. I'll continue to tap you for medical advice."

"Glad to help any way I can. Doctor Whitmire, my medical director, has also been around the scene. I'll leave his number, as well."

Major Gittings stopped Weaver as he was leaving the command post, "Danny, we have the team's food ready for you. Think you can hump all this back by yourself?"

Looking at the four stuffed bags, Weaver responded, "Not a problem, sir."

"Good. Let Phillips know we'll be sending the bomb squad's robot up with donuts for Nash. We'll give Jack a heads up when we're ready."

"Donuts? I thought he asked for eggs?"

"He did. And he's getting donuts. We send Nash eggs, he might get the idea he's controlling the situation. We're manipulating him, not the other way around."

Weaver nodded and picked up the bags to head back to the rest of the team. At the foot of Burkeshire, Weaver radioed Phillips. "Weaver to Phillips."

It took two more attempts before Phillips would answer. "Go ahead," he said in an agitated tone.

"I'm en route back to 58." *I bet he's not a happy camper to hear I'm coming back.*

CHAPTER 34

Nash wiped his eyes as he hung up the phone. Walking the few steps to where Christy lay, he bent over and ran his hands through her hair.

"Tell them, Christy," he whispered.

Christy shuddered at his touch. "Tell them what?"

"Tell them this is all a big misunderstanding. We love each other and just want to be together. They'll go away, and things can be like they were. Happy." Nash began to sob.

"Rick, are you okay?" Young asked.

Christy was relieved at the interruption. There was no way she was going to tell anyone that she loved Rick Nash. But she also knew he was volatile, and refusing his request could bring about another flurry of brutal strikes. She needed a plan in case he persisted.

Not wanting to admit he'd been crying, Nash answered, "I think I'm getting a cold or something."

"I heard you sniffling—you don't look all that good. Your eyes are pretty red, too."

"I'll be fine. It was cold out there waiting for you in the bushes yesterday—probably caught something."

"Take a shot of booze, it'll make you feel better. Probably kill some germs, too."

Nudging Jackie with the tip of his shoe, Young asked, "Got anything?"

Despite the pain, Jackie rolled her head back and forth on the floor twice, saying, "The strongest thing we have are a few bottles of beer in the frig and some wine downstairs."

"Yeah," Young said, "guess I shouldn't have expected a couple college pukes to have any JD around. I could've used a shot of ole Jack myself."

"That's okay," Nash interrupted, "I'll just close my eyes for few. Probably feel better with some rest. Keep an eye on those two. The cops are going to send up some food—watch for that, too."

Nash sat on the couch that graced the side wall of the living room opposite the staircase and door where they had entered. He sank into the soft, linen-covered cushions and plopped his right leg on the small coffee table. He used the leg to slide a near-empty pizza box out of the way to make room for his left. After adjusting his butt, he dropped his head back onto the upright cushion of the sofa. Within seconds, his eyelids became heavy, and he lapsed into a fitful sleep.

$$* * *$$

Weaver saw only a sliver of a teammate's left side in the doorway of 58 Burkeshire. It was difficult to tell who was covering him as he moved toward the forward staging area. With armor and helmet, most everyone looked the same, especially from behind. Even though it was daylight, Weaver felt more at ease than when he had made the trek the previous night; it had become familiar territory. Whoever was providing him cover had his M-4 raised and pointing toward 54—his undivided attention on the front of the house.

Nearing his destination, Weaver whispered a security word three times to let the person at the door know there was a *friendly* approaching from behind. Drawing closer, Weaver saw it was Runk holding cover—his attention never leaving his AOR.

Weaver slipped past Runk in the doorway and raised the bags of food to chest height. "I come bearing gifts." The food was spread out in the dining room, on a table that Weaver had cleaned earlier.

"Smells good, Doc," Gunny said. "Thanks."

"Egg sandwiches?" Lebo added. "We need to keep you around. We've never been treated like this on an op."

"There's also some Power Bars, powdered Gatorade, and fruit," Weaver said.

Phillips came down the stairs from the second floor and, spotting Weaver, said, "You're the last person I expected to see. But since you're here, get your ass upstairs and check on Mund. He's been in the bathroom for the better part of an hour."

"On it," Weaver answered.

Son-of-a-bitch doesn't ask what they wanted me for. Thanks for the food. Nothing. Just get your butt upstairs.

Weaver knocked on the door of the small bathroom at the top of the staircase.

"Hey, Mike," Weaver said. "Lebo's a little out of sorts. He wants to use the bathroom to shave his head. You okay?"

"Screw him, and no!"

"Okay... then what's going on?"

"Bad case of the shits. My stomach feels like it's in knots."

"Okay, I'll get you something. Be right back."

Weaver returned to the first-floor and stooped down to retrieve some meds from his STOMP bag when he spotted everyone grabbing food from the table.

"Stop!" Weaver yelled. "Did you guys wash your hands before touching any of that?"

The big muscular operators looked like small kids who had just been scolded. Through a mouthful of food, Jones mumbled, "No."

Tossing a bottle of hand sanitizer toward the group, Weaver said, "Guys. This place is a sewer. Don't put anything near your mouth without first washing your hands. That may very well be why Mund is stuck on the crapper."

Upon hearing Weaver's admonition, Phillips stepped toward the medic from his position near the front door.

"I thought you were here to prevent those kinds of problems?" Phillips barked. "I've got an operator down because of your incompetence? Damn it—get your shit together!"

Weaver stood and was no more than two inches from

Dennis R. Krebs

Weaver knocked on the door of the small bathroom at the top of the staircase.

"Hey, Mike," Weaver said. "Lebo's a little out of sorts. He wants to use the bathroom to shave his head. You okay?"

"Screw him, and no!"

"Okay… then what's going on?"

"Bad case of the shits. My stomach feels like it's in knots."

"Okay, I'll get you something. Be right back."

Weaver returned to the first-floor and stooped down to retrieve some meds from his STOMP bag when he spotted everyone grabbing food from the table.

"Stop!" Weaver yelled. "Did you guys wash your hands before touching any of that?"

The big muscular operators looked like small kids who had just been scolded. Through a mouthful of food, Jones mumbled, "No."

Tossing a bottle of hand sanitizer toward the group, Weaver said, "Guys. This place is a sewer. Don't put anything near your mouth without first washing your hands. That may very well be why Mund is stuck on the crapper."

Upon hearing Weaver's admonition, Phillips stepped toward the medic from his position near the front door.

"I thought you were here to prevent those kinds of problems?" Phillips barked. "I've got an operator down because of your incompetence? Damn it—get your shit together!"

Weaver stood and was no more than two inches from

250

Phillips' face. "An hour ago you didn't give a shit if I came back here, and now I didn't do my job? Pound sand up your ass!"

Runk jumped between the two. "Whoa, kids! Can't we all just get along?"

Turning to Weaver, Runk said, "Doc, go take care of Mund."

Weaver slid a small black satchel of meds from his STOMP bag and climbed the stairs to where Mund was making his mark.

Runk waited until Weaver was out of earshot and turned his back so the remainder of the team couldn't hear. "Jack, what the hell are you doing? Danny has done more for us and this agency in the past few days than any of us could have imagined. But you keep riding his ass."

"If he was so worried about us washing our hands, then he should have said something last night when everyone was pounding down donuts. Now we have somebody laid up. Admit it, he screwed up."

"I believe Weaver said it 'could' have been the reason for Mund being sick. He could have also been coming down with something long before taking a bite. But let's assume you're right, and he forgot to say something last night. He corrected it by saying something now and keeping the rest of us up and running. If he wasn't here at all, this entire team would be taking turns on the shitter right now—'cause none of us would have thought about it—and we'd really be up the creak without a paddle."

"He's a damn wannabee," Phillips countered. "At some point, you and everyone else will figure that out."

Phillips brushed past Runk and headed to the table for some food. Runk looked at the ceiling and shook his head.

Knocking on the bathroom door, Weaver said, "Mike, I've got some loperamide—Immodium—for you. Can you make it to the door?"

"Yeah," Mund answered. "I've got a lull in the action."

The door slowly opened—Mund was moving at a snail's pace. He was hunched over, one arm holding his stomach. His face was drawn—he looked like hell.

"You're not looking too good," Weaver said.

"Believe me, I'm not feeling great, either."

"When did you start feeling bad?"

"Started midday yesterday. It got worse during the night."

"Any nausea or vomiting?"

"Yeah, vomited about fifteen minutes ago."

"You've got a little more going on than just a case of the shits. I'll be right back." *Guess I should've brought my whole damn bag up to begin with*, he thought.

Weaver returned less than a minute later to find the bathroom door closed once again. He tossed his STOMP bag on the floor of the bedroom next door.

Standing in the doorway of the room, Weaver looked at the peeling paint on the walls and ceiling—*not the best place to treat a patient*. Taking in the posters on the wall—one of Kim Kardashian, the other a Budweiser beer advertisement—

Weaver began to reevaluate his original impression of the student occupants. They were slobs, but at least they had good taste in girls and beer. The crumpled sheets on the bed looked, and smelled, like they hadn't been changed in months. He rummaged through a chest of drawers and a closet before finding a sheet that looked reasonably clean. Ripping the sheets from the bed, Weaver tossed the soiled linens in the corner of the room. *Should just burn the damn things.* Next, he threw the clean bed covering on the mattress and opened his medical kit on the less than sterile treatment area.

"Hey," Weaver said. "When can you come over to the bedroom?"

"I'm not quite that easy," Mund responded.

"You're not that sick if you can crack half-ass jokes."

The door opened and Mund slowly walked into the room where the medic had set up shop. Weaver was just pulling on a set of black nitrile gloves as the ill cop entered the room.

Allowing the wrist of the glove to slap against his skin, Weaver said, "I'll fix you right up."

"Like hell you will!"

"Just lie down on the damn bed and shut up."

"You pull out a tube of KY, and I'm outta here."

"By my estimation, I won't need to," Weaver retorted.

"That's just wrong."

"All right, shutup. I'm going to take your pulse, blood pressure, and temperature."

Weaver wrapped the sphygmomanometer around Mund's arm and squeezed the black bulb to inflate the instrument. He slipped the earpieces of his stethoscope into his ears. Once the gauge on the cuff read two-hundred, he gently released the silver knob on the device, allowing air in the bladder to slowly escape. Weaver watched the needle on the gauge drop as he listened to the beat of blood flowing through Mund's artery come and go.

"One-twelve over sixty," Weaver said.

Weaver placed the index finger and middle finger of his right hand over Mund's wrist, near his thumb. Looking at his watch for thirty seconds, Weaver announced, "Pulse eighty-two."

Finally, Weaver slid the tip of an infrared thermometer into Mund's right ear.

"Ninety-eight point eight. You're not running a fever. Hopefully, this is just a short-duration viral thing. Here's two 2-milligram tablets of loperamide; it should help with the diarrhea. Take them and I'll be right back."

Weaver returned to the first floor to give Phillips an assessment of Mund's condition. His stomach seemed to knot each time he talked to the team leader. After their last encounter, minutes ago, he was even more reluctant to approach him. *If I lose my cool and go off on him, he'll shit-can me for sure.* Reaching the bottom of the steps, Weaver was caught off guard by Phillips making the turn to go up the staircase.

"I was just coming to see you," Weaver said, controlling his temper. Not allowing Phillips time to respond with any type of criticism, he quickly continued, "Mund's vitals are in normal ranges—even his temp. So this might be viral and not bacteria related. He said he began feeling bad yesterday. I gave him some Immodium for the diarrhea. I'd also like to start an IV on him and run about a thousand cc's of fluid to counter the amount he's lost. It'll keep him from getting further dehydrated. If he's not looking better after that, we may need to get him out of here. Can you afford to have him down for about an hour while I run the line and re-evaluate him?"

Phillips' eyes bore through Weaver, and he stared right back. After a few seconds Phillips responded, "Do what you gotta do," and turned on his heels to descend.

CHAPTER 35

Weaver returned to Mund's side. "Mike, I'm going to start a line on you and run about a thousand cc's of fluid."

"Doc, I'll drink some Gatorade," Mund responded. "I hate friggin needles."

"I've watched it being done dozens of times. It's not that big a deal—at least it didn't look hard."

"What!"

"But I did stay at a Holiday Inn last night."

"Come on! You're not making me feel very good.

Laughing, Weaver admitted, "I've done hundreds of them. Chill."

Weaver unzipped his large black STOMP bag and retrieved all of the supplies he would need. He first ripped open the opaque wrapper that contained the bag of intravenous fluid. He checked the markings to ensure it was the proper solution—Lactated Ringers—and to confirm the product had not reached its expiration date. Next he opened the administration set, which contained a forty-eight-inch length of tubing, a drip chamber, and a clamp that regulated the flow of liquid.

Weaver stretched out the tubing, then removed the blue

protective covers on both the administration set and the IV bag. Holding the bottom of the IV bag in his left hand, he drove the spike of the administration set into the appropriate port with his right. He raised the entire setup high above his head and allowed the colorless liquid to fill the tubing. After a few drops fell to the floor, he closed the clamp on the tubing and inspected it for any large air bubbles.

"Let me take a look at your left arm," Weaver said.

His gloved fingers slid across the inner aspect of Mund's left elbow—the antecubital area—looking for a useable vein. He cinched a blue constricting band around Mund's left arm proximal to his elbow. Within seconds, the basilic vein began to swell with trapped blood.

"Shit. That thing is as big as the Lincoln Tunnel. Should be able to hit that with my eyes closed."

"Yeah," Mund admonished. "Well, don't even think about it. You got one shot and only one shot."

"You know I'm really trying to have a good bedside manner here," the medic joked.

Weaver cleaned the site with two betadine swabs. After ripping the eighteen-gauge catheter needle from its wrapper, he inspected it for defects. The medic's facial expression changed; now it was all business—no more kidding as Weaver prepared to start the line on his comrade.

"You're going to feel a stick" Weaver said. "Try not to move."

He held the skin taught with his left hand, preventing the vein from rolling away as the needle penetrated the epidermis. He grasped the needle between the index finger and thumb of his right hand. Holding it at a ten-degree angle, a fraction of an inch above the insertion site, he quickly and smoothly pressed the sharp edge against the skin. Feeling a pop and seeing a small flash of blood enter the clear chamber at the rear of the needle, Weaver knew he had hit the vein. He slid the catheter off the needle, advancing it further into Mund's vein.

"Got it," Weaver said. "That's all there is."

Continuing to stabilize the needle in Mund's arm, he untied the constricting band. After removing the needle, leaving the catheter in place, he attached the IV bag and tubing. He slowly opened the clamp and inspected the venipuncture site, ensuring the vein had not blown. After taping the catheter and tubing in place, he increased the flow of fluid into the operator's arm.

"Don't move around too much. And don't bend this arm."

Weaver looked around the room for somewhere to hang the IV bag; it needed to be higher than his patient in order for the fluid to flow properly. Seeing nothing he could use, Weaver reached into a pocket in his medical bag and retrieved a roll of olive green hundred-mile-an-hour tape, what the civilian world called duct tape. He ripped off a twelve-inch piece of the tape with his teeth. After feeding the tape through the small hole in the top of the bag, Weaver smacked the tape onto the plaster wall about two feet above Mund's head. *Another use for that stuff—IV hanger.*

Weaver returned to the first floor to find the team donning helmets and gloves and checking weapons. Everyone was still wearing their heavy body armor; the protective garments were too difficult to put on in a hurry if things went awry.

"Gunny, what's going on?" Weaver asked.

"The command post is sending EOD's robot up with food for the bad guy and hostages. We need to be ready in case something goes wrong," Gunny said, referring to the Explosive Ordnance Disposal Unit—Bomb Squad.

Weaver threw his helmet on his head and his M-9 bag on his back and stood ready with the rest of the team. *I'll need to check Mund's IV in about fifteen minutes.*

Radios began to crackle to life through everyone's earpieces.

"Phillips to all sniper elements. EOD robot will be heading this way with food for the target. Acknowledge."

"Brett, ten-four."

"Davidson, ten-four."

"Tucker, ten-four."

"If our bad guy comes out to retrieve the food and we have a clear opportunity to snatch him without endangering the hostages, we'll do so. It'll be a short window, so everyone be on your toes. Brett and Davidson—I'll need continual updates on what you're seeing."

Phillips received nods from each operator and another radio acknowledgment from the sniper elements.

"Gunny, I want you holding long cover from the door. Runk and Davis will go hands-on with the suspect. The rest of us will have to maneuver quickly to cover any other threats from the target house. It's a long distance from here across the front of the adjacent house to the target. We aren't going to have the element of surprise for long, so I don't have high confidence in having a good opportunity. Nonetheless, I want to be ready."

The team watched as the MK3 Caliber EOD Robot rounded the corner from Burke Avenue. The device was nearly three feet long by two feet wide, with two robotic claw arms. It had rubber tracks, like a tank, which fit over rubber tires. Unlike many other robots, it did not rely on a hardwire tether that limited its range. The MK3 was operated over radio waves. The operator could maneuver the robot, using its onboard cameras, while sitting back in the bomb squad vehicle.

Its top speed only five miles per hour, the robot slowly rolled up Burkeshire Road. In the claw of the main arm was a blue plastic grocery bag. At the rear of the abandoned patrol car, the robot turned right and climbed the curb at the edge of the street—bobbing up and down after completing the maneuver. At the edge of the small, wintered plot of grass in front of the target house, the machine stopped. The blue bag of groceries swung back and forth as the robot sat, waiting.

* * *

A small bit of light shone past the edges of the drawn shades and curtains in the first floor rooms. Nash sat quietly, continuing to ponder his predicament and his options. He had been awakened moments earlier by a phone call from the cop—Tim—letting him know the food was being sent up by a robot. Before him lay two women whom he believed were his leverage with the police. A grin crept across his face. *They don't even have the guts to send a real person up here with the food —pansies. I've got the edge. The cards are all in my hand.*

"Rick, I hear something outside," Young said.

"Take a peak out the window. It may be the cops' little toy bringing our food."

Young peered through the fragment of an opening between the shade and the window frame. He began to laugh. "Hey, it's one of those bomb robots you see on TV. It's got a blue bag in its hand. You want me to run out and grab it?"

"No!" Nash yelled. "You walk out that door, you may not come back. Think, Randy—think. Who knows where they're hiding out there? The cops will put a bullet in you quicker than hell."

"Sorry, man. You're right, I wasn't thinkin'. What do you want to do?"

Nash heard a familiar voice coming from the speaker on the robot. "Rick, it's Tim. Your food is outside. Can you come out and grab it? Rick—can you hear me?"

"Yeah, my ass I'm going out there," Nash said to no one in particular.

Pointing at Jackie, Nash said, "Grab the girl. I got a plan."

Jackie began to kick wildly as Young approached. Christy yelled, "Leave her alone, Rick!"

Nash dropped to one knee, grabbing Christy by the throat and drawing back his opposite hand into a fist.

"Hit me, you bastard! Hit me!" Christy screamed.

Nash's eyes fixated on her. Christy stared back into the hollowness of his soul—there seemed to be nothing there but evil. After what seemed like an eternity to Christy, Nash released his grip and walked away.

Nash went to where Young was struggling to control Jackie. Reaching for her left arm, Nash said, "Grab her by the arm and get her the hell up." Young did as he was told, and the two slammed the young college student up against the wall near the front door. Tears streamed down her face as she began to sob.

"See if there's another extension cord around here," Nash ordered.

Young quickly scanned the first floor and, finding nothing, ran to the basement. In seconds, he returned with a six-foot-long brown electrical cord.

"Tie it around her throat—tight," Nash said. "I want her to know I'm here. We'll send her out to get the food."

Jackie, her head turned to the side and left ear buried into the wall, attempted to wrestle herself out of their grip. Nash grabbed the girl's hair, pulling her head away from the wall at an unnatural angle. Young synched the cord around her neck. The taut, plastic-covered wire cut into Jackie's skin.

"I can't breathe", Jackie squeaked. "Please, I can't breathe." "Shut-up, you're fine," Young retorted.

Nash said, "I'm going to open this door, and you're going to grab the food. Nothing else. Don't try to run. If I don't strangle you with this," Nash yanked tightly on the cord, "I'll put a bullet in the back of your head before you make it two feet."

"I can't," Jackie rasped. "My hands are tied behind my back."

"Well, turn around and grab it, you stupid bitch."

With his left hand on the doorknob, Nash grabbed Jackie by the collar of her shirt and pushed her toward the door.

"Screw this up, and you're dead," Nash whispered.

CHAPTER 36

Weaver's radio exploded to life. Listening intently, he pressed his first two fingers against the earpiece in his right ear.

"Davidson to Phillips. Target door's opening. Target door is opening," the sniper radioed from his hide across the street.

Everyone's attention piqued. With the exception of Runk and Davis, who would be the ones to reach out and touch their suspect and who were not carrying long guns, each operator instinctively completed a quick visual check of his M-4 rifle. Some lightly tapped the bottom of the magazine with the palm of their hand, ensuring it was properly seated.

"Phillips, ten-four," he radioed, eyeing the rest of his team.

"Davidson. I have a female exiting the house. She's tethered —looks like an extension cord tied around her neck. Hands are also secured behind her back."

"Shit," Phillips mumbled. "Ten-four."

"Davidson to Phillips. Female's early twenties, five-seven, five-eight. Wearing a light blue t-shirt and grey sweatpants. Subject still at the threshold of the door."

"Ten-four. That's the roommate. Nash's girl is shorter," Phillips said to no one in particular. "Phillips to Davidson and Brett. Do either of you have a visual on the suspect?"

"Davidson negative. He must be tucked behind the door."

"Brett negative. Do we have permission to take the shot if we get a clear visual?"

"Phillips to Command Post."

"Command Post, negative. Not at this time."

"Phillips, ten-four."

The two sniper teams acknowledged the command post's denial. Although not pleased, each would follow orders. Nash could do a dance in the doorway, and he would not be accosted.

What's he up to? Phillips thought.

"Phillips to Tucker."

"Tucker go," from the sniper hidden in the rear.

"Keep a tight eye on the Charlie side," Phillips said. "I would not put it past this guy to attempt an escape out the rear while our attention is on the front."

"Ten-four."

"Davidson to Phillips. Female now on porch, moving toward the robot. Still no sight of the suspect."

Weaver could feel warm beads of perspiration build on his hands once again. His heart began to beat faster in anticipation of what might happen in the next few seconds. And it would only be a matter of seconds. If the team attempted a rescue, it would be swift. In the blink of an eye, it would be over. The key to their own safety—and that of the hostage—would be to move quickly. Grab her and get back behind cover. That was if things went well. If they didn't, it could be a blood bath, with four or five of his teammates, and the girl, being hurt.

"You want to try to snatch her?" Runk asked.

"No," Phillips answered. "It would take too much time. We'd have to not only get to her, but cut that cord as well. Then there's the repercussions to the other hostage."

Weaver was disappointed. They had been sitting for hours with no progress—he wanted to get it over with. He was tired. So was everyone else; he could see it in their eyes. But even with his limited training and experience, Weaver knew it was the right decision by the team leader. Even though he disliked the guy immensely, he couldn't deny his respect for him as well.

* * *

Nash held the electrical cord tightly as Jackie advanced across the porch toward the robot. He stayed behind the door, well out of sight.

The cord suddenly went taught. Her head jerking back slightly, Jackie cried, "It's not long enough. The cord, it's not long enough. I can't make it to the food."

"Tell them to move the damn thing closer," Nash yelled. "I'm not letting go of the cord. They can hear you—tell them."

Jackie did as she was told—tears dripping down her cheeks.

A voice crackled from the speaker on the robot. "Stay

calm," Tim said. "I'll have the operator bring it closer to you. Everything will be fine."

The mechanical gears of the machine engaged and the small tracked robot bobbed forward. Jackie turned to her left in an attempt to get her hands—bound at the wrist—to the bag. Her fingers fluttered about feeling for the handle. Grabbing the bag, she heard a whirring noise as the claw on the telescoping arm opened.

"I have it," Jackie sobbed.

Nash said nothing, but merely yanked on the cord drawing the frightened girl back toward the door of the house. Once inside, Nash slammed the door shut and yanked the bag from the terrified girl's hands.

"Can't you take this from around my neck?" Jackie complained. "I can hardly breathe."

Nash looked toward his partner and nodded. Young untied the electrical cord and pushed Jackie onto the sofa.

"Randy, grab something to eat," Nash said tossing the bag onto the kitchen counter.

Finding ten to twelve donuts, the two rummaged through the bag to find something they liked. With a donut in each hand, Nash turned to lean against the counter. The fact that he was eating donuts and not eggs was completely lost on the hungry hostage taker.

For fear the police had drugged the food, Nash watched as his friend began eating, "How are they?"

"As hungry as I am, anything would taste good," Young

said. Nodding toward the living room, he asked, "You want to give them anything?"

"Screw them," Nash said. "Let 'em starve."

Young snickered, "Harsh dude. I love it."

Hearing Nash's words, Christy wanted to say something but knew it would merely result in more rough treatment. Jackie however, became enraged.

"You piece of shit!" Jackie yelled, "You send me out there to get this stuff and you're not even going to give me anything?"

Nash calmly retrieved one of the doughy confections from the plastic bag and walked toward the sofa. Bending over, Nash's demeanor quickly changed. His pupils dilated and the veins on his forehead bulged. With his right hand he yanked the girl's head back reflexively opening her mouth.

"Here bitch!" Nash yelled, shoving the donut down her gullet. "Choke on it."

Nash's right hand quickly came around to Jackie's throat. His fingers dug into the soft skin on either side of her trachea. He yanked back sharply, pulling her windpipe away from the vertebrae in her spine and drawing her face closer to his. Squeezing tightly Nash said, "You'll eat when I tell you to eat and you will breathe when I tell you to breathe. I own you! Screw with me and you won't be breathing at all."

Nash released his grip, throwing her head back to the couch. Jackie's face had turned varying shades of red. Coughing and gagging she spit the donut onto the floor. Her head hanging from the cushion, Jackie gasped for air.

"My, my, my," Young snickered. "Didn't your mother teach you not to waste food?"

Nash returned to the kitchen and quietly continued to eat. After a few bites the telephone began to ring. His mouth half-full of food, Nash snatched the phone from the wall and mumbled, "What!".

"Rick, it's Tim," the negotiator responded.

"Who the hell else would it be? It's not like I'm getting calls from family and friends."

Following an awkward moment of silence, Tim said, "Now that you've had something to eat, perhaps we can talk for a bit. Everybody still doing okay?"

"I have to keep reinforcing who's in charge and who's holding all the cards," Nash said, his voice raised.

Tim wanted to keep him talking and merely acknowledged the statement, "Okay."

"Stupid bitch thinks she can call me names because I didn't give her anything to eat. I don't allow people to talk to me that way, especially women. That kinda' shit pisses me off!"

"Who's that Christy?"

"No. The other one."

Tim saw an opening and calmly said, "Rick, I hear what you're saying. We all have those folks that we just don't gel with. Personalities are different. There's nothing wrong with that. Sometimes—like at work—you may not have a choice in the matter and you have to adapt. Other times you can just cut any ties and each person goes their separate way. If your personality and hers don't match, perhaps its time to just send her out."

"That's one option," Nash said softly. "And the other option is I cap her damn ass!"

Tim knew how volatile Nash was and did not discount the possibility he would shoot either hostage. A good negotiator had to remain calm and measure the impact of each word he or she spoke. They also had to be able to think on their feet, and quickly.

"Rick, if you do that she will still be in the house with you. You'll continue to have a certain level of angst every time you look at her. Why not send her out?"

"Well Tim... because I'm running the show not you."

"Rick, I'm not trying to *run* anything. I was just trying to help you with something that seemed to be a problem."

"I'll make the decision on when I want to get rid of her— and not anyone else."

CHAPTER 37

The surge of adrenaline that had coursed through Weaver's body was now diminishing—his pulse and respiration slowing. Days into this tragedy, he was surprised at his body's reaction. Seeing the young girl, bound as she was, had proved difficult. He was used to decisive action. Arriving on the scene of a fire or medical problem, Weaver was accustomed to undertaking some type of operation to mitigate the emergency. Over the years he had learned to control and focus that natural surge of adrenaline into the tasks he needed to perform—grappling with a hose line or performing CPR.

Standing here helpless was nerve wracking. As the events unfolded, he found himself wanting to run out, cut the cord, break the door down, and beat the snot out of the guy who had tied her up.

Weaver had known there would be long hours of waiting associated with the job. But this thing had now been going well over twelve hours and there was no end in sight.

Shit, Mund! Weaver took the steps to the second floor two at a time. Checking the IV bag, Weaver asked, "How're you doing Mike?"

"Crappy," Mund responded with half a smile. "I had to hit the head again while you were gone."

"You're a real comedian. Here's another 2-milligram tablet of loperamide. You know if I can't control the diarrhea, I'll need to recommend you be evac'd out of here."

"Bullshit, I'm not leaving," Mund said.

"Mike, you're not doing anyone any good if you're lying in here or sitting in there," Weaver said, pointing toward the bathroom.

"Well, Nurse Nancy, I'm not going anywhere."

Weaver shook his head. "I'll check on you in a few minutes."

Returning to the first floor, Weaver sought out Phillips.

"Mund's diarrhea hasn't been controlled yet," Weaver told the team leader. "I just gave him more medication. If that doesn't resolve the problem, I'd recommend he be evac'd out."

"Not going to happen, Weaver. I don't have sufficient personnel as it is; I can't afford to lose anyone from this team."

Weaver knew the team leader had the final call. As the medic, he was Phillips' medical conscience. He could make recommendations, but that was it. Phillips was responsible for the entire SWAT team and their portion of the incident. Like everyone else on the team, Weaver was only responsible for a small portion.

Phillips continued, "Fix him up and get him back on his feet. Because if he goes, you go. You're a waste of time and space to me if you can't take care of a simple case of the shits."

In a way, Weaver knew Phillips was right. He needed to get Mund back on his feet.

Returning to his patient's side, Weaver told Mund, "You got your wish. You're not going anywhere. Phillips said if you go, I go."

"He knows when he's got the best," Mund joked.

"Don't kid yourself. You're a place holder—a warm body to fill a slot. That's all. Besides that, there are other people downstairs that need to use the head," Weaver said.

Weaver closed the clamp on the IV line to discontinue the flow of liquid into Mund's arm.

"You have about a thousand cc's of fluid on board—the bag's just about empty. If you have any more bouts of diarrhea, let me know. I'll give you another dose of medication and, if necessary, I'll run another line."

Weaver pulled the catheter from the vein in the operator's arm, "You know, I was raised in a row house similar to this on the east side of town."

Weaver suddenly stopped and looked at Mund.

"What's wrong?" Mund asked.

"Shit! I just realized something. Be right back."

Weaver turned to leave.

"Hey, Doc! You know I'm bleeding over here," Mund exclaimed.

Turning back around, Weaver saw blood running from the puncture site where the IV catheter had been placed.

Throwing a couple pieces of four-by-four-inch gauze at Mund, Weaver said, "Here, put that over it. There's tape in the bag."

Weaver was out the door of the bedroom and halfway down the stairs before his teammate could say a word.

Hitting the first floor, Weaver saw Runk holding cover at the rear door.

"You diagrammed the layout of the house last night didn't you?" Weaver asked.

"Yeah, why?" Runk said.

"I grew up in a house similar to this on the east side. Our place had a small hatch that allowed access to the roof. And—"

"And our bad guy could access the roof, drop down into another house and possibly slip out unnoticed," Runk interrupted.

"You got it."

"Good catch, Doc. We need to brief Phillips and get a game plan."

Runk had Gunny take his place on the rear door and dragged Weaver over to the living room where Phillips was sitting.

"Jack," Runk said. "Danny realized there may be a trap door leading to the roof in these places. The roof is flat and there's a possibility our boy could slip out of here."

"That's all I need. Okay, check it out and let me know what you find." Phillips was not only worried about his suspect getting away, he was also frustrated the information had to come from, what he considered the most useless person on the team—Weaver.

Heading to the second floor Weaver noted, "The hatches

are usually in one of the closets. It may be difficult to see if there's a lot of junk in the way."

The two split up, each taking a room. Weaver opened the closet door in the front bedroom and found it jammed with clothes, shoes, and sporting equipment. *Damn, how much crap can you stuff into a three-by-five space?* He pulled a small black LED flashlight from a pouch on his body armor. Illuminating the ceiling of the small space, he pushed his way further into the closet.

"Got it!" he yelled to Runk.

Runk joined Weaver in the bedroom, and both began emptying the closet of its contents. Completing the task, Runk slid his .40 caliber Sig from its holster. The pistol had a Surefire LED light attached beneath the barrel and a touchpad on the grip, allowing him to focus light wherever his weapon was pointed.

The burly operator tossed his helmet on the bed and slowly moved into the closet. With the gun pointed at the ceiling, Runk lightly pressed the small black pad that completed the circuit to the weapon light. With the small space now illuminated, he raised his left arm and attempted to push open the hatch. The two-foot square piece of wood did not budge.

Runk re-holstered his weapon and kicked an old plastic milk crate into the closet.

"Doc, shine a light in here," Runk ordered.

Weaver, doing as he was told, watched his teammate step onto the crate and repeatedly attempt to open the hatch.

Runk finally gave up. "Son-of-a-bitch ain't going to open. No way, no how."

"The owner may have had a company tar the thing shut when the roof was last replaced," Weaver said. "Renting to a bunch of college kids—can you imagine these knuckleheads being able to get up there? They'd have rooftop block parties every weekend."

"Yeah, but we can't be sure the hatch in the target house is sealed shut. We're still going to need to get up there."

Runk and Weaver returned back downstairs to find Phillips talking to the command post on his cell phone. Ending the call, Phillips said, "What did you find?"

"There is a hatch," Runk said. "However, I can't get it open. Must be sealed shut."

"It'll still need to be checked, but I can't afford a body to monitor that hatch continuously."

"It's not much of an issue while it's light. Air One can keep an eye on it, and the snipers can watch the exit points on the other houses."

"I'll have the command post make that tasking to Air One," Phillips said. "Darkness is going to complicate things. I have an idea, but we'll need some additional equipment."

✳ ✳ ✳

After the telephone line went dead, Tim Bolz's head flopped backward, his eyes staring at the ceiling of the command post as if looking for the answer to his dilemma. This was the most difficult hostage situation he had ever encountered.

This many hours into an incident, the situation would normally have entered the holding stage. Although psychologically difficult for the hostage—having someone else control their every action—the hostage taker would have had time to fully comprehend his situation. He would have calmed and been less prone to violence.

However, Nash was not reading from a normal script. He was unpredictable. His emotions were all over the map—one minute crying, the next ready to kill.

Tim had consulted with a number of his law enforcement colleagues over the past hours. Even the on-call police psychologist could not predict how the situation would end. Their only advice was to keep talking and attempt to build rapport.

Tim stepped outside to stretch his legs, get some sun, and gather his thoughts. Standing with a cup of coffee in his hand —the fourth of the day—he spotted a patrol officer with a cigarette hanging from his mouth.

"Hey, can I bum one from you?" Tim asked.

He had stopped smoking over a year ago. *My wife and kids are going to kill me.*

As he lit the cigarette and took a slow drag, he thought about the lives Nash had already impacted—the families of the dead and injured, as well as the two girls he was holding. Not to mention all of the cops that were part of this sad situation. Before inhaling a second time, he threw the cigarette to the pavement and crushed it into the ground with the sole of his shoe. *I'm not one of the ones you're going to affect. Your destiny is yours.*

Looking up, he noticed a tall, lean man in his fifties heading toward the command post. The man wore a gray pinstripe suit with a button-down collar white shirt and paisley tie. He looked like a man on a mission; his pace was quick and his attention was straight ahead.

As the stranger approached the door of the truck, Tim asked, "Can I help you?"

"Are you in charge?" the stranger asked.

"No, that would be—"

"Then, no, you can't. And you can get the hell out of my way."

Tim put his hand on the door and retorted, "Sir, I need you to identify yourself and your business here."

"If you still want to have a job at the end of the day, I suggest you get out of my way."

Tim's fuse was getting short; it had been a long night. It would have been easy to lash out at this jerk and then throw him in cuffs, but he reached deep for what little patience he had left and said, "Sir, you are obviously upset about something. I would like to help you, but in order to do that I'll need to know your name and what this is all about."

"My name's Ed Benson. One of the girls being held hostage is my granddaughter. I spoke to the County Executive earlier, but I wanted to see firsthand what was being done to get her out. And I'm not leaving here until there are some answers." Benson had made it past the police line by dropping the county executive's name.

Tim recognized the man's name. He was the owner of a

sizable bank headquartered in Maryland. *My day just went from bad to worse.*

"Mister Benson," Tim said. "The incident commander, Major Gittings, is just inside—"

Benson took a step toward the door.

Holding his left index finger up and grabbing the door handle with his right hand, Tim said, "I'll have him step out to talk to you."

Tim opened the door and stuck his head inside, "Major, I think you need to step outside. There's a Mister Benson that wants to speak to the person in charge."

Gittings' head dropped ever so slightly, giving away his frustration. Stepping out the door, the Major extended his hand toward the banker. "Mister Benson," Gittings said. "Pleased to meet you. Sorry it's under these circumstances. The County Executive mentioned he had spoken to you; however, he didn't say you would be stopping by."

Ignoring Gittings' extended hand, Benson said, "Where's Chief Sherman? Why isn't he running this thing?"

Dropping his hand, Gittings said, "The Chief had to step away for a few moments. I'm in charge right now."

"What are you doing to obtain my granddaughter's release, and why is it taking so long?"

"Mister Benson, let me begin by introducing Detective Tim Bolz. He's the lead negotiator trying to gain Christy's release."

Tim didn't even attempt to shake Benson's hand.

"His team, and everyone here, have been working diligently to bring this thing to an end," Gittings went on.

"You were supposed to be protecting her," Benson said. "What was the cop sitting up there doing—sleeping?"

Tim couldn't contain himself. His eyes narrowed and he pointed his index finger at Benson's chest. "That officer—the one trying to protect your granddaughter—is in Shock Trauma fighting for his life. He was ambushed. His family is wondering if he'll be coming home."

Gittings quickly interjected, "Detective, why don't you check on how things are progressing inside?" It was an order not a request.

"Yes, sir," Tim said, staring at Benson.

"Mister Benson," Gittings said. "Once again, we are doing everything possible to bring this to a peaceful conclusion."

"Do you even know if she's still alive?"

"We believe she is. The hostage taker requested food for everyone and Christy's roommate—Jackie—came out to retrieve it. We've also been utilizing a highly trained paramedic to assess some of the information we've obtained."

"A paramedic! Why in the hell isn't a doctor here? Do you understand the influence I have in this community—the money I bring to this entire region?"

"We have a wide range of medical professionals working with us. This paramedic has some specialized skills that we've tapped."

"Major, it sounds to me as if you're covering your ass. Your time is running out. My next option is to step before those cameras over there and describe to the public what incompetent buffoons you are."

Benson turned and stormed off.

"Sir," Gittings said. "If you give me your number I will be glad to update you. Sir?"

CHAPTER 38

Phillips and Runk discussed the details of the plan they hoped would keep Nash from escaping across the rooftops. Weaver stood by silently.

After a few moments Phillips grudgingly asked Weaver, "Can you get us a ladder and some lights from the fire department?"

"Shouldn't be a problem," Weaver responded.

"Good. I'll contact the Major and let him know you will be making the necessary arrangements."

Turning to Runk, Phillips said, "Take two other people with you. Let me know when you're done on the roof."

Weaver contacted the area fire department battalion commander for permission to use the equipment. Within minutes a long red-and-white ladder truck arrived at the command post. Weaver, Runk, Davis, and Bones met the unit and gathered the items they would need.

Weaver and Runk slid a long, two-section ladder from the belly of the truck. They hauled the 114-pound piece to their shoulders for the long trek back up the street. Davis and Bones brought up the rear, carrying the lights, heavy duty electrical cords, and rope they would need to complete the task.

Arriving back at the side of the house where the team was staged, Runk wanted to run through the plan one more time before proceeding.

"You know," Weaver said, "these ladders are not exactly quiet when being extended. Will our boy think something's up?"

"That could be a problem," Runk said. "I'll have Air One do a low fly-by to cover the noise of the ladder."

As Air One arrived in position, the ladder was raised to the roof of 58 Burkeshire Road. Bones slung his M-4 across his back and began his ascent with Davis a few feet behind.

Two feet from the top, Bones stopped and drew his pistol. He had no idea if Nash was already on the roof. The trick would be getting his eyes and his gun over the parapet at the same time—but nothing more. If their suspect was up there, Bones needed to be ready to engage immediately without providing Nash a large enough target to return fire at. It was a dangerous maneuver.

Bones grabbed the top rung of the ladder—positioned inches below the roofline—with his left hand. He took a deep breath and slid the top of his body upward. His eyes scanned left and then right. "Roof's clear," he radioed.

Bones climbed onto the roof. In one smooth motion, he holstered his handgun and slid his M-4 around from his back bringing it up to eye level as he dropped to one knee. Within seconds Davis was on the roof bringing his own M-4 to bear. Both operators had the barrels of their weapons pointed at the hatch on the house where Nash was holed-up.

Weaver threw a coil of rope onto his shoulder and climbed

to the roof. Once topside, he held one end of the rope tight while tossing the other end over the side. The rope paid out down the wall. Runk gave a tug after tying a series of knots around the lights and cords. Hand-over-hand, Weaver hauled the fifty pounds of equipment to the roof. His shoulder and arm muscles were burning as he made the final pull on the rope.

Arriving on the roof himself, Runk motioned for Bones and Davis to cover his advance. The three moved cautiously across the rooftops—weapons trained on the hatch atop their target house. At their destination, Runk stooped and ran his hand underneath the tarred piece of wood. *Doesn't feel like it's been sealed shut. Couldn't be so lucky.*

Weaver remained at the roof's edge and began untying the equipment.

Using hand gestures, Runk had Davis move opposite him and, in unison, they attempted to lift the hatch cover. Bones moved to a position where, if Nash began shooting, Bones could return fire without hitting his teammates. The hatch moved freely as the two operators applied upward pressure. Stepping forward—his M-4 just below eye level—Bones quickly peaked into the now open hole. As he returned to his cover position, the other two slowly lowered the cover back into place.

With weapons still covering the hatch, the three retreated back across the rooftops to where Weaver was working.

"I've got two 1000-watt lights ready," Weaver told Runk, "I'll run the wire down the ladder as we descend."

"Good," Runk replied. "The lights will blind Nash if he

tries to exit the hatch. He won't know if someone is up here or not. We can have Air One fly over periodically. I just wish we had the equipment to get a live video feed from up here."

Turning to Bones, Runk asked, "What did you see below the hatch?"

"Looked like a closet. There were shoe boxes on a shelf just below the opening. Everything seemed to be neatly piled—undisturbed. He may not even know the hatch is there."

"We can only hope. Okay, let's get out of here," Runk said.

One-by-one, the squad slid over the parapet and down the ladder, hoping the maneuver would keep Nash off the roof.

✷ ✷ ✷

Randy Young raced down the steps. "Rick, Rick," Young barked. "There's somebody on the roof!"

More as an utterance of surprise than disbelief, Nash said, "What?"

"I was taking a dump and it sounded like there was somebody up there."

Nash bolted up the stairs to the second floor, Young close behind. In the hallway at the top of the staircase the two stood silently, looking at the ceiling.

After a moment Nash looked at Young and said, "Are you sure? I don't hear a thing."

"Rick, I'm sure. It sounded like something rubbing. I heard it twice."

"It could have been a tree branch."

"There's no tree branches anywhere near the house. Look for yourself. There was somebody up there. I'm telling you."

The blinds on the second floor were still up and Nash knew better than to get near any windows.

Suddenly, Nash heard talking and movement from downstairs.

"Shit! There's nobody watching them."

Nash bounded down the stairs, gun in hand, to find Christy and Jackie at the rear door in the kitchen. Jackie, her hands still bound behind her, was on her toes trying to unlock the deadbolt on the door.

Christy tried to block Nash as he entered the room. "Go, Jackie go!" Christy screamed.

Seething, Nash threw Christy into the side of the refrigerator as if she were a child's toy. In less than two steps Nash was within reach of the escaping girl. "You aren't going anywhere," Nash said.

Jackie spun and tried to head-butt her captor. Nash slammed the Glock pistol into the left side of Jackie's face. Blood splattered against the wall as a two-inch gash opened on her cheek.

"You think you can get away from me!" Nash yelled.

Jackie fell to the floor—crying. A small puddle of blood spread across the tile. Nash straddled the girl and pointed the gun at her head. "I ought to kill you right here."

"Rick," Young said from the dining room door, "if the cops hear a gunshot, they'll be in here in a flash."

Nash didn't move. His finger gripped the trigger of the gun. His eyes remained fixed.

Jackie could not look up. She closed her eyes, not wanting to see the thug's face in what could be her last moments on earth.

"Rick-," Young said.

"I heard you," Nash replied.

CHAPTER 39

A red LED light on the console in front of Tim Bolz began blinking; a buzzing sound could be heard throughout the command post with each successive flash.

Tim eyed Finessey and Mitchell with a look of surprise as he slipped his headset in place. This was the first time that Rick Nash had attempted to contact the negotiating team. Tim closed his eyes, as if to get in character, and pressed the button to open the phone line.

"Hey, Rick," Tim said. "What's up?"

"I've had enough of this bullshit," Nash said. "We're coming out."

Tim knew it couldn't possibly be this easy—Nash merely walking out and giving up. However, stranger things had occurred. If Nash wasn't planning on ending the standoff, Tim would at least attempt to coax him in that direction.

"Rick, that's great. I'm sure you're tired and hungry. We'll need to make a few arrangements, but then I'll personally make sure you get a shower, some clean clothes, and some rest."

"I'm not giving up, you idiot! Somebody was on the roof."

"I don't know what you're talking about," Tim interrupted. "Nobody was on your roof."

"I don't believe you. Not for one minute. We're getting out of here—I want a car. If any cops try to stop me, I'll kill one of these two."

Tim had known that Nash would eventually make some demands. He was surprised it had taken him this long.

"Rick, I can't make that decision. That's done way above my head. But I have to tell you, I don't know if my bosses will go along with the idea of you just walking away with the two girls."

"Well, Tim, I guess you better convince them."

"Rick, we don't want to see anyone hurt. That's the goal here. You and I talk through this, and we both agree on a solution. Again, I don't know if my bosses will agree to this, but I'll ask. I'm going to need some time. If they do agree, we'll need to get a car down here. I know you don't want to use a police car—they stand out and they can be tracked. We would need to get to a car rental place, and you know how they are with paperwork. I'll get back to you in a bit."

"You've got one hour," Nash said.

"Rick, you know that's not enough time to get this done."

"One hour," Nash said, and the line went dead.

Providing Nash with a car and what amounted to a free pass was a non-starter. That's where this whole thing began three days ago, with Nash taking Christy hostage and driving around the city of Baltimore.

Most hostage situations normally began with threats by the hostage taker that his captives would be killed if demands were not met. It was the negotiators' job to get past deadlines while reducing the list of demands. Although Tim himself had been able to eventually negotiate the release of hostages with as little as a hamburger and an order of fries, he had no illusion that this situation would be that simple.

Tim looked at Mitchell and Finessey while removing his headset. "Thoughts?"

"Obviously," Mitchell said, "he has no qualms with killing one of the girls. He's got quite a bit of blood on his hands already."

"Question is," Finessey added, "will he pull the trigger in an hour if that car is not in front of the house?"

"I don't know," Tim said. "Nash's been extremely agitated at times, but he's yet to pull the trigger. He's roughed them up a bit—but not shot them. That would lead me to believe he would not kill them. The problem is, he's exhibiting every type of emotion possible, and he certainly isn't playing by the normal script that we see with this type of situation. He could do almost anything and it wouldn't surprise me."

There was silence amongst the three negotiators as they contemplated their next move and its potential ramifications. It was like a chess game. They needed to think two to three moves ahead. Anticipating what their challenger—in this case, Nash—would do. The problem was that these weren't pieces on a board. The lives of two college girls were at stake. And one of them had a wealthy, influential relative. Tim could not get that tidbit out of his mind.

"I don't have an answer," Tim finally said. "We'll just have to wait. Let him call us—wanting to know where the car is. If we see he's ready to pull the trigger, we have the SWAT team initiate a rescue operation."

∗ ∗ ∗

Weaver was running the heavy-duty electrical cord from the lights on the roof to the inside of the house, where the team was staged.

Phillips ended a phone call and announced, "Command Post advises we have a deadline in one hour. We'll brief on the plan in three minutes."

Weaver looked at Gunny, who was standing nearby. "What's that mean?"

"It means our boy has probably made a demand and given the command post an hour to comply," Gunny said.

"And?" Weaver asked.

"Normally, the message is, the hostage taker will kill a hostage if the demand isn't met."

Phillips pulled Runk aside. Minutes later, the team leader delineated the situation as it had been relayed by the command post.

Everyone looked on—expressionless—as Phillips gave out assignments.

"The order to initiate will come with little-to-no warning," Phillips said. "We will need to move quickly. I want everyone geared up and ready ten minutes prior to the deadline."

Each member of the team readied themselves. The sounds

of metal moving against metal could be heard throughout the first floor as operators checked their weapons. Flashes were seen as lights were tested on handguns and rifles.

Weaver unzipped his M-9 bag, assuring himself there were sufficient supplies. His hands were once again wet with perspiration. His shoulders ached from the weight of the body armor. It had become painfully evident why the SWAT school had such an emphasis on physical conditioning. Without the endurance and the ability to compartmentalize pain, he would not have been able to last. Weaver also knew the adrenaline would soon return—bringing with it the warmth of surging blood—as the deadline approached.

Meantime, Phillips contacted each sniper team individually, by phone, to provide an update on the situation and Phillips' plan of action. Any hostage rescue would need to be coordinated between the entry team and their sniper overwatch.

At the appointed time, everyone began moving toward their assigned positions. Bones had point. He grabbed the ballistic shield as he headed to the front door, pressing the trigger on the handle to ensure the 50,000 watt candlepower light was operational. Weaver's position in the stack was just ahead of Mund, the rear guard.

"Mike," Weaver asked. "How're you feeling?"

"I haven't hit the head in the past twenty-minutes, if that's what you mean. Beyond that, I'm just tired. No different than everyone else."

Weaver gave Mund a thumbs up. Weaver was beyond

tired; more like exhausted. But he was not going to admit it to anyone.

Weaver checked his watch—two minutes to the deadline. The radio was silent. *That's good. The command post would be providing updates if things were deteriorating with Nash.*

One minute. Everyone's body language changed. Some stood more erect; others adjusted the grips on their weapons. Bones picked up the shield and balanced it on his thigh—ready to go if Phillips gave the order to initiate.

"Brett to Phillips," the sniper transmitted. "No change."

Weaver jumped. He had been so focused on the silence, the transmission had startled him. It felt as though he had jumped six inches off the ground. Weaver felt a hand rest lightly on his shoulder. He turned his head to see a smile on Mund's face.

"Ten-four," Phillips acknowledged.

The other two sniper elements radioed similar reports.

The team waited. Weaver noticed Phillips had never checked his watch. He knew they were well past the deadline. *He'll wait here all day until he's ordered to do something else.*

"Command Post to Phillips," Major Gittings radioed. "We're at H plus fifteen. Give it another five minutes and then stand down."

They were fifteen minutes past the deadline.

"Ten-four," Phillips radioed.

At the appointed time, Phillips announced, "I need two people to cover the front and rear doors again."

Moving to the doorway being vacated by Bones, Gunny said, "Gunny's got the front."

"Rice has the back."

It was now the middle of the afternoon. The team had been on duty for thirty hours. In all, this was their third day of dealing with Rick Nash.

Weaver removed his helmet and ran his hand through his matted hair. *I could use a shower and a shave. Can't imagine what I look like, cause I sure don't smell very good.* Finding an unoccupied, cushioned chair he plopped down and stared off into space.

"You okay?" Lebo asked.

Startled back to the present, Weaver shook his head and blinked his eyes, "Yeah, just out of it, I guess."

"Doc, you're falling asleep with your eyes open. Between going to the command post, treating Mund, and hitting the roof, you've been non-stop. Not to mention being ready to go just now. You're no good to us exhausted. Get a couple minutes shuteye."

"I'm fine."

"I know what you're worried about. Even Jack has gotten a power nap in. What did you learn in school? Rely on your teammates. That's not only related to fields of fire and areas of responsibility. That also means listening to more experienced operators providing guidance. This is your first operation with us. You don't need to prove yourself; you did that in the early hours of this thing. Get some rest. We need you one hundred percent if the shit goes bad."

Weaver did as he was told, rested his head against the wall and allowed his eyes to slowly close.

CHAPTER 40

"Where's the car, Tim?" Nash asked.

"You know the way the government is," Tim said. "The bureaucracy is mind numbing. I'm working on it."

"I don't believe you. What do I have to do to convince you I'm serious? You had an hour. Do I put a bullet in Jackie's head and push her ass out the door? Is that what it'll take, Tim?"

Tim allowed Nash to continue his rant without interruption. He hoped that by allowing him to vent, Nash might calm down.

The negotiator was getting worried. It had been nearly twenty-four hours; he was no closer to ending this disaster than he had been when it all started.

Tim tried to empathize. "Rick, I'm frustrated too. I would like to just snap my fingers, give you whatever you want, and end this. You're a smart guy. You know that's not the way things work."

"I tell you what," Tim continued. "It's been a long day; you've got to be getting hungry. What if I send some more food while we wait?"

"Fine—," Nash blurted. "Pizza, with pepperoni—I want pizza with pepperoni."

"Okay, Rick. I'll get that in the works."

"And, Tim," Nash said softly. "I'm not waiting much longer."

The statement sent chills up Tim's spine. He was about to answer when the line went dead.

Is Nash ready to kill—again?

Tim looked toward the rest of his team, each of whom had been monitoring the exchange. Chief Sherman and Major Gittings, having seen the worried look on the face of the lead negotiator, decided to join the group.

Letting out a sigh, Tim leaned back in his chair and rubbed his face with both hands. "What's he going to do?"

"We're forty minutes past the deadline," Sherman interjected. "You're over that hurdle. If he was intent on taking some type of action, hurting either of the hostages, he would have done so when the car was not in front of the house. Did he give you another deadline?"

"No," Tim said.

"Good," Sherman said. "We'll work on getting the food delivered. What's your plan at this point?"

"We need to re-examine our intel. Mitchell talked to Nash's mother yesterday. I'll have him interview her again. There's got to be a nerve we can hit that would get him to release the hostages."

"Talk to our psychologist again," Sherman added. "He may have some ideas, given the recent events."

Tim knew time was running out. He and his team had to

begin making real progress at winning the release of the hostages. Just maintaining the status quo was not the answer.

CHAPTER 41

"Mund," Phillips said. "The command post has some pizzas for us. You're low man on the totem pole. Get your butt in gear and get them back here before they're cold."

Grabbing his rifle, Mund leaped to his feet. "I'm on it. At this point anything that has to do with food—I'm there."

Weaver overheard Phillips' directive to Mund. *Not the most nutritious thing in the world. But, damn, it would sure taste good right now. Oh, no—food, dinner, Kathy. Maybe she was just joking; she knew I wasn't going to make it. No, not that lucky.*

He slipped his phone from his pocket and began typing with his thumbs. *Thank goodness for text messages. I don't have to listen to her yelling.*

Bad guy still not cooperating.

Weaver hit 'SEND' on the keypad and waited. Minutes went by as he sat staring at the phone. *Crap—what's worse than hearing her yelling at me? Silence. Never knew that could carry over to text messages. Didn't think of that.*

"You waiting for something?" Gunny asked.

"My wife had dinner reservations tonight for us and her parents. Just sent her a text that I wasn't going to make it."

"And—"

"She's not answering."

Gunny patted Weaver on the shoulder. "Been there, my friend. Believe me, it won't be the last time."

"Thanks for the words of encouragement, Gunny."

Mund stuck his head out the front door and, instinctively, looked right at the target house. Jones was holding cover for him as he darted down the street. Mund hugged the front of the row houses much as Weaver had done hours earlier. Passing the stone wall at the end of the street, he encountered a uniformed officer holding five pizza boxes.

"Dominos delivers," the officer said with a smile.

"Thought you guys had a thirty-minute delivery time," Mund said. "Hope you're not expecting a tip."

"Yeah, I know. Catch you next time."

Mund took the boxes and began his trek back. As he retraced his route to the staging area, the smell of cheese and pepperoni was overwhelming. Midway up the block, he lowered his face to the boxes and took a deep breath. *Damn, never knew a pizza could smell so good. If I had to go get these things, then I've got dibs on the first slice. Screw the rest of them. They'll have to fight me off.*

Suddenly, there was a bang. Startled back to the moment, Mund tripped and fell face-first into the pizza boxes. *That friggin' dog again!*

Weaver, Lebo, and Davis were near the front windows when Mund went down. None of the three could control themselves and began to roar with laughter.

Agitated, Phillips asked, "What the hell's going on?"

The only one who could get a syllable out was Davis. "Mund-," as the laughter continued.

Even Jones, still holding cover at the door, turned to see what was happening. He had to do a double take.

Arriving at the windows, Phillips saw the new guy still face-down in his dinner. The team leader merely shook his head and walked away.

"It's like something out of a Three Stooges episode," Weaver finally choked out.

Mund slowly got to his feet. He heard nothing beyond the barking dog on the other side of the glass window. *I don't even want to think about what these things look like. I'll blame it on the patrol officer. He's the one that screwed up the pizzas.*

The dejected Mund continued his journey back to where his teammates lay in wait. As he crossed the threshold of the house, all eyes were on the newest team member and failed delivery boy.

Looking around the room, Mund asked, "What?"

"I knew I shouldn't have given such an important assignment to the new guy," Phillips scolded.

Mund knew his plan to lay blame elsewhere was not going to work. "It was the dog. I swear!"

"Yeah," Runk said. "Blame it on a poor, little dog."

"Was that the same dog that scared the pants off me last night?" Weaver asked.

"Yeah," Mund said, looking for sympathy.

"When I went by that house earlier today," Weaver said, "I had common sense enough to keep quiet and not disturb the damn thing."

Gunny grabbed the deformed boxes from Mund's hands. Placing them on the table, he flipped open each box. All but the last had cheese and toppings stuck to the lid. Gunny pulled his twelve-inch, Marine-issued, KA-Bar knife from its sheath. He scraped the gooey mess from the cardboard and slathered it back on the sauce-topped dough. Before re-sheathing the deadly instrument, the former Marine ran his forefinger down the length of the blade and devoured the cheese that had been left behind.

"Shut up, and let's eat," Gunny said.

Mund nudged his way forward to grab a slice. With the KA-Bar still in his hand, Gunny raised the knife and said, "Don't think so, ass-wipe."

In an artificial show of sadness, Mund lowered his head, pushed out his lower lip and waited for the rest of the team to eat.

"Eat fast," Phillips announced. "We've got work to do. Just received word they're sending food to our bad guy."

Everyone stuffed a slice or two of pizza in his mouth.

Within minutes, Phillips was briefing the crew once again. "We'll keep the same line up as before. I'll assume Nash will again have the girl retrieving the food tethered. Should we get an opportunity to make a rescue, I'll cut the wire. Davis, get her out of the line of fire and back here."

The EOD robot started to roll up the street just as the team lined up inside the doorway of their staging area. The robot took the same route as it had before, making a right turn from the street and stopping only two feet from the front stoop of the target house.

Just as before, the robot sat waiting for someone to retrieve the sack hanging from the device's mechanical arm—this time a large McDonalds bag.

The minutes dragged by.

"Brett to Phillips," the sniper radioed. "Door's opening."

"Ten-four," Phillips acknowledged.

As had happened each time previously, Weaver noticed everyone's body language change.

"Brett to Phillips," the sniper said calmly. "Looks like the same female as before retrieving the food. Same clothing, same hair. She's tethered again. No visual on the suspect."

"Phillips, ten-four."

"Brett to Phillips," the sniper said urgently. "Female has visible injuries—left side of her face. Left eye appears swollen shut. Dried blood on her face and clothing. Try to get a visual on her from your angle."

Hearing the transmission, the hair on the back of Weaver's neck stood straight out. His adrenaline went into high gear. It was like a drag race where the funny car hit two-hundred miles per hour in seconds.

He strained to see around his teammates and get an eye on the girl. Phillips saw the medic in his peripheral vision as he acknowledged the sniper's transmission. Releasing the push-to-talk button, he raised the first two fingers of his left hand and motioned Weaver forward.

Weaver stepped out of formation and took a position next to Bones and the ballistic shield. He knew he only had seconds. Pulling his phone from his pocket, Weaver zoomed-in and began snapping images of the girl's face.

"Brett to Phillips. That's a significant change in the girl's status from her previous excursion outside."

"Affirmative," Phillips said. "Phillips to Command Post. You copy?"

"Command Post, ten-four. You still don't have a visual on the suspect, correct?"

"Brett to Command Post—affirmative. No visual."

"Davidson to Command Post—nothing here."

"Command Post to Phillips. Stand fast—we'll get back to you."

"Phillips, ten-four."

The girl took the bag from the robot and hobbled back inside the house.

After the team stood down, Weaver opened the images on his phone and examined them closely. Having more time to focus on the injuries, he was sickened. *How could someone be so brutal?*

CHAPTER 42

Chief Sherman grabbed Major Gittings as well as the two negotiators—Tim Bolz and Ray Finessey—for an urgent meeting. Pete Mitchell was still out gathering additional intel.

"Everyone heard the transmission regarding the girl's injuries," Sherman said. "I think you'll agree we have a clear escalation of violence against the hostages."

"Chief, if I may," Bolz interrupted. "We have clear escalation against *one* of the hostages. We don't even know, definitively, whether the other is even alive."

"Point taken," Sherman acknowledged. "Nash admitted to, using his term, roughing the hostages up, when he went through the door. This girl now has visible injuries. I think we need to re-evaluate our current strategy to confine and negotiate."

"I would tend to agree," Gittings added. "We are twenty-four hours in with no real progress."

"Not that I disagree," Tim said, "but I think we should talk to the medic guy, Weaver, and get his perspective on those injuries. Just so we have all of our ducks in a row."

Looking at Sherman, Gittings said, "I don't see a problem, do you?"

"Get him on the phone," Sherman agreed.

Tim dialed Weaver's cell phone number.

"Weaver."

"Danny, this is Tim Bolz at the command post."

"Yes, sir."

"I'm here with Chief Sherman, Major Gittings, and Ray Finessey. We were just discussing the injuries to the girl that retrieved the food. Did you happen to get a look at her?"

"Yeah, I was able to snap a couple of pictures from my phone."

"Fantastic. Any possibility you could forward them to the CP?"

Weaver agreed and immediately sent the digital images to the command post.

"They just came through," Tim said.

Finessey opened the images on his computer screen while the remainder of the group gathered around.

"What's your assessment of her injuries?" Tim asked.

"As you can see," Weaver said, "she has a two- to three-inch laceration on the left side of her face. Bleeding appears to be controlled."

"She lost a lot of blood don't you think?" Gittings said.

"Face and scalp wounds bleed profusely due to the vasculature in the head. They often look worse than they really are. The laceration alone is not that big a deal. She's going to need stitches, and if that doesn't happen soon, she'll have a nasty scar.

"I have two larger concerns. First, we can't tell how much damage has been done to her left eye—as you can see it's swollen shut. More importantly, she may have suffered another concussion. Coupled with the possible concussion, and period of unconsciousness last night, she may have some serious short- and long-term issues. Sustaining two possible concussions in such a short period of time is problematic. But we can't be sure without in-hospital tests."

Tim asked if any members of the group had questions. "Danny, I think that's it," Tim said. "Thanks for the information."

"What about the other girl?" Weaver asked. "Anything more on her?"

"Not a thing."

A loud knocking came at the door of the command post. Having been placed in charge of the coffee pot, Lieutenant Rambo was near the entrance. The lieutenant opened the door and immediately recognized the well-dressed banker standing outside.

"You're Ed Benson," Rambo said.

Trying to get his attention, Major Gittings yelled, "Lieutenant!"

"Come on in!" the lieutenant said; the words spewing forth before the major's bellow sunk in.

Benson entered the command post with an air of arrogance. Seeing Sherman, he said, "I'm glad to see you finally decided to get involved in freeing my granddaughter."

Major Gittings had warned the Chief about Benson's previous threats to go to the media.

"Ed, we're very busy," Sherman said. "What can I do for you?"

Everyone in the command post was distracted by Benson's raucous demeanor, forgetting to cover sensitive material.

Benson glimpsed at the computer screen to Sherman's right. "Is that my granddaughter?" Benson yelled.

Tim quickly closed the image on the screen. *Shit!*

"No," Sherman said. "That's Jackie, Christy's roommate."

"How did you get that? Did that bastard hurt my granddaughter, too?"

Sherman evaded the questions. He did not want Benson to know they had assets within feet of the hostages. And—he didn't have any concrete information on Christy's well-being. Giving Benson an overly positive response could come back to bite him. If he was too pessimistic, Benson would go berserk.

"Our goal is to end this safely."

Benson pounced. Pointing to the computer screen, he said, "You've obviously failed in that regard. I've got one concern here—my granddaughter. I don't give a damn about anyone else. Get her out of there, and get her out of there now! And I swear, if there is one hair on her head harmed, you will regret this day."

After Benson stormed from the command post, Sherman unleashed his frustration on Lieutenant Rambo.

"Lieutenant," Sherman said, "if you don't want to be busted back to corporal, walking a foot post in a cow pasture along the Pennsylvania line, then you better not let another unauthorized person in this vehicle!"

"Yes, sir," Rambo said.

"Major, give him a list of who can be in here and have him stand guard outside."

Gittings nodded and began to write.

Sherman closed his eyes, took a breath, and said, "Okay, let's get this cleaned up."

The team of hostage negotiators and command staff debated their options. Their present strategy was clearly not working.

Sherman sat listening to the discussion. Finally, he spoke. His words had a sense of decisiveness.

"Major," Sherman said, "find a way to get him to a window and end this."

With that, the Chief of Police rose and left the command post.

The group looked at each other, knowing the intent of the order, but not how to implement it. Something Nash had said early on, gave Tim an idea. Gittings thought it was worth a shot.

* * *

It was dusk when the armored personnel carrier rounded

309

the corner. The warm air of the day was cooling as the sun set behind the row of brick row homes.

"Murray to Phillips, turning onto Burkeshire now."

The APC's driver, Bob Murray, slowly made his way up Burkeshire Road. Tim Bolz, sitting beside him, reached down and pulled the PA system's microphone from its clip, mounted on the dash.

Phillips and his assaulters, as well as the sniper elements, had been briefed on the plan and stood ready.

The menacing truck stopped in front of 54 and sat idling. Tim looked to his right and saw the SWAT team operators standing in the doorway, ready to strike when needed.

Slowly, Tim turned his head left. He knew there were two sniper teams across from where Nash was barricaded. His eyes scanned the windows and doors, but he couldn't see the snipers. A chill reverberated up his spine. He knew they were out there somewhere – somewhere. That was the mark of a good team, being unseen. Snipers, good at their craft, could walk into the woods and disappear. You could walk on them and not know they were there. A person could look through a window and not see them looking back. Tim recalled Brett's admonition during one of the county's famed sniper schools: "Compromise is failure." The worst thing for a sniper was to be seen.

Tim's stomach knotted. He knew what he was about to do would generate a response. He just hoped the two girls wouldn't be hurt in the process. He wondered if Sherman's decision to change course had been caused by Ed Benson's intense pressure.

He brought the microphone to within an inch of his lips and pressed the push-to-talk button.

"Ricky," Tim announced over the PA. The sound reverberated off the brick houses. "Ricky, it's Tim. Why don't we end this? Give yourself up."

Tim released the button and the street fell silent.

Seconds later, he tried again.

"Ricky. It's been a long couple of days. I know you're tired. Just walk out—you can finally get some rest. Ricky, can you hear me?"

"Brett to Phillips," he radioed. "Movement first floor, front window."

"Davidson to Phillips. Drapes are moving—I've got someone at the window. Standby."

Tim pressed the PTT button again, "Ricky, just walk out the door—."

The street erupted with gunfire. Tim ducked as rounds began pinging off the armored truck. *I knew that was going to piss him off. He sure as hell doesn't like being called Ricky.*

Brett peered through the scope on his rifle. His breaths were controlled as the crosshairs swept the window. The sniper's right hand wrapped around the stock of the rifle just behind the trigger guard. The index finger of his hand—pointed in the direction of his target.

Devo, the sniper support, was inches above Brett's right shoulder, his eye glued to a spotter's scope.

"Brett to Phillips. No shot, no shot—suspect has an unidentified female as a shield."

The fusillade of bullets continued to hit the APC.

"You asshole," Tim mumbled, raising the middle finger of his left hand. "Screw you."

"Davidson to Phillips. I've got a sliver of his head. To close to the girl for a shot."

"He's got her around the neck," Brett said over the radio. "Right arm's over her shoulder—firing a pist-."

Brett's transmission was cut short. Within five seconds Devo was on the radio. "Devo to Phillips. Brett's been hit."

Weaver suddenly felt the color drain from his face. At the same time, the earlier slice of pizza began making its way up his esophagus. His close friend was hurt, and a hail of bullets prevented him from making it to his side.

Phillips lowered his head slightly and closed his eyes. After a second he spoke into his microphone. "Phillips to Devo," the team leader said calmly. "Give me a quick sitrep."

"Think we took a ricochet; it shattered the glass window. Brett's got a cut on his head and his arm. Can you get Doc over here?"

"Negative—too risky. You'll need to get him back to the command post."

Weaver held up his phone and mouthed, "I'll take care of it."

Phillips nodded and refocused on the continued gunfire outside. Weaver hit the speed dial for Devo.

"Doc," Devo said. "He's bleeding like a stuffed pig."

"I need you to be my eyes. Tell me what you see."

"He's got a cut on the right side of his head, just above his eye. There's another pretty good cut on his right forearm. The glass must have bounced off of his hard head—he says he's not leaving. He keeps repeating the Monty Python thing, 'It's just a flesh wound'."

"Stubborn jarhead. Is he still bleeding?"

"Yeah."

"Do you carry any type of first-aid kit?"

"No," Devo replied. "Guess we should, huh?"

"Don't worry about it. Find a couple of clean washcloths and towels. Put the cloths over the wounds and apply pressure. That should stem the bleeding. Once that's done, cut the towels into strips and use them to secure the cloths in place."

"Got it."

"Devo—if that doesn't work, he's got no choice but to come out. Either way he's still going to need stitches."

Weaver listened as Devo helped his partner.

"Doc, I found the cloths and towels. We have a choice between pink and green. What do you think? Right—pink it is."

"Always the clown Devo," Brett said. "Always the flippin' clown."

Weaver could hear Brett's flurry of expletives. After a few moments, Devo returned to the phone.

"Okay, everything's in place. I think the bleeding's stopped."

"Good. Keep an eye on it. Excessive movement could break the wounds open and cause them to hemorrhage further."

"Doc, the big words again—."

"Bleed!" Weaver retorted.

"Got it. You know, I should take a picture. We could submit Brett to the sniper's beauty contest. His little pink bonnet is over the top."

With another round of cursing from Brett, Weaver ended the call.

The APC pulled into the parking lot beside the command post. Tim was not a happy camper as he jumped from the armored black truck. Entering the command post, he was met by Major Gittings.

"Are you okay?" the Major asked.

"Considering," Tim exclaimed, "I couldn't get Nash in a position so we could end this, and I got one of our own guys hurt—no, I'm not doing okay, Major."

"Tim, it's not your fault. We knew there was a risk with that option. This whole incident is risky."

The phone that linked the command post to Nash began to buzz. Tim grabbed his headset and slipped it into place. He could not get a word out after pressing the button to open the line.

"I told you I can't stand to be called that!" Nash screamed.

"Rick, I apologize. I haven't had any sleep; I quite simply forgot. Again, my apologies."

"You said you wanted to end this. Well then get me the car. Christy and I drive out of here, and it's over."

"Rick, the rental company is throwing up some roadblocks."

"I don't want to hear about your problems!" Nash yelled.

"They want to know where the car will be returned to," Tim said. "If it's one way or round trip. Obviously, you're not going to give us that information. We just have to approach it from a different angle; it's going to take time. We're working on it."

"I'm no dummy, Tim. Do I have to put a bullet in someone's head?"

Nash disconnected.

Tim looked up to see Chief Sherman and Major Gittings looking on intently.

"He has no idea we were trying to take him out," Tim said. "He's threatened to shoot someone again if he doesn't get the car soon."

"Major," Sherman said. "Get Phillips on the phone. The mission's his. Anything he needs, he gets."

CHAPTER 43

Christy lay on the floor shaking as if having a seizure. She was taking fast, short breaths—inhaling more carbon dioxide from her exhalations than oxygen. She was panicked.

The gunfire, so close to her head, was more than frightening. The loud reverberations still rang in her ears. Hot bullet casings ejected from Nash's gun fell on her, causing small burns.

She thought sure the police would shoot back, hitting her instead of her captor. *The bastard is such a coward! If I could get to his gun, I'd put a bullet in his head myself.*

Nash slammed the phone down. "They're screwing with me. I know they are!"

"Rick, what's up?" Young asked.

"The cop says they don't have the car. That whole thing just now outside, wanting me to give up is bullshit!"

"Why don't we just try to slip out of here during the middle of the night?"

"No—they're probably watching. We get the car, or I whack the girl." Nash nodded toward Jackie.

"We're up," Phillips said as he returned his cell phone to its holder.

Heads turned.

"We need to finalize a plan and advise the Major of any resources we need," Phillips added.

Everyone's adrenalin kicked into high gear, including Weaver's. This was the type of mission they had trained for. It sounded corny as Weaver thought about it, but that's exactly the way he felt. Their training was hard. If they weren't exercising, they were on the range. And if they weren't on the range, they were running room entry and clearing scenarios.

Weaver looked around the room at the men gathered in the small space. They were all dead tired but, to a man, they persevered. Weaver was proud to be a part of such a group—true professionals.

Phillips began the briefing. "Bones will lead the stack with the shield. Rice, you're cover. I'm behind you. Then Lebo, Runk, Gunny, Davis, and Jones. Mund, you're rear guard. Weaver, you're in front of Mund, and for crap sake don't get in the way or get hurt."

Weaver was irritated by the comment, but let it slide. He realized both he and Mund were new, especially for this type of intricate operation. They could be liabilities if they didn't follow direction carefully.

Weaver's agitation vanished when Phillips made a subsequent request.

"Can you get two of those hooks the fire department uses to pull down ceilings?" Phillips asked.

"Shouldn't be a problem," Weaver answered.

"You and Mund are going to take out the two rear windows as a diversion when we hit the door."

Weaver and Mund looked at each other. Both raised an eyebrow. *Damn—I get to play medic and break shit. What a day; you can't ask for more than that!*

"I'll touch on the door breach momentarily. Once inside, I want Runk, Gunny, Davis, and Jones to peel off and clear the second floor. We'll leave the basement for last. As soon as we encounter the hostages, I want them cleared for weapons and booby-traps and taken outside.

"These are small houses, we should have both floors cleared in less than thirty seconds. After the hostages are safe, we'll conduct our normal secondary search."

"Remember your noise discipline," Runk interjected. "There's an open window pane on the first floor that our suspect blew out when he was shooting at the APC. If Nash hears us we'll have lost our element of surprise. Radio silence until we're through the door. We will use only hand gestures outside. The sniper elements will provide radio updates if they see any changes."

"Back to the door," Phillips said. "There are a number of different ways we can breach the front door. Each has disadvantages."

"I think the battering ram is not an option," Gunny said. "If the lock doesn't give on the first hit, Nash may have enough time to kill the girls."

The team discussed the other methods of entry and the

challenges each posed. After fifteen minutes, they came to a consensus.

"In order to maintain flexibility in the plan," Phillips said, "I still want Lebo to bring the ram and Rice to carry the breaching shotgun. If our primary means of entry fails, we have two backup options."

As darkness began to settle in, the team walked through their plan. The house where they had been staged for the past 24-hours was a mirror image of their target and served as a mock-up on which to train. Inside the house, away from prying eyes or long range camera lenses, the team practiced— slowly at first, then picking up tempo with each successive run. From just inside the front door the team maneuvered through their practice area as they would on their target.

Their fourth time through, Phillips shook his head and said, "I don't feel comfortable leaving Weaver and Mund, two new guys, at the rear alone.

He really enjoys pissing me off, Weaver thought.

"We can put Bones and Rice out there," Runk interjected.

"No. I need all the experienced people we have going through the front door and clearing that house.

"Have them take out the front windows. I would rather have their attention on the rear as we come through the front, but it should work none the less.

Phillips pondered Runk's suggestion. "Okay, we'll go with it."

Looking at Weaver and Mund, he added, "After taking out the windows, fall in at the rear of the stack."

After the rehearsals, Phillips phoned Major Gittings.

"Yeah, Jack," the Major answered.

"We have our plan," Phillips said. "We've run some rehearsals. We've made a few minor adjustments, but the overall strategy should work."

Over the next few minutes, Phillips provided his commander with the details. "One final thing," Phillips said. "Is Cliff Lind available? I want him to take out the door."

"Are you sure? What about your other options?"

"A few of the tools we could use might give our position away while we try to get them in place. Other methods are not guaranteed to get us through the door on the first attempt. We need to breach the door quickly—Lind can give us that."

"Okay. I'll get him up to you as quickly as I can."

CHAPTER 44

It was well past midnight. The team had once again been checking their gear. Flashlights flickered on and off to test batteries and bulbs. EOTech Sights were similarly examined to ensure they were operable. Extra ammunition magazines were inspected. Everything from radios to weapons had to work flawlessly.

As did the rest of the team, Weaver checked his .40 caliber Sig Sauer handgun, radio, and light. Then he moved on to his M-9 bag. He opened a small, black plastic case that contained his first-line medications and examined their expiration dates. If they were needed quickly, it would be one less step he would need to perform in the heat of things. He stared at the bag's other contents. *Is there anything else I might need?*

Weaver opened a pouch on his body armor. He withdrew the Combat Application Tourniquet, or CAT, stored on the exterior of his armor for rapid access. A quick check ensured it was ready for use. After checking the remaining contents of the pouch, he decided to carry an additional military-type gauze compression bandage. He unzipped his STOMP medical bag that carried additional supplies and pulled a bandage from within. After his first equipment check was complete, he went through again just to ensure nothing was missed.

He stopped for a second, closed his eyes, and said a silent prayer that God would keep him and his teammates safe. He also asked for the strength to meet the demands set upon him should he be needed.

Completing his appeal, Weaver slid his arms through the straps of his medical bag. He hopped up and down, listening for any clinks and clangs; racket that would give away his position. Anything that could possibly produce a sound needed to be taped down. Assured his equipment was secure, he pulled a black balaclava over his head. The nomex hood, although intimidating, was primarily worn, along with nomex gloves, as fire protection when deploying a sound and light diversionary device commonly referred to as a flash bang.

Weaver looked up to see a new face slip silently through the front door. The short, middle-aged man carried a rucksack over the standard tactical gear. He was also lugging two long, black poles with a hook on the end of each.

"Cliff," Phillips said. "Thanks for getting here so fast."

"Glad to help," the man said. "These are the fire department hooks you needed." He leaned the tools against the wall near the front door.

Cliff Lind had been on the force for over twenty-seven years, most with the Explosive Ordnance Disposal Team.

"This house is a copy of our target," Phillips told Lind. "We don't have any intel on major alterations that were done, so this should closely reflect what you'll see. Let me know when you're ready, and we'll move out."

Lind carefully examined some of the structural features of

the house, paying particular attention to the doors and frames. Minutes later he gave Phillips a thumbs up. With that, Phillips looked around the front room of their staging area and said, "Everyone ready?"

Without another word spoken, the operators fell into formation for the assault. With all of the previous false starts behind him, Weaver knew this time it was the real thing. Within minutes, they would be going through a door and confronting a killer. He took in a deep breath and slowly let the air escape from his lungs.

"Phillips to all sniper elements," the team leader radioed. "We're moving out."

"Brett, ten-four."

"Davidson, ten-four."

"Tucker, ten-four."

Mund squeezed Weaver's left leg, letting him know he was ready. Weaver did the same to Jones, the next man in the stack. The sequence continued.

"Brett to Phillips," Brett radioed. "No change—you're cleared to move."

After getting a squeeze-up from Rice, Bones raised the ballistic shield. He thrust his right hand, carrying his pistol, in front of the shield and snapped a right turn out of the house. As each subsequent operator in the stack rounded the corner of the door, his weapon sprang upward and covered an area of the target house.

As Weaver and Mund reached the front door, they each

grabbed one of the fire department's ceiling hooks. Stepping outside, Weaver caught a gust of chilled air.

The eleven dark, ghostly figures moved smoothly and silently the fifty feet to their destination. The moonlight cast strange shadows on the ground beside them. Periodically, Weaver heard a rush of air bristle past the straps holding his helmet in place. That was the only noise he heard—that and his heart pounding in his chest.

Bones stopped just before the small concrete pad in front of the door to 58, their target. He was like a hawk watching his prey—his eyes never leaving the door. If it suddenly opened, a split-second decision would be necessary. Friend or foe; shoot don't shoot. Rice was positioned so that Bones did not take a round to the back of the head if he himself had to open fire.

As the team stopped and readied themselves, Weaver's knees began shaking uncontrollably. He told himself it was just the cool air. Then his stomach began to knot. As much as he tried to convince himself otherwise, he was scared.

Phillips raised his left hand and motioned for Weaver and Mund to take their positions at the front windows. Weaver stepped to his left, out of the stack, and proceeded forward. Mund slung his M-4 behind his back and was on Weaver's heels.

Weaver passed Bones and his ballistic shield, ducking low as he passed in front of the side-by-side windows. He leaned against the warm brick wall at the far side. He brought the hook up to near vertical and stood ready for his order.

Mund took his position in the three-foot space between the first window and the door. Phillips had been emphatic, he had to stay close to the window and the brick wall. When the door went—he was not to be in the way.

His breathing heavy, Weaver thought for sure Phillips could hear the noisy respirations. Again his knees began to shake. With all his training, he remained unsure whether he would be capable of performing in the heat of battle.

Cliff Lind made his way to the entryway of the house—stepping up to the concrete pad that served as a small porch. He was in the kill zone. If Nash heard a noise, he could easily fire through the wooden door. Lind would be a sitting duck, his only hope being the strength of his body armor—that was, if he took a round to the small portion of his anatomy that was protected by the device.

The bomb technician quietly hung the charge on the door. He allowed the wires to pay out as he stepped back to the rear of the stack where he attached them to the trigger. The charge was now live. Lind signaled Phillips that he was ready.

The team crouched low. Bones brought the shield high at a forty-five-degree angle. Phillips raised his left hand, with his first three fingers extended.

Weaver's hands were sweating inside the nomex gloves. His heart still pounding, he brought the tip of the hook closer to the top of the glass window. He focused on Phillips' hand as the first finger dropped.

This is it!

The second finger came down.

Phillips dropped his third finger and closed his hand into a fist and yanked it down as if pulling the cord on a transit bus, signaling he wanted to get off at his stop. But there was no getting off this bus. It was rolling quickly down a highway that no one had a map to.

Weaver and Mund drove their hooks through the window. They both raked downward toward the bottom of the frame, shattering the thin glass. Nash's attention would be drawn to the windows and away from the portal where the team would enter.

With a delay of only seconds, Lind pressed the button on the firing device that initiated the explosive charge on the door. The resulting detonation blew the door inward.

Bones and the rest of the team were up and moving through the now open doorway even before the smoke had cleared.

"Police—get down!" Bones yelled. "Police—get down!"

Weaver tossed the hook he had used to break the window to the ground. Heading to the door, he heard two gunshots. They were immediately followed by eight to ten more. Weaver knew they all could not have missed their target.

* * *

Nash sat silently on the couch, his right index finger caressing the cool metal trigger of the Glock 9mm semi-automatic. His gaze was fixed across the room at the corner where the wall and ceiling met.

Young sat beside his friend, sinking into one of the overstuffed cushions nearest the window. He wondered what kind of insidious plan Nash was hatching in his cagey brain.

Whatever it was, Young knew it would be wicked. His eyes refocused on the two women lying on the floor in the dining room. The two had fallen asleep, their hands still bound behind their backs. Young chuckled to himself recounting Christy's reaction after Nash had used her as a shield when he opened fire through the window. *She was crying and shaking like a baby. It was great!*

The silence was broken as the two front windows crashed inward—shards of glass reigning down on the two hostage takers. Nash spun right, pointing the Glock toward the windows. Young reached for the Mossberg shotgun leaning against the sofa near his right leg.

The two girls, now wide awake, began screaming.

An explosion at the front door overloaded the senses of all four occupants of the house; their minds incapable focusing on any one thing.

The front room filled with smoke and the entry door—blown from its hinges—now lay against the staircase.

Young, shotgun in hand and cut by flying glass, rolled to his right and scrunched into a small cubby between the front wall and the sofa. *Son of a bitch!*

Nash saw dark figures stepping through the smoke at what had been the front door. His mind was still not able to comprehend what was happening. But his body reacted in the manner in which he had lived most of his adult life—violently. Nash pulled the trigger on the handgun twice. He didn't aim; the gun tracked his gaze and his muscles contracted without thought. Two rounds exited the muzzle and flew across the room.

The third cop in line went down. Immediately Nash could feel what seemed like hot pokers penetrating his body. He knew he had been shot and was surprised at the lack of pain. The voices he heard were distant—as if coming from a tunnel. He tried to fire again but could not command his muscles to contract and pull the trigger. Breathing was becoming increasingly difficult and he was feeling weaker by the second. Taking his last breaths, Nash knew it was the end. He hadn't given an afterlife much thought and really didn't care what might await him.

CHAPTER 45

"Shots fired! Medic up! Medic up!" came the radio transmission.

Weaver couldn't tell exactly who was speaking. The voice, although not panicked, was garbled. Weaver bolted for the door. Just inside, at the bottom of the stairs, lay one of his teammates—face down on the carpet.

The house was filled with smoke and the odor of burned gunpowder.

In the living room, just in front of the sofa, Nash lay face up. Peppered with bullet holes, his mouth was agape and his eyes wide open. Weaver noticed the gun still in his hand.

In the dining room, beyond the gunman's bloodied body, the two hostages were screaming as they frantically twisted against their bindings.

The radio was now alive with transmissions.

"Mund," Runk said. "Get the girls."

The rear guard stepped over Weaver, to grab the two girls. Seeing the imposing SWAT team member approach provided no comfort to the girls. The two continued to struggle and began kicking at the hooded officer. Mund slung his M-4 carbine around to his back and grabbed them under his arms, retreating to the door and safety. Bones and Rice had continued forward, clearing the dining room and kitchen. The remainder of the team had headed to the second floor. The assault continued.

Weaver dropped his M-9 bag to the floor while reaching down to roll the limp operator over. *You have got to be shitting me—Phillips!* He was immediately sprayed in the face with blood. Things went from bad to deadly. Everything was in slow motion. Things occurring in seconds seemed like an eternity. *Of all the damn people who had to get shot—the one that hates me!*

Phillips had been hit twice—once in the upper right arm and once in the very top of the right leg, millimeters from his armor. Uncontrolled, he could bleed out in a matter of two minutes. Probably less, since he was hit in both the brachial and femoral arteries. The femoral alone is the size of a person's little finger. Phillips looked like a fountain. Blood was now spilling out of the team leader at an amazing rate, pooling on the floor around his body.

Without thinking, Weaver dropped his right knee into the hole on Phillips leg, stemming the flow of blood from the femoral. His left hand was going for Phillips' other wound on the right arm when he spotted movement in his peripheral vision.

Weaver's head spun left. Someone was coming out of a small area between the sofa and the smashed window. Weaver could see what looked like a sawed-off shotgun in the man's hand. Weaver pulled his .40 caliber Sig from its holster and emptied five rounds into the man's chest. The tattooed gunman fell to the floor, blood oozing from his wounds.

"Shots fired! Suspect down!" Weaver screamed.

The cavalry was coming over the hill. Bones and Rice ran from the kitchen; the remainder of the team flew down the stairs from the second floor, making contact with only half of the steps. Weaver's hand shook as he tried to keep his weapon on the downed suspect.

"Doc—we got him," Rice said, kicking the shotgun from the man's hand. "Where the hell did he come from?"

Weaver rammed his side-arm back in its holster and dropped the palm of his left hand onto the hole in Phillips' bleeding arm. It was a reaction; he was back in medical mode. He looked across the room to see Nash take two, short agonal breaths.

Rice tossed their second suspect on his stomach and cuffed him.

Weaver's right hand unzipped the pouch on the front of his armor and pulled out the CAT tourniquet. He slid the device up Phillips' arm, just above the bullet wound.

Leaning over, Runk asked, "Doc, what do you need?"

"Get a chopper in here quick!" Weaver said. "We'll need the APC up here to transport him to the LZ. I also need an IV set up. I'll talk somebody through it. And then see if those other two are still alive."

Weaver cranked the metal rod on the tourniquet, tightening it against Phillips' arm. With the flow of blood stemmed, he turned his attention to the leg wound. His knee still compressing the bloody femoral artery, he pulled a pouch of Celox hemostatic agent and a wad of four-by-four-inch gauze from his M-9 bag.

"You're going to be okay," Weaver said.

"I hope you're right," Phillips said through clenched teeth.

Phillips' injury was too high on the leg to use a tourniquet. This was the same devastating wound suffered by Corporal James Smith in Mogadishu, Somalia. Hemostatic agents like Celox had been developed as a direct result of the Army Ranger's death. The powdered substance bonds with red blood cells to form a gel-like clot.

Weaver put the top of the bag between his teeth and ripped it open with one hand—spitting the top portion on the floor. The next few steps needed to be both quick and flawless. Weaver pulled his knee from Phillips' leg and rammed a wad of gauze deep into the wound. Phillips jerked in pain. The excess blood needed to be sopped from the bullet hole in order for the hemostatic to work.

Weaver pulled the now bloody gauze back out a mere second after plunging it in. Immediately, he poured the Celox into the wound. He pushed a second wad of gauze into the hole. Again Phillips jerked. Weaver formed a fist and pressed on the dressing, holding it in place for three minutes.

"Talk to me, Phillips. You still with me?" Weaver said.

"Pain, lot of pain."

Weaver grabbed Phillips' left wrist and felt for a peripheral pulse. If one was felt he'd be relatively confident his patient had a palpable blood pressure of at least eighty. *Got it!* He held his fingers in place for another few seconds to be sure.

"I'm going to get a line going and then I'll give you something for the pain."

Phillips nodded.

Weaver instructed Gunny how to set up the IV while he gathered the other supplies he would need.

"I'm going to use a large bore sixteen-gauge needle," he told Phillips. "It's going to hurt—they're not fun. You've lost a lot of blood; I need to get some fluid back in you."

He hated using such large catheters; it was like trying to push a pencil through the skin. After cleansing the insertion site, Weaver took the needle in his hand.

"You're going to feel a stick. You've got large veins so it should be quick."

Weaver punctured the skin with the needle and slid the catheter in place. Phillips winced. After attaching the tubing, Weaver ran a roll of surgical tape around Phillips' arm and the tubing and catheter four times. He didn't want to have it infiltrate the vein and lose the IV. *It's not the pretty tape job you see in the hospital… but screw 'em.*

He then reached into his bag and pulled out a fentanyl lollipop. The drug, a synthetic narcotic, was about one hundred times more potent than morphine.

"This is fentanyl. I'm going to put it between your cheek and gum. It'll relieve your pain." He turned. "Gunny, attached to the bottom of my bag is a litter. Can you roll it out for me?"

"Got it," the former Marine responded.

The litter was a black PVC tarpaulin with two handles on each side.

To Runk, Weaver said, "We're going to need some hands getting him on the litter and out of here."

Runk said, "Gunny, Jones—give us a hand getting Jack on the litter. Doc, the one you shot is dead. Nash took a few gasps of air, but stopped breathing."

"Can you have a medic unit confirm that once you feel things are secure?"

"Will do."

"Command Post to Runk."

"Runk, go."

"Trooper One ETA is three minutes."

"Doc, did you get that?" Runk asked. "The helicopter will be on the ground in three."

"Yeah, let's get him out of here," Weaver said. "One person on each corner of the litter. Phillips, you're going to be okay. Chopper's almost here."

Weaver grabbed his medical bag and threw it on his back, then put the top edge of the IV bag between his teeth. Runk, Gunny, and Jones, along with Weaver himself, each grabbed a corner of the litter and headed out the door.

Murray, along with the APC, was waiting as the four hurried down the sidewalk. Overhead Weaver could hear the medevac helicopter as it circled on its final approach to the LZ.

Reaching the open rear doors of the armored truck, Runk and Weaver lifted their end of the litter into the crew compartment and climbed inside. Gunny and Jones followed suit and, once inside, slammed the doors closed.

"Go!" Runk hollered.

The truck sped the short distance down Burkeshire Road heading for Towson University, where Trooper One had landed the previous night.

The truck bounced and swerved; the heavy vehicle was not built for comfort. Still wearing his helmet and armor, Weaver knelt beside his patient and checked both wounds. He was concerned that the clot made by the Celox hemostatic agent might not have held during jostling of their evac. *No hemorrhaging. Celox and the tourniquet are holding.* He turned his attention to the IV, scanning the venipuncture site where the catheter entered Phillips' arm. *Line's still patent.*

Weaver's fingers once again searched out a pulse in Phillips' wrist. He moved his fingers back and forth searching. *Nothing —he's bottoming out!*

"Hang in there," he told Phillips now searching for a carotid pulse in his neck.

Weaver's eyes met Runk's and, without a word spoken, conveyed the direness of the situation.

"Murray. Step on it!" Runk yelled to the driver of the APC.

Laying a hand on Phillips' shoulder, Runk said, "Come on Jack. Fight; don't give up."

Turning into the university grounds, Weaver looked out the front window of the APC. Dust filled the air as the chopper set down. The roar of the turbines changed pitch as the wheels set firmly on the ground.

When the truck stopped, Gunny and Jones threw open the rear doors. The medic from the chopper ran toward them with his folding stretcher in his right hand. Weaver was relieved to see his friend Gabriele.

335

"Danny, what do you have?" Gabriele shouted .

"Jack Phillips, our team leader," Weaver yelled over the engine noise of the chopper. "He's hit once in the left brachial and once in the left femoral. Both controlled. CAT on the arm; Celox in the leg. Blood loss moderate. He's lost consciousness and I no longer have a peripheral pulse; just a carotid."

After receiving the patient turnover report, Gabriele said, "Let's get him loaded in the chopper and get him out of here. I'll get an airway in and put him on O-two when he's inside."

The team slid Phillips onto the helicopter's stretcher. Gabriele grabbed the front left corner of the stretcher and led Weaver, Runk, and Gunny the seventy-five feet to the aircraft.

After loading the stretcher inside, Gabriele secured the door and the pilot immediately spun up the engines. The rotors turned faster as the whine of the engines increased.

Weaver made his way back to the side of the armored vehicle. He silently watched as the helicopter lifted from the grassy plot; red and white strobes flashing brightly. Weaver recited a quiet prayer for his team leader. Even though the guy had been a pain in the rear end, he didn't want him to die.

With its nose dipping slightly, Trooper One picked up speed and headed south to Shock Trauma in Baltimore. As the noise of the rotors cutting through the early morning air diminished in the distance, the team climbed back into the APC and returned to Burkeshire Road.

It was over. Weaver had survived something few outside

those in the military would ever experience—a major gun battle. He had taken a life—he was sad about that—but he had also survived a potential disaster and he had perhaps saved the life of a teammate.

But Phillips was deteriorating quickly when he was loaded into the back of the helicopter. His blood pressure was dropping and he had lost consciousness. In medicine, trends were everything. Phillips was trending downwards; his chances of survival were dropping as quick as his pressure.

Weaver was exhausted. But, as he returned to Burkeshire Road to retrieve his equipment, he was already questioning his performance. As he walked back into the house where the assault had taken place the smell of coagulated blood hung in the air. He noticed the pool of blood from Phillips' severed arteries and wondered if he had done everything possible to keep Phillips alive. *Did the fentanyl cause the drop in his blood pressure? Could I have gotten an airway in him before we got to the LZ?*

Reaching down to pick up equipment he had left behind, Weaver noticed the lifeless bodies of Nash and his collaborator. He knew the military's philosophy about treating friendly forces before combatants. He had heard that lecture during his medical training a week earlier. However, this was the civilian world and Weaver wasn't sure how it would all shake out in the end. He hadn't even made an attempt to treat them or the two girls. *I completely forgot about them!*

Another day was beginning to dawn as Weaver gathered the last of his gear. Although he was looking forward to a good breakfast and some much needed sleep, he was worried about what the coming hours would bring.

CHAPTER 46

Weaver stepped off the elevator on the fourth floor of the R. Adams Cowley Shock Trauma Center in downtown Baltimore. He had come to check on Christy. She had been transferred to the trauma center minutes after arriving at the local hospital that was a stone's throw from where the standoff had ended the previous night. Christy's grandfather, Ed Benson, had intervened and insisted she be moved. Jackie had remained behind at the local facility—Weaver had checked on her prior to the trip downtown.

One part of a tactical medic's job was to act as a patient advocate—being an intermediary between the hospital staff and the sick or injured and both their family and law enforcement. Weaver felt uneasy as he walked the long hall to where Jack Phillips was recuperating. The previous night Weaver treated Phillips just like any another patient. His treatment modalities were based on the injury or illness and not on whom you were. Today however, he was checking on Jack Phillips, the one man on the team who seemed to hate him. Weaver could not get that fact off his mind.

It was late in the day; Weaver had not made it home until noontime. The entire team had to undergo an exhaustive review of their actions during the siege. Every step of the assault and gun battle was picked apart *ad nauseum* by Internal Affairs and Homicide detectives.

Kathy had heard of the yet sketchy events on the morning news. Although still upset her husband had missed the previous evening's engagement, Kathy showered him with kisses as he crossed the threshold of their small suburban home. Within minutes he was asleep on the couch.

Weaver hadn't given her the entire story of his involvement. That was for another time. He merely noted Phillips had been seriously injured and was in Shock Trauma.

Cops filled the hallway outside Phillips' room. As Weaver neared, heads began to turn.

"Doc!" Brett said. The sniper grabbed the medic's hand with his right and embraced him in a hug with his left. "You saved quite a few lives today — thanks," he whispered into Weaver's ear. Weaver's eyes were now wet and red. "Thanks Brett."

He continued past the throng of SWAT team members and department brass, many shaking his hand or patting him on the back.

Weaver stuck his head through the door of Phillips' room. Phillips had been in surgery for a number of hours and was still groggy from the anesthesia. Weaver was about to leave when Phillips saw him and nodded for him to come in.

"How're you feeling?" Weaver said.

"Not too awfully bad, considering," Phillips said slowly.

"I'm glad you're going to be okay."

Weaver could see Phillips' eyelids starting to sag.

He turned to leave.

"Doc!"

Weaver had not heard that term pass the lips of Jack Phillips before. He turned with a look of disbelief on his face.

"Thanks, Doc," Phillips said. "You saved my life twice today; once by treating my wounds and once by pulling the trigger. Don't ever second guess your actions today. In my book you are every bit an operator as anyone on this team."

"Jack. I never thought I would hear you use that term. Maybe you aren't as stubborn as I thought."

"No, I'm still stubborn. I just know when to admit I'm wrong."

Weaver stepped closer to Phillips' bed, intending to shake his hand.

"Hey," Phillips said. "Don't go getting all lovey-dovey on me."

Weaver stopped short. Whereupon Phillips cracked the slightest of smiles.

Being called *Doc* by the one man who despised his presence on the team came as a shock to Weaver. As Phillips closed his eyes, Weaver quietly left the room his own eyes now wet and red. As he exited the large glass doors at the main entrance of the hospital, Weaver was bathed in warmth. Partly from the afternoon sun, but mainly from feeling a sense of complete acceptance by Jack Phillips and the team.